The
Five-Step Plan

by

Elizabeth Welsford

The Five-Step Plan

Cover Art by *Debbie Taylor*

The Wild Rose Press, Inc.
PO Box 708
Adams Basin, NY 14410-0708
Visit us at www.thewildrosepress.com

Publishing History
First Mainstream Historical Edition, 2015
Print ISBN 978-1-62830-776-4
Digital ISBN 978-1-62830-777-1

Published in the United States of America

"Dr. Vorago! Man, I've done it!

I've *really* done it! Tell me you have some hysterics scheduled this morning for pelvic massage! You have to let me at them!" Dr. Whitcraft was still breathing hard. He had run all the way from his office after his second hysteric, Mrs. Fussock, had been successfully dispatched...and in such a grand fashion!

"Well, no, I only do mine in the afternoons, to save the wear on my—"

"Oh, well, you won't have to worry about that anymore! I'm coming back after luncheon and you have to let me do it! I did *two* this morning already, and they each took *less than ten minutes*!"

"Oh, now, come on..." The loose skin under his chin wagged as he shook his head.

"I'm telling you, you've got to see it! The Whitcraft Maneuver! It's going to revolutionize this whole business!" Dr. Whitcraft clapped his hands together, rocked forward on his toes and then back onto his heels, beaming with the sheer delight of it all.

Dedication

To my loving and supportive family

Chapter One

"Where is she, then?"

"Can't you hear, Doctor? Just follow the screaming up the hall and to the right. She's destroyed every piece of furniture in her dressing room and has moved on to Mr. Wedfellow's study."

"Good Lord." Dr. Whitcraft quickened his pace. The butler followed closely behind. Now that he was deeper into the house, he could make out the ravings of his patient, unquestionably in the throes of a hysterical rage. It was likely going to be a difficult morning.

"Where is Mr. Wedfellow?"

"I would guess he has stepped out, sir." The butler rushed past and stopped in front of the closed study door. Inside, it sounded as though a team of laborers were rearranging the room.

Dr. Whitcraft stepped forward, flattened his palm against the door, and leaned in to listen. He grimaced at a profoundly unfeminine string of curses—and then there was a monumental crash.

The two men drew breaths and looked at one another with wide eyes. Dr. Whitcraft pursed his lips and placed his hand on the knob. It was locked, of course. "Is there a key?"

The butler's frightened countenance turned contemplative. "I believe there may be, sir. In the pantry. I'll have to see."

"Splendid."

The butler scurried away. Dr. Whitcraft turned back to the door. What was the best way to go about managing this difficult situation? He had diagnosed this unfortunate woman with hysteria only a few months back, but it appeared that the rigorous treatment regimen he had devised was not exactly doing the trick. A bland diet followed by purgatives, pelvic massage on alternating days, cold water plunges—it was all time-tested, thoroughly researched, and professionally unquestionable.

Still, something would have to be altered, but before he could attend to that, he had to address her immediate symptoms. Irrational behavior, violence, and rage: all typical manifestations of the disease. What a pity. He knocked on the door.

The rumblings from within fell silent.

He cleared his throat. "Mrs. Wedfellow, this is Dr. Whitcraft. Could you please let me in? It is necessary that I—"

A blast of immense force exploded against the other side of the door.

"Good Lord," he whispered, stepping back.

He collected himself and approached again, bringing his lips up to the door. "Mrs. Wedfellow, you are ill, and this behavior simply won't do. If you do not let me in...why, you are only going to exacerbate an already dangerous situation. Can you unlock this door, please?"

"I suppose *he* sent you? I suppose *he would* send you!" Her muffled agitation was followed by a horrific ripping, which Dr. Whitcraft surmised to be the end of Mr. Wedfellow's upholstery. He sighed and stepped back, pleased to note the butler's hasty return.

"Sorry for the delay, sir." He knelt and began fumbling through a large ring of keys. "It's one of these. I'll need to try a few…"

"Certainly, certainly," Dr. Whitcraft said, and then inquired, "Do you have any idea what prompted today's bout of…unpleasantness?"

The butler shrugged as he shuffled from one key to another. "Mr. Wedfellow puts her on a pedestal, you know that. She doesn't lift a finger around here, he doesn't let her. She spends her days in a quiet, dimly lit room, as per your orders. Of course her wardrobes are filled with only the latest fashions. She has every bauble and trinket her heart desires, but still, she's miserable!"

"Hmm." Dr. Whitcraft nodded, his eyes searching the floor.

"Ah…I think…yes…this is the one!" The lock disengaged with an authoritative snap. The butler scuttled back on his haunches and watched the doctor from the floor.

Dr. Whitcraft grasped the knob once again. "All right, Mrs. Wedfellow, I'm coming in."

The door swung wide, revealing what had once been a gentlemen's well-appointed, wood-paneled study. Now, it resembled a shipwreck of splintered wood bobbing in a sea of shredded paper. Furniture was overturned, the upholstery was torn, and its stuffing strewn about. Book bindings were cracked open like walnut shells, exposed, and cast aside in piles. And there, in the very center, directing the mischief, was the apoplectic Mrs. Wedfellow.

Her long black hair was undone and swinging in

tangled ropes. Her white dressing gown billowed and twisted with every sweeping movement. She looked like an Olympic goddess wreaking havoc on the mortals who had displeased her.

She stopped moving and glared, her eyes hotly lined in red. "How the hell did you get in here?"

Dr. Whitcraft stepped over a mound of shattered crystal and set his bag on the floor. In his usual calm and scholarly delivery, he said, "I would have been happy to wait for your next appointment, Mrs. Wedfellow, but your husband felt I should be summoned—"

"Oh he did, did he? Is that what *he* thinks?" She clawed at the pillow in her hands.

"I think he has judged the situation correctly, Mrs. Wedfellow." He studied her over his spectacles. "You are distraught and have let your hysteria get the better of you. You *must* try to calm down."

"So it's my fault?" She flung the pillow at the wall, then lunged toward him, her skirt raking an assortment of debris as she moved. "All of this?" She made a grand gesture. "This is *my* fault?"

"No…no." He took a step back. "Of course not. You are the *victim* of an illness, Mrs. Wedfellow, clearly. I am merely suggesting…why don't we sit for a moment?" He reached for her shoulder, hoping to steer her toward what was left of the couch. "Let's try to—"

A sharp crack rattled the room as Dr. Whitcraft's spectacles sailed from his face and landed in a flutter of paper shreds that took to the air like frightened birds.

Mrs. Wedfellow stood motionless, her hands covering her open mouth as bits of paper drifted to the floor.

Dumbstruck, the doctor massaged his stinging cheek and slowly turned back to gape at his patient.

"Oh! Oh my! I'm...I'm so sorry," she blurted, and watched in helpless horror as her doctor dropped to his knees and rummaged about for his glasses.

She burst into tears, but Dr. Whitcraft paid her no mind as he patted this way and that, trying his best to assuage his rising panic. He had only just purchased the eyeglasses, and the thought of them being damaged in this foolishness was enough to make his heart rate triple.

Finally, he brushed against their familiar steel frame and fished them up through the rubble. He blew the dust from their lenses and held them up to the light. Just as he was about to replace them, Dr. Whitcraft was flattened to the floor. His unhappy patient had draped herself across him like a net.

"Mrs. Wedfellow." He flipped himself over and squinted at the back of her sobbing head. "Mrs. Wedfellow, please, you must try—"

"What the devil is going on in here?" a voice bellowed from above. It was Mr. Wedfellow, of course, clutching the door frame, surveying the madness.

Mrs. Wedfellow lifted her head from the doctor's lap at the sound of the offending voice, and through tears extended her arm stiffly. "There's the man...there! Is it not enough that your intrigues in London include every last under-aged gutter-slush, but now you've moved on to include *society women* in your *disgusting* parade of debauchery?"

The man's pallor blanched. After a moment or two of inward reflection, he muttered, "Well, that's preposterous. She's mad, that's all there is to it." He nodded for emphasis, although perspiration dotted his forehead.

"And he's spent it *all,*" his wife cried from the floor. "All my father's money, filling this house with ridiculous nonsense! Did you see his latest acquisition?" She pointed at the fireplace.

Dr. Whitcraft noted a large porcelain statue glowering from the mantel. It was a rather striking interpretation of Poseidon wielding his trident, posing atop a cluster of sea creatures.

"God knows how much he paid for that grotesque atrocity, and I have no say in any of it!" She threw herself back to the floor and wept, near exhaustion.

Dr. Whitcraft replaced his glasses and smoothed his wrinkled frock coat as he climbed to his feet and stepped over his patient. Mr. Wedfellow was speechless.

"Do you have any spirits?" the doctor whispered.

"Oh, well, yes, of course, some brandy, I believe."

"We need to give her a significant amount. She must calm herself. She's very vulnerable right now to the female anatomy's dangerous machinations."

"I see." Mr. Wedfellow dabbed at his forehead with a handkerchief.

"It appears that I may have to reevaluate my treatment plan for your wife," Dr. Whitcraft said. "The purgatives, the pelvic massage...it simply isn't enough for a case this severe."

Still regarding the prone figure of his wife, Mr. Wedfellow nodded with a cough of understanding. "Yes. Yes. Of course."

"You know, Mr. Wedfellow, it is common for women stricken with hysteria to be...shall we say, rather fanciful in their imaginations. It is quite fascinating, really. The vapors of the afflicted hysterical uterus are dangerous to the mind, often creating delusions that are very real to these women. They are liable to imagine any number of things. You must not take her accusations personally. With the proper treatment, she'll return to herself—not overnight, of course…but in time, God willing."

Mr. Wedfellow adjusted his collar and inhaled. "Well, thank heaven for that."

Chapter Two

Dr. Whitcraft dropped himself down at the table. "I'm sorry I'm so late." He grimaced as he opened and closed his right hand.

Dr. Vorago arched his brows as he chewed. "Not at, not at all." He swallowed and nudged his friend on the shoulder. "Good to see you. I'm afraid I started without you…"

"Oh, I'm glad you did." He sighed, signaling the barmaid in the far corner with his undamaged hand. "This week has been an absolute nightmare, and it's not even half over. Beginning Monday with Mrs. Wedfellow, which I already told you about. Now today—three hours! I've just come from performing three hours of pelvic massage on Mrs. Brabble. Look." He held up the sore hand. "I've nearly crippled myself." He wiggled his swollen fingers as proof. "I have another hysteric scheduled a mere hour from now. *Her* last treatment took over *two hours* before a paroxysm was finally obtained. I suppose given the state of my hand I should cancel her outright."

"Or you could engage a midwife, just to assist—"

"Yes, but that would cost me nearly half my fee. It's ridiculous."

"Hysteria is the scourge of our age, I'm afraid." Dr. Vorago pawed through the basket of rolls. "What the devil are you doing scheduling two of them back to back? It's your own fault, you know. I only schedule pelvic massages in the afternoon. Otherwise I would be ruined for the rest of the day." He put the bread aside and reached for his colleague's hand. He studied his fingers, gingerly articulating the tender second proximal interphalangeal joint.

"Ouch." Dr. Whitcraft jerked his hand away.

"Terrible, just terrible." Dr. Vorago shook his head, picked up his fork, and plucked another oyster from its shell. He let it dangle before dropping it into his mouth, closing his eyes with ecstasy. When he recovered himself, he continued. "The workings of the feminine anatomy are a mystery, dear sir. Why, I've had patients who achieved a paroxysm in less than an hour in one appointment, and in the very next took double or even triple that time. It's ridiculous." He waved his tiny fork for emphasis. "You, my friend, are a casualty of your profession."

"Tea?" The rosy-cheeked girl behind the counter held the kettle in one hand and an empty cup in the other.

Dr. Whitcraft nodded. "Yes, please."

"And give us another half-dozen, my dear. Two left, William. Have at them. They're delectable." He dabbed the corners of his mouth while eying the survivors of his previous dozen.

"Oh no. I'm in the first week of a dietary experiment. For the next hundred days, I will only allow myself roasted fowl and two servings of bread per day."

"Why what the devil for?" Dr. Vorago was positively appalled.

"I'm toying with a theory that these alterations will

be beneficial to one's regularity and general constitution. I have all the relevant data outlined on a graph in my office, should you be interested in my results."

"Well, surely you haven't given up your nightly glass of brandy and water?"

"Indeed, I have. Only through the course of my experiment, however."

"Ah, the denials and sacrifices we make for our art. How is your hand?"

Dr. Whitcraft glanced down, wiggling his fingers. "I believe there has been some improvement. You know, I read an article the other day disputing the necessity of pelvic massage in the treatment of hysteria altogether. It went so far as to compare the female paroxysm to that of the male reproductive crisis—"

"Preposterous!" he sputtered, nearly spitting out his oyster.

"It even went on to imply that contact of that nature should be reserved exclusively for a spouse…in the course of…well, you know. Can you imagine?"

Dr. Vorago wrinkled his nose. "I can guarantee that article was written by a stodgy old academician partitioned off from the real world. Novel academic theories are all well and good, but a hysterical patient must be offered a therapy that will provide her immediate relief. I have seen pelvic massage work time and time again. Ah, here they are."

The girl had returned with another plate of oysters, setting it between the men, but slightly closer to Dr. Vorago.

"You know," he said thoughtfully, "you're a clever man. What you *should* do is give up that dietary nonsense of yours, have one of these sinfully decadent oysters and concoct a method whereby practitioners like ourselves can be relieved of *our* suffering. Develop some kind of machine, or better yet, some type of method that would cause a consistent, successful paroxysm. Although, if it could be achieved, someone probably would have done it by now."

Dr. Whitcraft brought the teacup toward his lips, blowing at the curls of steam before daring to take a sip. All the while, a new sense of determination took hold of his heart.

****

Dr. Whitcraft walked steadily up Bruton Street, back toward his office. This time of day, London's Berkeley Square bustled with activity. Carriages and wagons shuddered past, their drivers deftly dodging pedestrians, sedan chairs, and bystanders alike. The passing conveyances stirred up an enormous amount of dust. It hung in great billowing clouds among the populace.

Every class of character could be seen on these streets, but Dr. Whitcraft didn't pay the slightest mind to any of them as he stepped over a pox-ridden pauper huddled in a doorway, or when he grazed the frockcoat of a beaver-hatted Lord. Rather, the doctor was lost in his thoughts as he recounted his luncheon conversation with the esteemed Dr. Vorago.

A consistent method for pelvic massage that would ensure a rapid paroxysm every time—was it even possible? Such a discovery could revolutionize the lives of women suffering with hysteria and would quite possibly be the most important advancement in recent medical history. He giggled at the thought.

Dr. William Whitcraft was a slight man but stood very straight, elongating his person with a confident posture. He had a habit of holding his chin in front of him, particularly when trying to gauge the tenor of any situation. He wore his spectacles low on his nose and contemplated his subjects with thoughtful brown eyes under brows furrowed with deep concentration.

He wore a dark blue, double-breasted frockcoat overtop a grey waistcoat. His white linen tall-collared shirt was tied at the throat with a grey-patterned cravat. Brown trousers and black shoes completed his outfit. Even in the most casual of circumstances, he wore a different version of this exact same ensemble.

He bounded up the steps to his narrow townhouse and saw through the glass that Miss Faffle hadn't yet returned. He dug into his waistcoat pocket and produced his key, unlocking the front door with practiced ease.

Miss Faffle's abandoned desk, two plain wooden chairs, an area rug, and empty hat stand completed the sparse, no-nonsense professional décor. One never knew what one might find upon returning from luncheon, and he felt pleased to see that everything seemed well in order.

Last week, after another meal with Dr. Vorago, he had found an ashen-faced young fellow slouched on his steps cupping his dismembered hand in the crook of his elbow as he waited for the doctor's return.

"Good God, man! Why didn't you go to hospital? You are bleeding out!" he had yelled, dashing up the steps and fashioning a makeshift tourniquet out of his own waistcoat to stop the torrent of blood.

"Oh, it seemed like too much of a bother, you

know," the man had replied, his tongue thick, and his eyes half-opened. That poor intoxicated soul had turned out to be the calmest, most reasonable patient of the day.

Dr. Whitcraft eyed Miss Faffle's desk for any messages and, finding none glanced into his small examining room, which was also empty for the moment. Satisfied with the current state of his business, he strolled into his office.

Books upon books crowded the shelves encircling the room, making it feel smaller than it actually was. Bundles of journals lined his desk, spilling onto the floor in tall but organized stacks. Behind his desk, among the sagging stacks of academic ephemera, stood a large wooden cabinet tucked into the corner.

To a visitor, his office must have appeared rather haphazardly arranged, but to Dr. Whitcraft, the scheme was systematic and organized. He could lay his hands on any article within his collection, and when finished, would dutifully return it to its proper designation. Even the trusted Miss Faffle rarely entered this place, knowing he'd be frantic if a single item were mishandled or lost.

A narrow stairway against the back wall led up to his residence, a small flat consisting of two tiny rooms. It was all rather austere, but comfortable enough. With the exorbitant prices in London, he was lucky to be able to afford any accommodations at all, especially in a neighborhood as desirable as Berkeley Square.

Unlike many doctors in London, Dr. Whitcraft did not have access to familial money. His father had been a school teacher, and had raised his only son with constant admonitions regarding the merits of making one's own way in the world. "Wit and perseverance" had been the man's refrain, and Dr. Whitcraft had indeed earned everything he had by hard work and determination.

He rose to the tips of his toes and reached to the highest shelf, gliding his hand over three identically bound volumes before he fixed his grip on just the one. In faded gold leaf, the title read: *Treatise on the Study of Diseases Affecting Women, Including but not limited to the study of hysteria, hypochondria and nervous disorders.*

He pulled it down and at once began flipping through its thin pages, stepping over a pile of journals as he made his way back to the desk. Thoroughly engrossed, he barely noticed the sound of the front door, followed by the familiar scrape of Miss Faffle's shoes. But there was something else…was it *singing*?

In the eleven months that she had worked for him, he had never seen the nervous Miss Faffle joyous about anything. And now she was singing? Curiosity piqued, he set the book aside and wandered out into the reception area.

She had her nose buried in a bouquet of purple primroses. "Did you have a pleasant meal with Dr. Vorago, Dr. Whitcraft?" A rare smile quivered on her lips.

"Why, yes. Thank you, Miss Faffle."

The only extraordinary feature about this girl was her uncanny ordinariness. Her mouse-colored hair matched her sallow complexion, and when dressed in one of the drab beige dresses she often wore, the poor girl disappeared right into the wall, unnoticed by even the most observant patients. But today, she almost looked appealing as the primrose petals reflected shades of lavender and pink on her chin.

"It seems you are in good spirits this afternoon, Miss Faffle," he said.

"Oh yes," she whispered. "I've had the most wonderful luncheon. Mr. Gamon, the greengrocer from up the street, took me. I'm sorry I'm late."

"Oh, no bother. It appears Mrs. Snaggs is running behind as well." He took out his pocket watch and frowned. Her treatment was liable to take hours, and now she was late. He turned back toward his office. "Let me know when she arrives, then."

Good for Miss Faffle, he thought as he settled back down behind his desk, though Mr. Gamon did seem an unlikely choice as a suitor. He was a rather coarse fellow, unattractive to say the least, and known for grumbling at customers who mishandled his fruit. And wasn't he known to be a frequenter of disreputable publick houses?

Miss Faffle, on the other hand, was more of the bashful sort. Dr. Whitcraft had met her in the hospital when he had tended her dying father, and was impressed with her calm demeanor in the midst of the ward's gruesome conditions. After her father expired, he had offered her a job.

Now she lived a cloistered and dreary life sharing a tiny flat in Holborn with her mother and three younger siblings. Was Mr. Gamon planning on wooing and whisking away his assistant? He wasn't sure what to make of this development.

The front door opened, followed by the rustle of crinoline.

"Hello? Dr. Whitcraft? Is anyone in?"

Chapter Three

Every few months, The London Society of Physicians sponsored a dinner party. This evening's gathering was more lavish than usual, as it honored Dr. Charles Smatchet, who had recently been named 1829's Physician of the Year. Each new arrival gushed over the doctor, patting his back and offering their most hearty congratulations. Dr. Whitcraft was no exception. With his lovely young fiancée Miss Catherine Reave on his arm, he waded through the crowd toward the man of the hour.

After some appropriate words to Dr. Smatchet and his wife, Dr. Whitcraft grasped Miss Reave by the wrist and pulled her toward the center of the party. It appeared to be an excellent turnout, every room filled with physicians and their spouses, all exchanging pleasantries, sharing amusing medical anecdotes, and commiserating with one another about the details of their practices.

"Where on earth are you taking me, William?" Miss Reave asked, watching the party guests as they, in turn, watched her.

"Just looking for a colleague, my dear." He searched the crowd.

Miss Reave was a beautiful young girl, thin of frame, and tall enough to be mindful of heel height when selecting her shoes for an evening out with the conservatively statured Dr. Whitcraft.

She dressed fashionably, usually in something lightly colored and high-waisted, which accentuated her long lines and pleasing figure. She had fair skin, dark eyes, and rich, chocolate-colored hair sculpted into a still life and set upon the top of her head. Two delicate ringlets on either side of her forehead framed her face like a theater curtain drawn to the sides. She had dark eyebrows and rather a narrow nose that terminated just above her full, lightly shaded lips.

Dr. Whitcraft had known Miss Reave since she was a gawkish girl annoying him with her blushing attentions as he worked alongside her father documenting the hazards of breathing bad air.

Her father had encouraged the attachment, however, often commenting how a sensible, self-made man like Dr. Whitcraft would one day be an ideal match for his whimsical young daughter. Over the years she had bloomed into such a lovely young woman, the captivated Dr. Whitcraft had only recently gathered his courage and asked for her hand. To his delight, she accepted three months ago, days after her eighteenth birthday.

Escorting his fiancée to social occasions also meant keeping track of her rather questionable chaperone, Mrs. Anile. In her heyday, Mrs. Anile had been Miss Reave's governess, guiding her through childhood as an unrelenting taskmaster. A series of apoplectic episodes in her sixties, however, had robbed the woman of her higher faculties and previously unquestionable judgment. Now slow and easily distracted, she had developed a taste for card playing and hard drink. More than likely, Dr. Whitcraft and Miss Reave would spend the latter half of the evening interviewing the servants about the woman's possible whereabouts.

"Ah, there's the man." Dr. Whitcraft guided Miss Reave toward a musty looking gentleman with white whiskers standing by the fireplace and gazing out the window.

"Dr. Forspent, how nice to see you! Miss Reave, I'd like you to meet Dr. Eugene Forspent, one of my mentors from The London Hospital Medical College. He is a renowned expert in the art of bloodletting and humorism. I owe him a great deal."

"Oh nonsense, young man." Dr. Forspent raised his arm and patted Dr. Whitcraft across the shoulders. "Nonsense!" The humility was as false as his teeth.

"And how is *Mrs.* Forspent?" Dr. Whitcraft inquired with a smile, looking around for his wife.

"Oh, she is here somewhere—went to find our hostess I presume. She is well. You know, it will be forty years for us this September."

"Well. How about that."

"Say?" Dr. Forspent inched closer, his face wrinkled with confusion.

Dr. Whitcraft blinked and cleared his throat. "I said…well, how about that!" he shouted as pleasantly as possible at the man's ear.

Dr. Forspent burst into a smile of recognition as Dr. Whitcraft's words penetrated his withered auditory canal. He wet his lips and turned to Miss Reave.

"Miss *Reave* did you say?" He drew himself toward her in anticipation of a reply. "I believe I may have instructed your father, Dr. John Reave."

"Of course you instructed Dr. Reave. He speaks about you all the time," Dr. Whitcraft enunciated in his ear.

Dr. Forspent kept his eyes on Miss Reave. "Yes. How charming to finally meet you, my dear." The ancient physician squeezed the tips of her gloved-fingers with his gnarled blue hands. He hunched over, got very close to her face, and spoke with much gravity. "William Whitcraft was one of the most promising students I ever had the good fortune to instruct. So full of promise, this one. The kind of mind that can offer a real contribution to our field...a problem solver, you know."

Miss Reave smiled and turned to see her fiancée blushing, but not at all displeased with his mentor's affections. "Oh we are lucky to have him," she said, eyes wide and impish.

"Yes. You certainly are. Am I to understand that you are engaged to be married, then?"

"We are indeed." Dr. Whitcraft stood a little straighter and stole another glance at Miss Reave. "Next spring."

"Why that's splendid. Every young physician needs a loving wife by his side, supporting and doting on him. Ah, the hours may be difficult my dear, the sacrifices great, but the rewards will be substantial. The good Lord remembers those who endeavor to comfort the suffering."

Miss Reave nodded, looking past the old man. "Excuse me," she said before leaving the doctor's side to make her way through the crowd toward the champagne and hors d'oeuvres.

"Charming young lady."

"Yes. I am a lucky man," Dr. Whitcraft agreed. "Dr. Forspent, I was hoping I'd see you here today. I have been thinking about you lately. I am toying with a new pursuit, something rather ambitious. I'd be interested to hear your thoughts."

"Certainly, my boy." Dr. Forspent's cloudy blue eyes brightened slightly.

"The use of paroxysm in the treatment of hysteria," Dr. Whitcraft pronounced with a dramatic sweep of his hand.

The mere mention of the object of his research was enough to extinguish the old man's piqued interest. Dr. Forspent rolled his eyes and pursed his lips.

But Dr. Whitcraft remained undeterred. "I'm keen to develop a standard method whereby a physician can elicit a paroxysm in a more reasonable amount of time. Surely it must be possible."

"Ah, that's where you are wrong. In my younger days, when I practiced, I tried method after method, with erratic results. I know it is lucrative, my boy, but leave that business to the midwives. They have much more success."

Dr. Whitcraft frowned. "The midwives I've had the misfortune to encounter are little more than mystics and magicians. They aren't scientists. They don't have the capacity for careful judgment and restraint in dealing with an illness as confounding as hysteria."

A tall, stylish gentleman approached, nodding furiously. "Oh, I couldn't agree with you more. Midwives have no business with these types of patients. I myself have been called in time and time again to right their wrongs. Excuse me, gentlemen. I didn't mean to interrupt your conversation. I am Dr. Edward Marplot."

Dr. Whitcraft extended his hand. What an

impressive individual—rather thin, almost concave, and was at least a head taller than Dr. Whitcraft. His hair, styled into dramatic, lolling waves atop his head, was that certain shade of light brown that towheaded children often acquire as they age. He had cool blue eyes, set perhaps a little too close together atop a rather dignified, patrician nose.

"Very nice to meet you, sir," Dr. Whitcraft said. "Forgive me, but are you the same Marplot who authored an article in *The Lancet* last week regarding the use of hands to divert the body's magnetic fluid?"

"Why yes! One never knows if anyone actually reads those silly academic journals. I'm impressed, Mister..."

He straightened himself. "*Doctor*. Dr. William Whitcraft."

"Oh excuse me, of course. *Doctor* Whitcraft." Dr. Marplot bowed his head, smirking.

Another gentleman appeared from the crowd and gripped Dr. Whitcraft on the shoulder. "Hello! I wondered if you'd be here! Good to see you! And Dr. Marplot and Dr. Forspent." The rather stubby man held a napkin in one hand as he balanced a small plate of savories in the other.

"Ah, Dr. Scamble. How nice to see you, as well." Dr. Whitcraft patted him on the back, nearly toppling his plate.

Dr. Scamble could barely contain his excitement. "Did you sample any of the shrimp? They have them by the bucketful over there. Just delightful! Those little pies with the cream and caviar? Outstanding! Oh, you know, Dr. Whitcraft, I read your paper on the potential uses of the voltaic pile in the treatment of muscle paralysis. Very enlightening, to say the least. I think you're really on to something, there. Very original thoughts, indeed."

"Why thank you," he replied with appropriate academic gravity, glancing over the speaker's shoulder for a glimpse of Miss Reave.

"Have any of you gentlemen seen our host?" Dr. Scamble asked. "I have yet to pay my respects."

"I met him when we arrived. Charming man," Dr. Whitcraft said. "Such a good reputation in London as well."

Dr. Scamble leaned in and whispered, "I guess administering to those society women is paying off. He's got the wives and daughters of at least a dozen earls as patients. Not to mention that he bleeds that lord from parliament, what's his name...oh I can never remember...but anyway, he bleeds him every other week for his indigestion! Imagine the revenue! And look at this house! How much do you think this townhouse cost him?"

"I haven't any idea." Dr. Whitcraft found the talk of money in situations such as this to be vulgar, but the other doctors seemed very interested. It could not be denied that it was an impressive home, however, furnished with all the trappings any professional man might hope one day to possess. "It is certainly lovely," he admitted, glancing around.

"And in this neighborhood, too. Positively the most desirable neighborhood in London," Dr. Marplot added.

"Look at his furniture. I don't know, maybe he's got family money." Dr. Scamble pointed across the room. "Did you see that he's got a collection of over fifty decorative crystal boxes, all imported from France,

I believe. Over there, next to the shrimp."

"Dr. Smatchet told me that a single one is worth over *fifty* pounds," Dr. Marplot said.

"Why that's more than half of what I made all last month!" Dr. Scamble gasped.

"Crystal boxes?" Dr. Whitcraft asked.

"Yes, over there." Dr. Forspent pointed with a crooked finger. "Look, there he is…hovering over them as he pontificates about each one's provenance."

"Hmm," Dr. Whitcraft whispered.

****

As Dr. Whitcraft climbed out of the Hansom cab, the driver hurried back from the house, breathing heavily and looking bedraggled.

"Dr. Whitcraft, Mrs. Anile was really a handful tonight. You'd better look in on her, Miss Reave." The man took her hand and helped her descend from the carriage. "She may need your help to get into her room. And oh…here's her eye patch. She threw it at me. Y'know…I don't think she even knew where she was."

Miss Reave rolled her eyes as she jammed the wadded eye patch into her bag.

"Thank you, sir." Dr. Whitcraft said. "I appreciate the extra effort." He produced a small stack of coins from his pocket and handed them to the driver.

"Why thank you, sir." The man looked into his hand with much approval. He bowed to the pair and jumped atop his cab. With a quick word to the horse, he clopped away into the night.

The moonlight cast a riot of shadows over the empty street. Miss Reave swayed playfully, clinging to Dr. Whitcraft's arm as they walked toward her father's steps. Her bag swung from her wrist and thumped him in the ribs with each step.

She hummed a nondescript tune as they walked, but quieted suddenly. Then she dropped his arm and bounded up the steps, giggling all the while. Dr. Whitcraft wondered how many glasses of champagne she had managed to drink while he wasn't looking.

"Did you enjoy yourself this evening?" he called, noticing her bare neck. She should be covered in this cold evening air.

"Why of course I did. I find all that doctor talk to be *so* enlightening."

"Splendid." It crossed his mind that her words could be construed as sarcasm, but he was quick to dismiss the notion. He climbed the stairs and stopped. She towered over him from the top step. She was blinking slowly, hypnotically flashing her eyes at him.

"I want you to kiss me," she whispered.

Dr. Whitcraft swallowed hard. Propriety dictated that this request must be refused outright. They were in public after all, and he certainly wouldn't want her reputation sullied should anyone observe such a careless moment of abandon. But he glanced around anyway, noting that they were indeed alone.

Truth be told, he had only kissed her twice since their recent engagement; once when she'd accepted his proposal of marriage, in private, of course, away from the eyes of her father, and again when she had entrapped him unawares in a darkened hallway. Not that he was averse to her feminine charms, however. Quite the contrary. Dr. Whitcraft was instead tormented by the fear that even the slightest waver in his resolve may lead to a cascade of animal carnality, unthinkable if directed at an incorrupt flower like Miss Reave.

These fears lingered still as he looked up into her dark eyes…so bewitching, her fair skin flushed with the chill of the night air. He could feel his rationality disintegrate, dispersing into the ether only to be replaced by the basest of male desires. He followed the sublime lines of her cheek down to the nape of neck, enrapt all the while by the slow rise and fall of her chest.

Suddenly, like a starving man lunging on a crust of bread, he cast his walking stick aside and leaped up, gathering her surprised form in his arms and delivering a most sinfully lustful kiss. She moaned in approval and returned his fervor, wrapping her arms around his neck, and pulling herself in closer still.

The proximity of his fiancée's unfamiliar curves was intoxicating. She was so immediate, so willingly pressed against his body that Dr. Whitcraft's excitement had been most discernibly stirred.

Both actors froze, and Miss Reave pulled back, revealing wide eyes as she glanced down at the urgent development now between them; a presence not unlike that of a third person. A look of devilish thrill settled onto her face, and she lifted her eyes to meet his.

The sight of his young fiancée betraying the knowledge of his compromised condition so embarrassed the doctor that he catapulted himself away and would have fallen down the stairs had he not managed to grab onto the scrolls of the cast iron railing.

Breathlessly, he declared, "Oh…oh, I'm so sorry." He pulled a handkerchief from his waistcoat pocket and mopped his lips. "How…how absolutely *inappropriate* of me." He glanced at the front window certain he would see her enraged father glaring at them from within, or worse, soaring out of the front door to thrash him on the spot. Mercifully, however, the window was empty and the front door remained still.

"*William...*" she purred in a coquettish singsong, smiling once again as she stepped closer, her fingers grazing his arm as they traveled up, tickling their way to his chin.

He spun away. "You know," he coughed, retreating backwards down the steps avoiding her eyes, "you really shouldn't drink so much."

She frowned at this, and then looked careless. "Well, is this good night, then, my darling doctor?"

"I think so…yes…yes." He brought his hand to his temple, squinting up at her.

"Will you call on me tomorrow?" she asked with the sweetness of an innocent.

"Yes, of course." He lowered his voice and inhaled. "Please tell your father I finished his paper this morning. I've had some thoughts—"

But she had disappeared into the house, leaving him standing on the steps alone. Dr. Whitcraft sighed and descended the remaining stairs. He tugged at his frockcoat and gingerly bent to retrieve his discarded walking stick. After one more look back at the Reave's front door, he turned and walked toward his home less than a mile away.

Inside the house, Miss Reave smiled to herself as she stumbled down the darkened hallway, making her way to the parlor where her father had been kind enough to leave a lamp burning. She fell onto the couch, tossing her bag aside. She stared at it for a moment, and then pulled it onto her lap. When she tugged at the drawstring, its contents spilled out—a mother of pearl hair comb, Mrs. Anile's wadded eye-patch, a house key, and an exquisite little crystal box.

Chapter Four

Dr. Whitcraft had hoped the brisk walk home would help coax his perturbed humors back into their proper state, but alas, it hadn't worked. Striding faster and counting his respirations had done little to dismiss the image of Miss Reave from his mind. Distracted, he approached his front steps with key in hand, but stopped suddenly. After a moment's reflection, he turned and headed to an entirely different destination.

He now found himself on Upper Newman Street in the Covent Garden, gripping his walking stick a little tighter. If things got out of hand in this rather infamous part of London, it might be necessary to use it as a weapon.

There were many lurkers out tonight, their numbers visible under the street lamps recently added courtesy of *The London Society of Manners*, an organization to which Miss Reave enthusiastically belonged.

But the gaslights, rather than dissipating the disreputable element, seemed to make them collect like moths, bathing under the green glow, waiting for whatever untoward rendezvous might be negotiated under their blazing night watch.

Tonight's collection of miscreants appeared occupied by their own distractions, however, paying Dr. Whitcraft little notice as he approached the modest but well-kept house number 3. The light burning in the front window was obscured by gauzy white curtains, its presence like a beacon of welcome. He stepped to the unremarkable front door and engaged the knocker five times—not more, not less. After a moment, an angel-faced young woman appeared.

"Ah, come in, come in." She stepped aside to let him pass, a cup of spirits clutched crookedly in her hand. She ambled behind him as he made his way into the parlor, which was more quiet this evening than usual.

"Brandy and water, right?"

"Nothing for me, thank you. Does your mistress have an engagement this evening? I thought perhaps she'd be at the theater."

"Oh no, she's in. She's been out of sorts, though. Is that why you came by?" The girl gave him a mischievous wink that the doctor chose to ignore.

"Out of sorts, how?"

"Ask her yourself...she's in bed." The girl yawned and went out of the way to brush herself against him as she passed.

Dr. Whitcraft watched the girl glide down the hall and turn into one of the rooms at the end. Adjusting his spectacles, he followed her path but stopped at the first door and knocked.

"Yes?" a hoarse voice answered from within.

"Mrs. Minnock? It's Dr. Whitcraft. May I come in?"

A dry cough followed a faint, "Come in...come in."

He opened the door and a dim flicker from a single candle illuminated a weary looking Mrs. Minnock. She had a nightcap pulled over her fair hair and her face was flushed pink with fever. She smiled, but coughed again at once.

He tossed his walking stick aside and hurried over. "My goodness! Why didn't you send someone to get me earlier? You are unwell." He dug a handkerchief out of his pocket and handed it to her. She dabbed her mouth as he rested his hand on her cheek. "How long have you had this fever?"

"I've had the cough all week, but the fever started today. I knew if you came here you'd want to bleed me."

"I should leave and get my bag this instant."

"Send one of the girls to go get it."

"At this time of night? No…" He paused, contemplating that for a moment. "No, I won't take long."

"I don't even know what time it is. Oh my…" She sat up, squinting at him. "Didn't anyone get you a brandy and water?"

"I'm taking a leave from spirits."

"Only spirits?" She grinned and placed her hand on his thigh.

He furrowed his brow. "Are you coughing anything up? Blood? Bile?"

She sighed. "Such a disgusting question. No, I don't think so."

"Eating?"

"Yes, of course." She studied him. Even bloodshot with fever, her eyes still shone a pleasing blue. "You look so dashing, all dressed up. Have you just come from a gathering?"

"Mmm hmm. Physician of the year dinner."

"Ah yes." With that she broke into another fit of

deep coughing.

After she quieted, he picked up an empty glass from the side table and gestured at her with it. "It is crucial you drink water, do you understand? Get one of the girls to make certain this stays full. Which one of them should I tell—"

"You don't usually come here on a *Friday*," she said, her eyebrows raised. "Are your humors out of sorts this evening, Dr. Whitcraft?" She grinned as if not particularly expecting an answer. Not getting one, she shrugged and pointed to the decanter of brandy on her dressing table. "You are abstaining, doctor, but I'm not. Pour me some, if you please."

"Just a moment." Frowning, he set the glass back down and leaned over her, placing his hands under her chin. With a light touch, he palpated her neck. "Hold still, now," he whispered. Satisfied, he sat on the bed and placed his ear next to her chest. "Take in a deep breath, if you please."

"Brandy, if *you* please," she whispered.

"Yes, yes." He pulled back with stern eyes. "I don't want you receiving any visitors until this fever clears up, do you understand? Let the girls manage their own affairs for the next few days, as well. They need to let you rest."

She turned her mouth under and cast her eyes toward the sheets. "I barely see any 'visitors' as you say," she muttered. "But I think you are aware of that, doctor."

He softened his professional countenance, and put his hand on hers. It was very hot. "I'm sorry you're not feeling well, Mrs. Minnock."

She smiled and laced her fingers between his. He

squeezed back, and the two sat in silence for a time. Finally, he let go, stood and poured her a small dose from the decanter.

"I'm going to my office to get my stethoscope. I'll find you something for that cough, as well."

"Wait. Would you like me to call one of the others for you?" she teased, taking the glass of brandy from his hand. "Before you go, Lilly or…"

Dr. Whitcraft felt himself redden as he reached for the door. "Don't be ridiculous. I'll be back within the hour."

****

Dr. Whitcraft was exhausted. It had been a late night at Mrs. Minnock's house. In all likelihood the poor woman had bronchitis. She was quite ill, so he had stayed up most of the night with her, applying cold compresses for the fever and lavender oil to her chest to ease her breathing. It was dawn by the time he made it back home.

When Miss Faffle arrived this morning, she discovered him asleep at his desk with his head in the middle of a treatise on hysteria, still sporting last night's dress clothes. But he had summoned his reserves, put the reading aside, and ascended the stairs to clean himself up for the new workday. So far, it had been a busy morning.

He replaced the lid on the mercurial ointment with a firm twist and proceeded to rinse his hands again in the washbasin. Mr. Brim sat on the edge of the examining table looking vulnerable in his long, blousy shirt while his legs dangled over the edge. His waistcoat had been removed and draped to the side and his trousers and small clothes hung in a bunch around his ankles. Oddly, however, he had neglected to remove his top hat.

"May I pull up my trousers now, doctor?" the patient said in a whisper.

"Give the ointment another few minutes to dry if you please, sir."

Mr. Brim glanced down at the creamy sheen. He took a deep breath and pursed his lips.

"No, no! It's oil-based. Blowing on it won't help," the doctor said. "Let it soak in...just another few minutes."

Mr. Brim's shoulders slumped even lower.

"Reapply the ointment several times a day, after meals would be best...taking extra care with the discolored areas. I must reemphasize that there is to be no—"

"Yes, I know. No contact with the opposite sex. I understand completely."

"For the next several weeks. Minimum."

As Mr. Brim nodded at the doctor, his wadded trousers and small clothes slipped over his shoes and landed on the floor with a soft thump. He stared at them, close to despondency.

"Now, Mr. Brim..." Dr. Whitcraft began in a serious tone. "This is the third episode in a relatively short time, and today's variation is a serious one. Perhaps your wife should come see me as well."

"This doesn't concern her," he whispered, looking up from the floor.

"I see. Well, as your physician, I hazard to say, without judgment of course, that in the interest of preventing future unpleasantness, you may want to consider confining your *activities* within the boundaries of your marriage."

Mr. Brim shifted his weight. "That option has been unavailable to me. You see, my wife…well, she has been away visiting, uh…her sister, with consumption." He stared at Dr. Whitcraft, offering a resolute nod with each additional detail.

"Well, I'm sorry to hear that." The doctor rose and walked toward his patient, ducking to take a closer look. "I believe the matter is quite dry now. You may reclaim your trousers at your leisure, sir."

Mr. Brim hopped down from the table and fumbled with his small clothes.

"You know, if marital activity isn't possible, and you sense that…well, that a release of certain, tormenting masculine humors is in order, prudence must still be the guiding factor."

Mr. Brim danced one leg into his trousers. "But you warned me at my last visit against… against handling the matter *myself*—"

"Good Lord!" Dr. Whitcraft cried. "Sir, it is an unquestionable medical fact that the manipulation of one's *self* in order to achieve that particular outcome is terribly, terribly dangerous, not only to one's general constitution, but to the soundness of one's mind."

"Then, what am I to do?"

"Well…" Dr. Whitcraft shrugged and tried to measure his tone. "Perhaps a more judicious selection of candidates is in order." He hated to sound as if he were scolding his patient. No one would ever be honest with a doctor who scolded them, after all.

"I understand that, but how am I to tell which ones are…up to snuff?"

"As I believe I advised you at your last visit,

sometimes a visual inspection can be helpful. I'm fairly certain that in this latest episode, had you taken the time to inspect the young lady's, er…well…gave *her* a good once-over, why you may not be in this predicament."

"Hmmm." Mr. Brim's eyes roamed the floor. "It was very dark, doctor."

"Uh…you could've used a lantern, to take a quick look."

"That crossed my mind, I do say, but I was afraid that the light would attract the police."

"The police?"

"Quite. I was in an alleyway, against the back wall of the stables—in the rookery. The clattering of the pitchforks made enough noise. The light would have been like a beacon."

"Well, good Lord!" Dr. Whitcraft's insides tightened in revulsion.

"I wasn't alone, you know. There were several other fellows."

"Any female who does not have access to the inside of a building should not even be considered for such an enterprise."

"A *building*? Well that could get rather pricy, I'm afraid," Mr. Brim replied, indignant.

"Your health may well be worth the indulgence, sir, not to mention that disreputable characters of that sort would likely not think twice about knocking you over the head and making off with your money." Dr. Whitcraft had recently been forced to attend The London Society of Manners symposium regarding the decay of morality in the city of London, specifically detailing the bloom in prostitution and its aftereffects over the last several decades. The horror stories shared at that meeting had shocked and thrilled its attendees.

Now fully dressed, Mr. Brim adjusted his top hat, dropped his arms to his sides and stared at the door as if yearning to pass through it.

Taking the hint, Dr. Whitcraft stood as well. "Sir, I hope I have given you something to think about." He walked to the door. "Caution, prudence. If money is the issue, perhaps saving for a few weeks might be worthwhile. Perhaps then you could afford an up-grade. Maybe discover an offering with a bit of privacy, at least." He opened the door.

A heavy-set woman with a bonnet choked around her larynx stood at Miss Faffle's desk surrounded by a collection of small children. She turned and her eyes widened in delight. "Why Father Benison, how wonderful! I almost didn't recognize you without your vestments. Look children, it's Father Benison. I had no idea you were a patient of Dr. Whitcraft. You're not ill, are you, Father?"

Dr. Whitcraft heard the air leaving the lungs of his patient.

"Why, no…Mrs. Pursy. No." He spoke as if someone had a vice-grip on his middle.

The children giggled, picking at and pushing one another; a few of the younger ones peeked from behind their mother's skirt.

"Well then." Dr. Whitcraft took a breath as he glanced around the room. "Miss Faffle, please schedule…*Father Benison,* here for a follow-up appointment two weeks from today, for his…*cough.*"

Even the unperceptive Miss Faffle sat open-mouthed, managing to grasp the rather delicate nature of this situation. At the doctor's words, however, she remembered herself, dipped a pen in the ink and scribbled on the schedule.

"Mr. Brim", donning a well-rehearsed expression of benevolence mixed with dread, forced a not particularly convincing cough. Dr. Whitcraft leaned close and rapped him on the back with one hand while tucking the mercurial ointment into the man's waistcoat pocket with the other.

He grunted an acknowledgement to his doctor, and promptly gathered speed toward the door. "Mrs. Pursy, lovely to see you. Children…mind your mother."

"See you Sunday, Father," the oldest boy called after the slamming door.

Dr. Whitcraft was certain that the Pursys did not notice Father Benison breaking into a cold sprint the moment his feet hit the pavement, or that his hat had been sheared off and was tumbling in his wake. The doctor, however, shook his head at the sight, and supposed he would likely never see the man again.

Mrs. Pursy, meanwhile, scolded her youngest boy, and pried Miss Faffle's paper knife from the chubby clench of his fist. Miss Faffle took the knife back and tucked it in her desk. "Why don't you all have a seat while I prepare the examining room."

Miss Faffle hurried around the swirling children. Dr. Whitcraft followed closely behind. Once inside, she dabbed at the stray drops of mercurial ointment on the table. "My goodness, Dr. Whitcraft, that was…"

"Yes, it was. Quite. I wouldn't have taken him for a papist, let alone…well, no matter." He picked up a bottle and studied its label. "I need to straighten out Mrs. Pursy's purgatives. We should have a break after that, yes?"

37

"Oh no, doctor. There's another pelvic massage scheduled straight after Mrs. Pursy. Mrs. Fussock."

Dr. Whitcraft winced. Last time Mrs. Fussock was on the table for over two hours before she herself got fed up and left.

"Miss Faffle, I will be undertaking a new endeavor. I simply must do something to improve this pelvic massage business."

"Oh, sir, that *would* make a difference, wouldn't it?"

"Unquestionably. I have some ideas, perhaps new ways to address the anatomy. Or, better yet, maybe I can craft a device to aid with the matter. Regardless, I'll need some test subjects eventually. I know it's rather awkward, but do you think you could possibly find me some subjects—females who would be willing to undergo pelvic massage while I work out a new process? I would pay them a small incentive, of course…"

"Oh. Why, yes, sir. I could try to find some women for you." She was so eager to please him.

"That would be splendid. Just splendid. Let me know if you get any takers. The sooner I can begin the better."

Chapter Five

Dr. Whitcraft adjusted his glasses and licked his lips in anticipation. With the voltaic pile in place, and everything in order, all he had to do now was gather his courage and engage the damn thing.

Several years ago, he had become fascinated by the exciting new work with electricity being done by Italian physicist Alessandro Volta. The man had discovered that by placing discs of alternating types of metal in a stack and then submerging the whole business in saltwater, an electrical stream would be generated out of the top and bottom contacts. The invention was called the voltaic pile.

The moment he had read about it, Dr. Whitcraft planned to make one of his own. The science behind electricity fascinated him. He had always suspected something that powerful may have a medicinal application, as long as it could be thoroughly controlled and consistently managed. He had even published a paper regarding potential medical uses for electricity that had been very well received.

After collecting the necessary parts and spending a few hours tinkering with it, he had indeed been successful in building his own version of the voltaic pile. But, like any other new toy, eventually he grew bored and tucked it away in the bottom of a cabinet where it stayed, all but forgotten.

But this morning, after reading yet another article regarding pelvic massage, it had occurred to him that perhaps the voltaic pile's electrical stream could somehow aid in the generation of a consistent paroxysm. Perhaps electricity was the key! Thrilled with this possibility, he dug out his old experiment. It had been necessary to refit the housing and make a new solution of brine, but within an hour he had managed to get the thing back into working order. Now, it was up to him to test it.

As he stared at his handiwork, he surmised that bringing the two contacts together on his skin might smart a bit, but he had to see what the sensation would be like. Goodness knows he would never do anything to cause his patients undue discomfort.

The anticipation was terrible as he looked down at the X he had drawn on his arm, but after reflecting on the sacrifices one must make in a life dedicated to medicine, Dr. Whitcraft took a deep breath, shut his eyes, and jammed the two ends together.

There was a sizzling snap, and a shower of sparks burst from the contacts, simultaneous with a vibrating sting that pierced his arm like a railroad spike. He shrieked, falling backwards through the smoke, landing hard on the floor where he heard himself deliver a most unprofessional staccato of profanity.

Miss Faffle appeared over top him. "Oh doctor! Doctor? Are you all right?"

But it wasn't his stricken assistant that had captured his attention, but rather the dancing orange glow growing atop his desk behind her. Luckily, she saw it too, and grabbed a hefty volume from his shelf with both hands, smacking down the pyre with a thud.

Smoke curled into a cloud and hovered over the scene.

"Well done, Miss Faffle. Well done," he whispered.

"Are you all right, sir?" She fanned the toasted treatise over his desk. The burnt binding smelled acrid.

"Yes, yes, I'm...just give me a minute." He skimmed his fingers over his singed arm.

"Oh, that gave me such a fright!"

"Yes." Dr. Whitcraft got to his feet and dropped back into his chair. "I wasn't quite expecting that either. I forgot how *powerful* this *damn thing* is."

He straightened his glasses and watched the smoke enrobe Miss Faffle as she exited his office. With trembling hands, he shuffled his papers, dismayed to see the majority of his notes were now peppered with tiny black holes, some of which were still smoking. He shook his head and groaned.

****

Mrs. Brabble pulled at her gloves as she marched toward Miss Faffle's desk. Dr. Whitcraft trailed behind, massaging his right hand.

"Again, Mrs. Brabble, I assure you...even though th-the *resolution* in question was not obtained on this particular occasion, I can say with the utmost confidence that the very *process* of the treatment does indeed offer a therapeutic effect." But his words sounded hollow even to himself.

"Did you expect me to stay on that table for the entire day, Dr. Whitcraft?" She smoothed out her dress and straightened herself. "I had an engagement over an hour ago. I'm sure that my fellow members of *The Society for the Prevention of Our Ruin* were at a loss wondering what became of me. And *I* was to give the closing remarks, after all! Frankly, I am beginning to wonder about this treatment of yours. Are you even capable of doing it correctly?"

Dr. Whitcraft felt his face flush. "Madam! You yourself know that it has worked in the past. Feel free to seek a second opinion if you like. Any other physician in London is likely to have the same difficulty." He tried not to sound as desperate as he felt.

But Mrs. Brabble remained unconvinced. "Regardless, I shouldn't be required to pay for today's appointment. My husband's finances should not have to suffer because of your incompetence."

"Madam..." He struggled to maintain himself. "The terms of our agreement have always been clear. When you gave your consent for this treatment, it was with the understanding that...it can sometimes be rather tricky—"

"It didn't work! Simple as that! Do you deny it?"

"I am not denying anything, Mrs. Brabble, but you must realize that I have invested a significant amount of time and professional resources on your treatment today. You cannot expect me to just waive my fee."

Nearby, Miss Faffle tracked the conversation like it was a particularly gripping match of tennis.

"Are you seriously telling me that I should be required to pay for a result that you could not achieve? Really? My husband will be unhappy to hear this...very unhappy indeed."

Dr. Whitcraft winced. Her husband was a prominent businessman and fixture of London society. Perhaps this argument wasn't worth it. He glanced at Miss Faffle, who responded with a shrug.

"Perhaps...perhaps we can agree to a *reduction* in

my fee…on this occasion, because you did miss your engagement after all."

"Only a reduction?" Mrs. Brabble tugged at her gloves again with a smirk, sensing an imminent victory.

The unpleasant Mr. Buzznack, who had been waiting in silence for his appointment, chimed in, "Well, if *she* doesn't have to pay, I don't see why I should. Nothing you do makes this gout any better."

"Sir, this matter does not concern you," Dr. Whitcraft snapped.

Another hysteria patient approached his front steps now, and Mrs. Snaggs was even older and meaner than Mrs. Brabble. Dr. Whitcraft grimaced at the sight. This matter needed to be resolved and quickly, too before Mrs. Snaggs could overhear it.

"Yes. All right," he whispered like a beaten man. "I'll refund your fee, for goodness' sake. Miss Faffle will see to the details...I need to step away, to make some notes and such." He shut his office door and leaned against it. He would hide in here until that woman left, he decided, dropping his head in defeat. After a moment he looked up. His eyes traveled across his desk and settled on the ugly, black scar left from the voltaic pile disaster. He shook his head and then stiffened as the booming baritone of his next hysteria patient floated through the door.

"Over two and a half hours? Good gracious! The man's an amateur!"

****

Given that his first crack at crafting a device to assist with pelvic massage had nearly put him out of commission, Dr. Whitcraft decided to be a bit more cautious with his next endeavor.

Miss Faffle peeked into his office from the doorway. "What are you doing, doctor?"

He sat behind his desk with his sleeves rolled up; a variety of parts and mechanisms cluttered his desk, all surrounding a wooden housing that he had constructed earlier. He grunted while attempting to fit together several parts taken from a nonfunctioning timepiece.

"Well, Miss Faffle," he adjusted a particularly stubborn gear, "I'm attempting to devise some type of…arrangement if you will, something that would make the whole pelvic massage experience easier on the physician. Something that will require a different subset of muscles, a different type of dexterity, perhaps…reducing the fatigue." He hunched over further still as he tinkered, stopping periodically to consult a drawing he had made.

"What's that crank for, Dr. Whitcraft?" She inched closer.

"I was considering attaching it to this, but now I'm not sure. I think I may need some more gears, on the flip side, there. And I'll need a smoother surface for that articulating flat part."

"I see."

He picked up a screwdriver and tightened another gear, but something snapped off of the device. Several ball bearings rolled across the desk and bounced onto the floor.

"Damn," he whispered. "Excuse me, Miss Faffle. That keeps happening."

"One of your little flippers has fallen down there, too, doctor." She knelt and pointed under his chair just as the front door clapped open. She stood back up and gestured at someone. "You can just sit over there, miss." She turned to Dr. Whitcraft. "The last of your test subjects has arrived."

"Ah, yes." He put his invention aside and got to his feet, rolling his shirtsleeves back down. His device might not be ready to test yet, but there were other possibilities he had planned to consider. He smoothed his hair then strode around his desk, but stopped in the doorway to observe his reception room with a pleasant, but academic air.

Three female test subjects were indeed waiting, most certainly enough to keep him busy all afternoon. A closer inspection, however, revealed that these women were not exactly the cream of the crop. In fact, each one looked more haggard than the next.

The girl closest to the examining room wore an age-yellowed cap atop her wiry bramble of hair. She beamed at him, and her smile revealed a scant collection of teeth jutting from her gums like shards of brown glass. Dr. Whitcraft silently contemplated her, and then turned to the next subject. The second girl slouched in the seat and appeared unconscious, her chin doubling as it rose and fell on her chest.

The third subject made a sudden *hmpf* sound and shifted her weight from one hip to the other, glaring at him as if he had already wronged her. Her face was full, her cheeks distended to such a degree that her eyes were barely visible, although her scowl was unquestionable. Her large blousy shirt tented over her belly, which hung low and heavy over the top of her skirt. Was it even advisable to attempt his experiments with pelvic massage on a woman who was with child?

Miss Faffle, meanwhile, had returned to her desk, humming whilst she arranged and rearranged the flowers she had brought back from her luncheon date.

"Ladies, thank you all for coming!" He clasped his hands in a prayer-like gesture. "I'm not certain what Miss Faffle here has told you—"

"She 'asn't told us anything," the standing-girl exclaimed, shifting her weight again.

Dr. Whitcraft drew in a breath, looking at her over his glasses. "Miss, you are expecting a child, I believe it may be best to disqualify you from being a subject."

"Wot the...? I'm bloody well not expectin' a child!" She looked down at her front, and then back at him with outrage. Her face turned dark. "At least, I don't fink I am..." She glanced at the other women while chewing on her lip.

"I see. Well, then..." Dr. Whitcraft cleared his throat. "The reason you are here is because there is a new procedure that—"

The one who had been asleep sat up and brought her knees together. "Is it gonna 'urt?"

"And 'ow much are yer gonna pay us?" the other added right before she spit an unsightly blob on the area rug.

"Oh dear," he whispered under his breath as he looked at his floor. "Uh, no... it shouldn't be that uncomfortable, and yes, you will be compensated for your time. I suppose we should just begin, then. I'll need to see you one at a time. I suppose that would be the best way to proceed."

The woman with the brown teeth stood up and walked past him toward the examining room. "I'll do it first. I 'ave to be back by two."

Dr. Whitcraft followed, but paused in the doorway. He turned back to Miss Faffle. "I shouldn't be more than a half an hour."

She nodded, but then stopped him, "Oh, Dr. Whitcraft, the phosphorous bottle and the pocket matches are already in there, by the basin, but—" she lifted a wooden box from beneath her desk—"here are the rest of the items you asked me to collect."

"Oh, why, thank you. I almost forgot." He rummaged through the box. A magnifying glass, a concave mirror with a candle fixed to the front, and a stopwatch were at the ready. "Capital," he said.

He gave a final acknowledgment to Miss Faffle and balanced the box in one hand while pulling the examining room door shut with the other. He turned around, a smile of nervous anticipation on his lips, and then gasped. His volunteer was stark naked—arms and legs spread wide as she gracelessly scaled his table.

"Oh! Ma'am...my goodness." He averted his eyes. "Let me get you a dressing gown, please! To preserve your modesty." He set the box aside and hurried toward the washbasin, plucking a linen gown from atop a stack. With his head turned away, he unfurled it and sidled toward her with an arm extended. "Uh, miss...here is the—"

It was snatched out of his hand. From the strange, stale smell hovering in the air, it seemed this young woman was a complete stranger to soap and hot water. He would have to remember to tell Miss Faffle to use extra rosemary when freshening the room, but for now, he tried not to breathe in too deeply.

"Now, madam." He took the magnifying glass out of the box and rolled his sleeve back up, "Let me explain what I am after here."

****

"Miss Faffle, honestly." The last of his test subjects disappeared into the street. "Where in heavens name did you find such a disgraceful lot of women? Two of them were syphilitic and the other had symptoms I've never seen in all of my days as a clinician. I can't begin to describe what…" He shook his head; the vision of it all was too fresh.

Miss Faffle looked stricken, more so than usual. "Oh no! I am *so* sorry, sir!" She stood up, wringing her hands as she walked around her desk. "Well, I didn't know how to go about finding you any subjects for your study, so I mentioned it to Mr. Gamon at luncheon the other day." She looked down at her hands and twisted her fingers in a knot. "He told me he would take care of it."

"Good Lord," Dr. Whitcraft muttered, walking back into the examining room to give his hands another thorough dousing with the lye soap.

****

"Water pressure?" Mrs. Minnock laughed. "Like with a hose?"

"Yes, and I fail to see why that is so amusing to you. The implement directs a constant stream of water toward the patient's nether region. A French fellow invented it, I believe. They've been using it for years in France and here in England as well, but of course it requires expensive equipment, not to mention a spa-like shower setting to get the job done. It's impractical, of course, for all but the most solvent patients."

She laughed even harder now. Tears streamed down her cheeks. Dr. Whitcraft quit speaking and frowned. "You know, I never would have brought this up if I'd known you would react this childishly. Usually you are unaffected by my professional talk."

She shook her head, wiping the tears from her eyes. "I'm sorry, but I had no idea this was even an issue. How long have you been working on this?"

"For the better part of three weeks now, and I'm afraid I'm no closer to a solution than when I began. I've read everything on the subject, conferred with other doctors, I've had female test subjects queued up in my office, but still...no results to even speak of. The contraption I built to manage the job fell off of my desk and is in pieces. I don't think I can bear to reconstruct it, as it never seemed to work, anyway."

"Well, you have been going about this all wrong. The first person you should have come to when you began this endeavor was *me*."

"You?"

"Yes. Me." She threw off the sheets and stepped out of the bed making no effort to cover herself. She walked to the dressing table and poured herself a glass of brandy. She held out an empty glass. "Are you still abstaining?"

"Where is your dressing gown? You just got over a serious illness and now you are parading around without a stitch of clothing on! Good Lord!"

"I've been perfectly fine for at least two weeks...and do you know that out of the few gentleman acquaintances I see, you are the only one who complains about my candid nature. You are really very stodgy for a young man," she teased, with one hand on her hip.

Mrs. Minnock was a petite woman, fair and freckled, unquestionably impressive for her natural, unembellished beauty. It seemed impossible that someone so young was already a widow. She couldn't have been more than twenty-eight years old.

She shook her head before taking a long sip. "I can solve your problem, you know. I happen to know how to guarantee a successful…what did you call it, again?"

"Paroxysm?"

"Yes. That. I know how to assure one every time, and in less than *ten* minutes."

Dr. Whitcraft laughed and shook his head. "Would that were true…"

"I'm serious." She dropped her hand from her hip. "Hasn't it occurred to you that I make it my business to know such things?"

"We are talking about medicine, for goodness' sake. Medicine! Not the amorous pursuits that are within your domain of expertise."

"Oh, I see. Isn't *medicine* the reason you're here? Don't you love to tell me that you partake in my services out of a medical need to keep the humors of your body in balance?" Mrs. Minnock rolled her eyes then walked to her door. She leaned out into the hall. "Lilly? Would you come in here, please?"

After a moment, a sleepy young girl wearing nightclothes entered the room, completely unfazed by the nude state of Mrs. Minnock.

"Lilly would you object to being part of a demonstration here for the good doctor?"

Lilly shrugged, watching the red-faced doctor pull the blankets up to the underside of his chin. She giggled. "I thought he was a conventional sort of fellow."

"Oh, it's nothing like that. This is *medicine*, right Dr. Whitcraft?" Mrs. Minnock winked and turned to

Lilly. "Have a lie down next to the doctor, dear, so I can show him something."

****

"Extraordinary!" Had he been clothed, Dr. Whitcraft would have jumped to his feet. "You are telling me that with those five steps you can achieve this exact result *every time*?"

"Of course. I said you should've come to me first. Lilly, my dear, you can leave us now."

Lilly's face was still flushed. She swallowed hard before sitting up on the edge of the bed. She tossed her hair back and staggered her way to the door, picking up her discarded dressing gown and dragging it behind her.

As the door shut, the doctor blurted, "Where on earth did you learn that?"

"From my husband, of course," Mrs. Minnock sat herself down on the bed. "I've told you about him. He was a sea captain and traveled extensively, the darling, all over the world. God only knows where he picked it up, but he returned from an expedition one year and surprised me with *that*." She smiled at the remembrance. "Most men would have brought back a trinket of some kind, I suppose... I never dreamed it had a medical application."

"My goodness! How often did he do that to you? It could have been dangerous! Something as forceful as *that* could put the inner workings of the female anatomy into complete disarray. Repeated paroxysm in an otherwise healthy patient could induce strangulation of the uterus and possibly *cause* hysteria. You are lucky to have escaped your husband's whimsy intact."

"Oh please! There's nothing dangerous about that. You saw Lilly. She's happy as can be. She's probably going back to bed."

Dr. Whitcraft sat up, his bare chest exposed now, his hands interlocked while he puzzled and calculated. "Regardless, I must be able to reproduce those steps. Frankly it looked a bit complicated…but you must teach me to do it!" He shook his head. "You get that same result every time? In *less than ten minutes*?"

"Of course. I can get the job done under five, actually, but that would require the introduction of an object—one your society women may not appreciate."

"Oh good Lord, no!" He reduced his tone to a whisper. "If I were to attempt this…there must be no….*infiltration,* you see…of *any* kind."

"You saw for yourself, there was plainly no inner access. Good gracious.*"* Mrs. Minnock climbed back under the blankets. "Give it a try on me if you like…I'm not afraid of the dangers." She brought herself closer to him. "Oh, you're right. I was cold."

She shivered, but the doctor's expression was impatient. "All right, all right…" She threw off the covers and looked at him with a bemused smile. "Give me your hand, and I'll show you…"

****

Dr. Whitcraft dashed into his office and flung himself into his chair. He had knocked over a stack of books on the floor, but he didn't care because he must begin writing at once, while it was all still fresh in his mind. He scribbled a few crude diagrams at first, with a paragraph of explanation after each. But he must make certain to accurately delineate each of the five steps. He could go back and redo the drawings, adding more detail later.

As he wrote, he laughed out loud in the empty

office. It was too good to be true! It would change the practice of treating hysteria...it would change his entire life. But he had to test it, and rigorously, too before he dared publish anything.

He must reproduce the maneuver on his patients tomorrow. He had two hysterics already booked as it happened, but he needed more. Perhaps he could call on Dr. Vorago and Dr. Scamble. They would certainly give him a crack at their hysteria patients if he let them keep the fee...oh he couldn't wait! He paused, tipping his chair back to gaze up at the ceiling. After a moment of giggling, he spoke out loud with deliberate enunciation.

"The Maneuver. *The Whitcraft Maneuver.*"

Chapter Six

Dr. Whitcraft smiled at his first hysteric of the morning. She was a rather thick woman in her late forties who had been cursed with melancholy since the sudden death of her husband several years ago.

"That's it, Mrs. Junters." He spoke in his most cheerful voice as he helped her onto the table. The woman had a tendency to be suspicious of anything novel, so he would have to approach her with extra sensitivity. "There you are. Now, Mrs. Junters, your treatment is going to be a little different, today."

"Different?" Her eyes followed him as he made his way around the examining table. "Should …should I be nervous, doctor?"

"Why no, not at all." He pulled the drape over her legs, struggling to couch his excitement in well-rehearsed professional detachment. "There's a little something new I'd like to try…something that may make this whole business go very much faster. But remember, relaxation is key." He sat at the foot of the table and took a deep breath. "So let's just give it a go, then, shall we?"

Truth be told, Dr. Whitcraft was even more nervous than she. He desperately wanted this to work on an actual patient like it had so astonishingly well last night on Lilly and Mrs. Minnock.

He began to roll up his sleeves, but then stopped. It

was all there, right in front of him, but the five steps. What if he got them out of order? Once you began you couldn't stop, and starting over could ruin the whole process.

"Just a moment, please, Mrs. Junters." He jumped to his feet and hurried to the basin where he had left his notes. He shuffled through them, mouthing out each step. Yes…that was it, he thought, glancing at his patient who was staring at the ceiling.

Then an idea occurred to him. Surely she would never know if he cheated and used his notes. He only needed one hand for the maneuver, and perhaps it wouldn't be too unprofessional if he held his notes with the other. From her vantage point, she couldn't see what he was up to, anyway.

Decision made, he tucked the notes behind him and strode back to the table. He leaned over and smiled at his patient, even as his heart thundered within his chest. "All right then, Mrs. Junters. Let's have at it."

He sat down, studying the first page. With renewed confidence, Dr. Whitcraft drew in a breath, reached out and began step one, which was probably the easiest step. Step one was never the issue. Step two had him more concerned, but regardless, the first step appeared to be going exactly as it had last evening. He glanced at his notes and then back to the patient. Those elaborate diagrams had really paid off.

He couldn't see Mrs. Junters' face. Her silence had him a bit concerned. Nevertheless, a few more goes and it would clearly be the moment to commence step two.

He needed to flip the page, but managing the notes with a single hand proved to be more difficult than he had imagined. Not knowing what else to do, he grabbed the first page with his teeth and then eased it free with his little finger.

He exhaled and leaned around for a quick peek at his patient. All appeared well in order. Then, just as Mrs. Minnock had showed him, he silently counted out four beats, and with quick inversion of his wrist, began step two. Perfect.

He brought the notes to his mouth again and bit at the top page, but it crumpled between his teeth, and the two sheets behind it slipped away. One went right…the other left, both drifting underneath his chair. He cursed to himself. Now when it was time for step three, he may have to play it by ear!

All right, he breathed, trying to calm himself. He could do this, but he had to relax. It was all going so well. He just needed to focus.

****

"Dr. Vorago! Man, I've done it! I've *really* done it! Tell me you have some hysterics scheduled this morning for pelvic massage! You have to let me at them!" Dr. Whitcraft was still breathing hard. He had run all the way from his office after his second hysteric, Mrs. Fussock, had been successfully dispatched…and in such a grand fashion!

"Well, no, I only do mine in the afternoons, to save the wear on my—"

"Oh, well you won't have to worry about that anymore! I'm coming back after luncheon and you have to let me do it! I did *two* this morning already, and they each took *less than ten minutes*!"

"Oh now, come on…" The loose skin under his chin wagged as he shook his head.

"I'm telling you, you've got to see it! The

Whitcraft Maneuver! It's going to revolutionize this whole business!" Dr. Whitcraft clapped his hands together, rocked forward on his toes and then back onto his heels, beaming with the sheer delight of it all.

Chapter Seven

Dr. Whitcraft had been performing *The Whitcraft Maneuver* for nearly three weeks, and had already acquired ten new hysteria patients. He purchased four additional reception room chairs, as the women had begun complaining about the standing-room-only condition of his office. It was an extraordinary expansion of his practice, and he and Miss Faffle were only just managing to keep up.

There had been victims of his success, however. Mr. Lask, one of his original patients, struggling with severe gastric distress, had appeared in his office without an appointment. Because the doctor had been fully booked with hysteria patients, Mr. Lask was forced to wait for his paregoric. The man's discomfort became so urgent that he had no choice but to make a run for it and relieve himself in the street.

He had returned to the waiting room shame-faced, pale and dejected, his hosiery irreparably soiled. All the strewing herbs in Miss Faffle's possession were of little use to adequately freshen the lingerings of Mr. Lask's inner disharmony, and the mood in the doctor's office had become dour, indeed.

That situation aside, Dr. Whitcraft managed remarkably well. In addition to his mornings filled with hysterical women, he still had responsibilities in The London Hospital every other afternoon. Any free moment in between was reserved for house calls, often to even more prospective hysteria patients. It was a frenetic, yet exhilarating pace.

On this afternoon, he had just entered the house of another such patient: a hysteric recommended to him by Mr. and Mrs. Wedfellow.

"Would you care for anything, doctor?" Mr. Pannade stood in an open posture as if on stage, a hand placed on his right hip while he swirled a brandy glass with the other.

"Oh, no thank you, sir," Dr. Whitcraft said, surprised he'd been asked. He selected the most reasonably placed chair in the parlor and sat on its edge. He smiled and nodded at Mrs. Pannade.

She was a bony, colorless woman dressed in a bland, high-necked frock and sat with her knees locked together. Her eyes darted from her husband to the floor, then into her lap and finally to Dr. Whitcraft, until agitation forced them elsewhere.

Her husband, in contrast, strode across the room while his brandy splashed over its brim. He sank his large frame into the settee and smiled at their visitor, cocking his head just enough to make his wavy blond mane ripple. His frockcoat, waistcoat, and blousy shirt were in descending shades of violet; a patterned green and yellow silk was tied around his neck and bundled into a bloom, obscuring his double chin. He grinned at Dr. Whitcraft.

How had this unlikely couple ever found their way into matrimony? Dr. Whitcraft adjusted his spectacles.

"Now, Mr. Pannade. I understand that your wife has been under the care of a physician for the last several years, is that correct?"

"Yes, the man's name is Hurple. In fact, I feel almost dishonest having you here, like we are going behind his back, but I am at my wit's end with Mrs. Pannade's suffering."

"There's nothing wrong with seeking a second opinion, Mr. Pannade. I'm not personally acquainted with Dr. Hurple, but I'm certain that any man of science understands the necessity of seeking different opinions. He has diagnosed Mrs. Pannade as suffering from hysteria?"

"Yes, of course. A most severe case."

"I see. How long has she been ill?"

"Hmm. I believe the symptoms began at least five years ago, isn't that right, dear?"

Mrs. Pannade nodded almost imperceptibly.

"The man has tried numerous remedies. She has a specific diet that she must follow, and the purgatives, of course. Pelvic massage treatments and such. She's even taken in the waters at Tunbridge Wells, which seemed to lift her spirits, I'd say, but that ended shortly after she returned."

"And you accompanied her, then?"

"No, of course not. I have important business that keeps me in London," he said into the glass just before draining its remaining drops.

Dr. Whitcraft looked at Mrs. Pannade. Her agitation seemed to have waned, but now her shoulders hung in a listless slump. Poor woman. She looked exhausted.

"Please explain, as best you can, what symptoms you have observed in your wife, Mr. Pannade."

"Take a look at her now and see for yourself. She's miserable. Cries day and night, you know, over nothing at all, although I do believe she has headaches on occasion. Believe me when I tell you that she takes no joy in life. No joy at all." Mrs. Pannade's pale features shrank into her face as her husband spoke.

"No joy?" Dr. Whitcraft's brows furrowed.

"If I wish to partake in even the tamest social occasion, I must go alone. I do have many male friends of course. I'm an avid theatergoer, you know…historical recitations and reenactment. Pantomime, mimicry…dumb shows and whatnot. Of course I never turn down a late evening soiree." He seemed wistful as he described these events, looking off to the side and pausing at their remembrance. His smile diminished as he refocused on the doctor. "Not that I enjoy leaving her behind, mind you, but if she would make just the slightest effort, maybe I'd consider bringing her along a time or two. Oh, but I shouldn't judge." He drew in a breath as he studied his wife. "Isn't it true, dear, that you've also had difficulty sleeping? She cannot seem to sleep, doctor—at least that's what she's told me."

"That is correct." Her voice sounded brittle, as if it hadn't been used in ages. "I can't recall the last time I had a good night's sleep."

"How is your appetite?"

"I have no appetite." She looked at the floor.

"How long has that been an issue?"

"Oh, since I've known her." Her husband rolled his eyes and adjusted the lace around his right cuff. "And she's liable to expel anything she does manage to get down."

"I see." The doctor rose. "If it would be all right, Mr. Pannade, I'd like to have a moment to speak to your wife…in private."

"Oh. Why of course." Mr. Pannade stood as well. He set the empty glass on the side table. "I know she'll be in excellent hands." With that, he turned and sauntered past his wife, exiting through the double doors.

Dr. Whitcraft followed his path and pulled the parlor doors closed. He turned and watched Mrs. Pannade pick at the handkerchief in her lap, lacing it in between her fingers.

"Mrs. Pannade," he began in his most gentle tone. "I want to reassure you that I'm very familiar with women suffering these types of symptoms. There is nothing you could tell me that would shock or surprise me. If I am to take you on as a patient, you must feel absolutely free to be honest with me about your symptoms, or anything else, for that matter."

She focused on him from some far off place. "Why would you be able to help me when Dr. Hurple could not?"

He smiled and approached his prospective patient, lightly patting her on the shoulder. She jumped under his touch. "As I said, I'm not familiar with Dr. Hurple, but from what your husband has said, the doctor has suggested perfectly reasonable treatments for your illness. Tell me about the pelvic massage treatments he administered. Did you find them helpful?"

She shrugged. "Not really. He spent hours with me, I'm afraid, insisting I wasn't concentrating properly on the treatment. He recommended a midwife, but I never contacted her. I'm starting to feel rather hopeless, I'm afraid." Gazing up into Dr. Whitcraft's eyes, her own were now lined red and filling with tears.

"Nonsense. There's a new treatment I'm using. I suspect it will do wonders for you. Today I would like to do a cursory examination, and then with your consent and that of your husband, I'd like to see you daily, either here or in my office, although I do believe the short walk to my office would do you worlds of good. The treatments won't take long, and I believe you'll see a difference in your mood in under a week's time."

She didn't seem convinced, but managed a small smile.

"I'll also need you to keep a detailed journal. I want you to write down everything. What time you wake, what you eat for breakfast, what activities you engage in...everything. Bring this journal to our appointments and we'll discuss it together. With that, in addition to your treatments, I believe we'll be able to move toward resolving this problem for you. How does that sound?"

She shrugged and strained a whisper, "All right."

"Splendid," Dr. Whitcraft said.

****

As soon as Mrs. Minnock shut her door, a giggling Dr. Whitcraft swept her off her heels and danced her around the room. He paused in his merriment and looked serious as he held her suspended for a moment, but then broke into laughter once again. "I'm going to toss you now," he warned.

"You are?"

After one, two and three swings in the air, he tossed her onto the bed, and dove in next to her.

"My, my, my," she giggled. She sat up, peeling off a glove. "You're in a wonderful mood this evening, aren't you?"

"I'm sorry, I'm just giddy." He sighed, grazing her cheek with the back of his hand. "Honestly, I haven't any idea how I can possibly thank you."

"Oh, don't be silly." She slipped off the other glove. "You don't have to thank me. You are my only client who pays six months in advance and stocks his own brandy and tea here. How could I ask for more? You're out of brandy, by the way."

"I'm abstaining...I'm abstaining." He waved his hand. "I'll bring more when my experiment is over, but seriously, I *have* to do *something* for you, Elizabeth!" He grabbed her bare hand. "Should I buy you a necklace, a bracelet? What is it that you want? I'm not very good at those sorts of things."

Mrs. Minnock patted his cheek. "I'm pleased you are so grateful, but you certainly don't need to buy me anything."

"Yes, but you have *no idea* how that maneuver you showed me is changing my life! It's only been a few weeks and already my practice has nearly quadrupled. I've got hysterics queued up...I just picked up another one this afternoon, a society woman, so pitifully stricken. You should have seen her, the poor soul!" He tossed his frockcoat to the floor and turned back to her with delight. "Oh, I just can't wait to get her up on my table!"

Mrs. Minnock pulled at her bodice. "So you're telling me that you have women, *society* women, queuing up in your office."

"Of course!"

"Help me understand this, if you please." She squinted as if conjuring the vision. "You put them on your table, and they just lie back and...and let you..."

She made the unmistakable sweeping gesture of step five.

Dr. Whitcraft frowned. "Why, of course they let me. Where would they be if they weren't on my table? I can't very well do it to them while they are standing."

"Oh. Well, actually you could." She reached around and patted the back of her dress for the hidden hooks and eyes. "But you'd have to attain a rather unprofessional posture, I'm afraid."

Dr. Whitcraft stopped moving, and stared at her. "It can be done standing?" he whispered, and looked off to the side. "Fascinating. I hadn't thought of that." He plucked at button after button on his waistcoat while envisioning this previously unconsidered possibility.

He shook his head. "These women...they are diagnosed hysterics, Mrs. Minnock. Deeply troubled women, and yes, they gladly let me do it. And you wouldn't believe their improvement."

"Well, I should expect so. I would think it would do wonders for most women, especially if they are grumpy."

He stopped unbuttoning his cuffs and looked up. "You're skeptical then, aren't you?"

She raised her eyebrows with a grin but said nothing. She reached around and unhitched some final complication. The top of her dress gave way, exposing one freckled shoulder and then the other, her bare neckline now scalloped by a lovely lace corset, looped and tied with a slim powder-blue bow.

But Dr. Whitcraft remained philosophical. "If you are skeptical because...well, because the maneuver appears to elicit a rather agreeable sensation, then you must also be skeptical about the proven benefits of rest and exercise, because they are enjoyable as well."

"You're joking."

"I'm telling you, the women who have received this maneuver daily for at least a week have, for the most, part shown a remarkable improvement in their symptoms—therefore, the maneuver is obviously working."

"I wouldn't say that I'm skeptical, Dr. Whitcraft." Mrs. Minnock wiggled the loosened dress over her lower curves. She climbed out of the empty garment and onto her knees, wrapping her arms around his neck. "I just feel like you and I have something in common now. I feel like you haven't realized it yet, but *you* are working *my side* of the street." She shrugged.

For a moment, agitation flashed upon his face. But he shook off his waistcoat and combed his hand through her curls.

"Mrs. Minnock, I know why you are saying that, but I promise you, there's nothing *untoward* about it at all. In order to restore a woman's health in certain cases of hysteria, her nether regions *must* be perturbed. This is a known medical certainty and has been since the time of Hippocrates."

She withdrew her arms and grasped his chin, studying the earnestness in his eyes all the while.

"It may seem silly to you, Elizabeth, but I really want you to believe me."

A soft smile bloomed on her lips. "Yes…well I suppose when one remembers about *Hippocrates*…it makes perfect sense, then, doesn't it?"

Dr. Whitcraft dropped his shoulders with a smile, pulled her close and tugged at the crisscrossing laces on her back.

She rested her chin on his shoulder, rolling her eyes just the tiniest bit.

****

Mrs. Pannade edged forward watching Dr. Whitcraft flip through her journal.

"Splendid." He nodded. "No headaches for the last few days. I see you kept down a coddled egg and toast yesterday morning. Capital! How did you feel afterwards?"

"I was afraid of becoming ill, of course, but I did all right."

"Did you enjoy it?"

"The meal? I don't know."

"Hmm." He jotted something down in his notes and then handed the journal back to her. "You are doing very well. Fewer incidents of unpleasantness after mealtimes and you slept through the night twice this week. Do you feel pleased with your progress?"

"Oh yes. Coming here this week and last...it's made me...well, I feel like I have something to look forward to." She smiled and bit her lip, blushing.

"Is your husband pleased with your progress, as well?"

The very mention of her husband obliterated her pleasant expression. "I suppose you would have to ask him," she mumbled.

"He hasn't said anything, then?"

"He doesn't take the slightest interest in me, or my condition."

"Really?" Dr. Whitcraft dipped his pen back into the ink and made an additional note. "What doesn't—"

"He's barely a husband anyway," she whispered under her breath.

"What do you mean?"

She looked down at her lap and fidgeted. "We've been married for six years...and in that time... Let's say, it's no accident that we don't have any children."

Dr. Whitcraft stared at this woman for a moment before he could bring himself to ask. "You've been married for six years. Are you telling me that, well...marital relations are *infrequent*?"

Blushing, she began to cry, and shook her head.

"Mrs. Pannade, it's normal during the course of a marriage, a certain diminishment in frequency."

She looked up at him with a desperate wildness. "I'm telling you that we have *never* had marital relations. Ever! I-I have *never*..."

Dr. Whitcraft sat dumbfounded, and then recovered himself enough to make a note of this dramatic and not unimportant piece of information. "I see."

He tried to sound nonchalant as he underlined this particular note four times, drew stars on either side of it and, after some reflection, made arrows pointing toward it from all four corners of his paper.

He looked up at his patient who was still shaken by the revelation. He set his notes aside and rose to get the pitcher of water by the basin. He poured a glass, and casually offered it to her. The gesture of kindness brightened her countenance at once.

"I'm sorry." Her eyes were fixed adoringly on him as she took the water.

"Not at all. There is no need to be embarrassed. Your candor is critical. Sometimes that includes discussing, well...any marital idiosyncrasies. The more information you provide to me the better."

There was a sudden male shout through the wall,

unintelligible up to the point when the man declared, "NOW!"

Dr. Whitcraft flipped open his pocket watch. "Oh dear. I have a feeling that my next appointment has become a tad impatient. We were about finished here anyway, I believe. Mrs. Pannade, I am delighted with your progress."

"Oh, as am I!" She stood, smoothed out her dress, and smiled warmly at him. "I'll see you tomorrow, then. Ten a.m. sharp."

"Indeed." He ushered her out and saw that among the three other hysterics, the unshaven Mr. Buzznack sat waiting. His naked right foot was propped against the wall. He was grumbling at Miss Faffle.

"I'll put my damn shoe back on when he gives me something for this gout!"

Mrs. Pannade winced as she scuttled past the untidy display, but recovered herself and looked back at the doctor with devotion. She waved to him again and passed through the door.

Chapter Eight

"Miss Faffle, we've had a bit of a mishap." Dr. Whitcraft dashed into his packed reception room. "Mrs. Junters has dropped her water glass. I'm afraid her hands were rather shaky after the maneuver. Could you fetch another if you please, and then sweep up?"

"Oh dear. Of course, doctor." Miss Faffle jumped up and circled around the women standing in front of her desk before rushing into the examining room.

He glanced back in at poor Mrs. Junters. She sat on the table, still wrapped in the drape and puffed away as Miss Faffle handed her another glass of water.

The other ladies in the reception area had become intrigued by his sudden appearance, and craned their necks to get a peek at his current patient. He extended his leg and kicked the examining room door shut, turning then to acknowledge his audience with a polite smile as he attempted to walk through the crowd toward his office.

One of the ladies, a large, heavy-bottomed sort dressed in layers of black ruffles, placed her foot in his path. She stuck her chin in the air and introduced herself with much gravity. "Sir. How wonderful to finally see you. My cousin, the Earl of Arundel, has recommended you to my husband, who wishes to engage your services on my behalf. Apparently you have all but cured his unfortunate sister's hysteria."

"Oh, why yes, madam. How uh…flattering. I'm afraid you've caught me on a rather busy morning."

Undeterred, the woman slid closer to his ear, breathing the hot, sour breath of one whose false teeth were chronically unkempt. "I don't know what these *other sorts* are paying you, but I can guarantee that my husband takes my health very seriously, if you understand what I'm getting at."

Dr. Whitcraft nodded, the beginnings of panic rising in his chest as he caught the glances of the other women, all probably intent on making their own cases directly to him as well. "I actually have a standard fee, you see, given the professional demands of the…uh, you know. Miss Faffle will most certainly schedule you when she returns."

He pivoted around the woman, disappearing into his office to fetch another chair. "Here is at least one more chair, ladies." He struggled to cram it in between Miss Faffle's desk and the wall. "Miss Faffle will schedule you all, I assure you."

"Oh she doesn't have to schedule *me*. I'm next," a younger lady in a fashionable blue dress announced looking up from her book.

"Yes, and *I'm* after you," called a woman with a narrow face and protruding eyes.

"*You!* Just look at you." A stout woman standing at the desk pointed her lace umbrella at the woman in blue. "I've been diagnosed with hysteria for over four years now, but by the looks of you, I'd say that you've only just gotten it. He should prioritize us, in order of urgency."

"Well! How astonishingly rude!" the woman in blue said. "Why don't you just keep to yourself and wait for your appointment like the rest of us?"

Dr. Whitcraft's insides tightened as he looked from face to face. "Uh, ladies, it's quite all right. I promise you all—"

"Who do you think you're talking to, you underfed, common house-trollop?" the stout woman shrieked, waving her umbrella at the woman in blue.

At that, a waifish, middle-aged lady who had been watching the fray in stunned silence, dropped her head into her gloved-hands and began sobbing. A third young lady turned her mouth under in disgust and heaved her journal full-force, missing the stout woman's chin by the narrowest of margins.

"Oh! How dare you!" She wielded her umbrella with renewed fervor at the entire collection of women.

"Ladies? Ladies!" Dr. Whitcraft picked up the errant journal from the floor. "For God's sake let's remember ourselves! I will see to all of you, but you must try to be patient." He glared at the stout woman, snatched the umbrella from her and hung it on the hat stand. "There is to be no more of this chatter! You will all sit quietly until you are called, is that clear?"

Seething glares and frightened glances abounded. Just then, Miss Faffle opened the door and cleared her throat. "She is much better now and will be out shortly." She dashed back to her chair. Several women crowded toward the desk and loomed over her.

"Which one of you was next?" She glanced wide-eyed from woman to woman.

Dr. Whitcraft flipped open his pocket watch. He had just enough time before his next appointment to take in some fresh air and get his thoughts straight. Because the maneuver made his treatments so quick, he scheduled appointments every twenty minutes now. If he had another examining room, he might even be able to double that. But he was getting exhausted.

He stepped out onto his stoop and sat down, marveling at the extraordinarily busy street. The air that he had hoped to find so refreshing was instead rather oppressive with all of the odors and noises of London.

As the wagons and carriages passed by his attention was captured by a woman across the street. She appeared to be staring at him, most intently too, but it was difficult to tell because she only came into view for a fraction of a second between the passing chaos. He adjusted his spectacles and waited for another glimpse, leaning forward just in time to see the back of her skirt disappear into a vestibule. Hadn't Mrs. Pannade been wearing a dress in that color when she'd turned up early this morning—a visit from which he was still reeling.

He had found her in the reception area before 6:30 a.m., long before Miss Faffle came in. He had been shocked to see her, of course, and demanded to know how she had gotten in. She didn't answer, but instead handed him a freshly baked pie.

Flummoxed, he took the pie and offered to give her the maneuver so she wouldn't have to return for her regular appointment. She had heartily agreed. But now, it must have been nearly 11 a.m., yet she appeared to be still lurking about. How odd.

A firm knock sounded from above. He turned to see Miss Faffle rapping on the glass. She gestured for him to come back in at once. Several restless female faces popped up behind her, one after the other. He sighed and stood back up, wriggling his fingers in anticipation.

****

Dr. Whitcraft bent over the sideboard and adjusted the oil lamp; its flame flickered and rose in the glass chimney, illuminating the darkened room with a pleasant golden glow. He straightened and strode past the slumbering Mrs. Anile. She was slumped in the corner armchair, her white curls tufted under her kerchief like cotton wool, her knitting tangled at her feet.

"You are going to become famous!" Miss Reave gushed as he sat beside her. "Julia's father is so pleased with her improvement, he thinks she may be well enough to attend a few parties this season. Their whole family is telling everyone how that maneuver has saved her!" She threw her arms around his neck and draped herself across his lap.

Dr. Whitcraft blushed. "Once I finish my paper and get it published, I would guess the fervor will increase exponentially. But it was never about the notoriety, of course."

"Yes, yes, it's all about helping those poor hysterical women. No reason to enjoy any of the glory for yourself." She rolled her eyes, but then brightened. "Papa says all the other doctors in London will be worried about their patients flocking to you when the word gets out. Oh, you know, if that happens…maybe then you could afford a proper office, one that doesn't double as your flat." She grabbed his hand and squeezed hard. "Maybe then we could get a *house* like we talked about. Oh wouldn't that be just splendid?"

Dr. Whitcraft couldn't help smiling a little, although he tried to stifle his reverie. It didn't seem appropriate, somehow. "Yes, well, we'll have to see about that."

Miss Reave got up from his lap and tucked herself beside him, studying her hands for a moment. She was thoughtful, her dark eyes cast down, as if there were something else. But she hesitated.

"You look like you were going to say something," he said.

She turned to him and leaned in closer, lowering her voice. "You know, William, Julia told me about it."

He blinked. "She told you?"

"Well, you know. She told me how you *did it* to her." Miss Reave scooted in closer still, reading his face all the while.

"Did she now?" Dr. Whitcraft felt himself blush; his mouth went dry, although he could not say why Miss Reave's query had had such a visceral effect on his ganglionic nervous system. How awkward it was to have a patient discussing such a personal treatment with his fiancée.

"Yes, she told me," Miss Reave continued in a purr. "Do you know what she said? She said *it was amazing*. That's exactly what she said. *Amazing*." Miss Reave's eyes were hypnotic, but she blushed and looked away. Finally, she whispered, "She even said…that I should get you to do it to *me*."

"That's absurd." He leaned back and glanced at the comatose Mrs. Anile.

"Why is it absurd? I am going to be your wife."

"That has nothing to do with it. It's a medical treatment. Doing the Whitcraft Maneuver to someone who is not afflicted could be dangerous. It would be liable to upset the delicate balance of a healthy woman's constitution. A paroxysm is a powerful tool in the arsenal of dealing with hysteria, and is nothing to administer with carelessness." He patted her on the knee before standing up. "I'm glad that Julia is feeling better." With that, he walked out of the room in search of Dr. Reave.

****

"Mr. Pannade is here to see you, Dr. Whitcraft," Miss Faffle whispered from the doorway.

"Ah, thank you." His shoulders slumped and he flipped *The Lancet* shut. He'd only had a few moments to catch up on his reading before luncheon, but now it would have to wait. "Please send him in."Dr. Whitcraft had been at a loss regarding Mrs. Pannade's revelation. After a great deal of thought, he had reluctantly concluded that a face-to-face meeting with Mr. Pannade was necessary, and had sent him a letter requesting an interview at his earliest convenience.

And there he was, appearing both surprised and delighted from the doorway. He opened his arms with a wide sweep, and strolled past Miss Faffle with long, lazy strides.

"What a pleasure it is to see you again, sir. I was so pleased to receive your summons!" He lowered himself into the chair.

Dr. Whitcraft clasped his hands together, studying the man on the other side of his desk. He wore a shining gold frockcoat lined with red piping and a peculiar patchwork design at the shoulders that reminded one of epaulettes, making the entire outfit resemble a military dress uniform of some small, strange country.

"I appreciate you coming, Mr. Pannade. I thought it best that I give you an apprisal of your wife's progress.

She is doing much better, of course. I had also wanted to inquire about something else."

"By all means. Our lives are an open book. I, for one, am at your service." He spread his hands open like he was conducting an orchestra.

"Why thank you. That should prove to be most helpful." Dr. Whitcraft straightened his spectacles and leaned forward. "Sir, I know you care deeply for your wife. Your attention to her medical care, the hiring of me, well it shows that you are concerned for her well-being."

"Mmm." Mr. Pannade glanced off to the side, and ran his hand over his neck, as if to iron away his double chin.

Dr. Whitcraft continued. "It is not my intention to be intrusive into your lives, but the very nature of hysteria makes all aspects of your marriage relevant to me, in attempting to determine the causes of your wife's problems. Do you understand at all what I'm getting at?"

Mr. Pannade shrugged and looked back at the doctor with childlike innocence.

Dr. Whitcraft sighed, and began again. "A woman's body...there are certain stagnations of fluids, humors, blood and the like, that when not properly...*dislodged*, if you will, can disturb the organs, torment them, leading to a variety of symptoms, many of which your wife is suffering. One treatment which has been recommended by physicians for generations, the best and perhaps the most beneficial for women in your wife's state is to be *married*."

"Well, obviously *that* isn't working because she's already married, isn't she?" Mr. Pannade wrinkled his nose with a small giggle.

"What I mean is, it's not just the legal certificate of marriage that is an issue, sir. It is the other, more intimate component of marriage that is in question."

Mr. Pannade sat in silence and seemed mystified by what the doctor was getting at. Finally, Dr. Whitcraft grabbed the edge of his desk and blurted, "Let me be frank, Mr. Pannade. The vigorous motions that accompany marital intimacy can be most beneficial, and I truly feel as a physician for me not to tell you this would be doing you and your wife a terrible disservice, although I certainly don't want to be intrusive…"

Mr. Pannade raised his hand. "A question, doctor."

"Yes, of course."

"These *vigorous motions*. Are they only beneficial for women, or would they also be advantageous for *men like us*, as well?"

The question was not at all what he had expected, and Dr. Whitcraft was completely thrown. "I'm not sure what you mean."

Mr. Pannade had gone silent, but his expression seemed to contain great import, although Dr. Whitcraft was at a loss to determine its meaning.

So he cleared his throat and took on his most pedantic tone. "Let me explain. Women have a uterus. In some cases hysteria develops in women who are not…shall we say, *active*. The male anatomy is entirely different, of course, but the same principle applies. The human body, when left to its own devices, uh…humors can stagnate and release becomes crucial for the proper function."

Mr. Pannade sat forward and smacked his hand down on top of Dr. Whitcraft's hand, meeting his eyes with a reassuring grin.

Flummoxed, the doctor jerked away, stood up and walked to the window. "Frankly, the both of you would benefit if engaging in marital relations became a priority."

A gentle knock made both men turn to the door, where Miss Faffle peeked in.

"I'm right in the middle of something here," Dr. Whitcraft snapped.

"I'm so sorry doctor, but it's Miss Reave. She and Mrs. Anile have arrived for your luncheon and she's getting very impatient. She told me to come in and—"

"Yes, yes. Please tell her I'll be right out." He sat back at his desk. "My apologies, Mr. Pannade, it seems my fiancée is getting restless."

"Your *fiancée*?" The man furrowed his brow and looked off to the side. "Hmm."

"Regardless, has our talk—has it inspired you at all, sir?"

Mr. Pannade stood up, and shrugged. He held out his hand rather stiffly. "Frankly I'm a little less inspired than when I came in."

Dr. Whitcraft shook the gentleman's hand, mystified. "That is unfortunate. I apologize if I haven't made myself clear."

"Oh no, you have. I understand completely. Good day, Dr. Whitcraft." Mr. Pannade bowed deeply, threw his shoulders back, and proceeded on his way.

****

Ah, the tranquility of being able to relax without a single hysterical woman in the vicinity, Dr. Whitcraft thought.

"Have you ever heard of a grown woman, a

married, grown woman that has never engaged in amorous relations with her husband? They certainly seem to be rather mismatched as a couple, but still... It was quite an extraordinary revelation she made to me, and after speaking to her husband today, frankly I am more confused now than before."

Mrs. Minnock had deposited herself in between the crook of Dr. Whitcraft's raised arm and his chest. After a moment of contemplation, she said, "You are telling me this woman has never been intimate with her own husband?"

"That's what she told me, yes. And she was very upset about the matter."

"Of course she was. Hmm." She inhaled, deliberating on the issue as she traced a figure-eight lightly on his arm. "How long have they been married, do you know?"

"Six years, I believe."

After a few moments, she said, "I would say that there are two possibilities. First, the husband has another woman tucked away somewhere. Someone he's known since they've been married and is more devoted to than his wife. So there's that. But I believe, from what you've described, if they've never been intimate, *ever*, then the most likely explanation is that the husband in question just doesn't fancy women. Simple as that."

"What the devil do you mean? He got married after all."

"Of course he married her...for money, or social position, or maybe even for access to other men, who knows? I'm rather surprised that a mind as deductive as yours hasn't considered the possibility that the husband prefers men rather than women."

He was quiet for a moment. "In our first interview with his wife there, he did mention that he has a great deal of male friends with whom he attends parties and other such nonsense. But the man prefers to be around men rather than women, it still doesn't explain their lack of intimacy."

Mrs. Minnock sat up on her elbows and stared at him. After a moment, she threw her head back and laughed before jumping atop her client, kissing his face in between fits of giggling. "My poor, naïve Dr. Whitcraft."

"Wait a minute. Do you mean…as in *prefers*?" He inhaled as her meaning became clear.

"Of course that's what I mean." She looked down at him, smiling sadly as one does at an innocent child who finally learns an important truth about life.

"My goodness. He, he came to my office, and tried to hold my hand."

At that Mrs. Minnock collapsed, burying her face in his shoulder in convulsions of laughter. "He, he…tried to…he tried to hold your hand…and you still didn't guess?"

"Oh sit up, sit up, will you! That's enough of that!" Red-faced, he gave her a gentle shove. She rolled onto her back and bit her lip to stop herself from giggling.

After a few seconds of contemplation, Dr. Whitcraft spoke. "Well, I hadn't anticipated *that*. What a confounding set of circumstances, I tell you. Now, the question is, what do I do about her treatment? The lack of marital activity is an aggravating factor in her disease, I'd gather. I don't know, perhaps more treatments are in order."

"Well." Having regained herself, she arched her back in a long and extended stretch. "They certainly wouldn't hurt."

Chapter Nine

The King's Theatre vibrated with excitement. Its expansive, classically appointed lobby buzzed with opera lovers and cultural pulse-takers from the elite of London society. Elaborately costumed ladies mingled about the lobby with their corresponding escorts, each making certain that their attendance at the premiere of Gioachino Rossini's newest opera, *Le comte Ory*, was duly noted.

Dr. Whitcraft enjoyed the opera but could rarely withstand the significant expenditure required to attend. Tonight's performance, however, hadn't cost him a penny. A grateful patient, suffering from the unfortunate aftereffects of an ill-advised amorous congress, had offered him tickets in exchange for clandestine treatment behind a bookshop.

Religious about his patient's discretion, he had happily accepted the payment, knowing how delighted Miss Reave would be to attend such an important social occasion. And there she was, crossing the lobby, stopping to speak to this gentleman or that lady, a vision of stylish grace. Even among the other ladies in their lavish gowns, Miss Reave stood apart. She wore a simple, but elegant, peach-colored gown with great puffy sleeves that terminated just below her shoulders. Its sculpted neckline left the top of her chest bare, save for the tight string of pearls encircling her neck.

She beamed with pleasure, completely in her element. "Oh, I am so excited to be here," she exclaimed, approaching him on soft feet and speaking directly into his ear. "Absolutely everyone is here!"

"We should take our seats, I'm afraid. I don't want to be one of those ill-mannered cretins who come in late to the—"

"Why, Dr. Whitcraft!" Dr. Edward Marplot stepped from behind a pillar, his long arms opened wide. He gave them a small, tranquil smile. Formal dress seemed to suit him—fitting the man just a little bit better than the other attendees—as if his ancestors and their ancestors before them had existed wearing nothing else.

"A devotee of the opera, I see. Well done, old man! I'm a music lover, myself. But you *must* introduce me to your lovely companion."

"Oh." Dr. Whitcraft frowned and glanced at Miss Reave. "How rude of me. I thought you had already met. Dr. Edward Marplot, this is my *fiancée*, Miss Catherine Reave."

"Ah. Miss Reave." He bowed, raised her gloved-hand to his lips, and kissed it softly. "I studied under your father at The Barts. A learned man who has produced a remarkably lovely daughter whom I have always admired from afar. I'm enchanted to finally make your acquaintance."

"Oh. Well. How charming," she breathed, transfixed by his most pleasant face.

Dr. Marplot straightened, still holding Miss Reave's hand. "You both are in for a treat. I saw this premiere in Paris last year, and I know you will just adore it!"

Dr. Whitcraft frowned again. How the devil could he have seen this in Paris? The tickets, the cost of the trip; it must have been staggeringly expensive.

"It is the most charming of farces. Oh, I just love a good farce." Dr. Marplot raised an eyebrow at Miss Reave. "And I have to say that I'm anxious to see how the French libretto will compare with tonight's Italian." He squeezed her hand for emphasis, but caught a sharp glance from Dr. Whitcraft, and released his catch.

"Oh, then you speak French *and* Italian?" she asked.

"Of course! All lovers of language speak French, and I would think most men of science have at least the basest familiarity with Italian, given our need for Latin, don't you agree, Dr. Whitcraft?"

Dr. Whitcraft felt his face redden. "Latin is necessary for our profession, yes of course." With that, he interlocked his arm with Miss Reave. "We should be getting to our seats, you know."

"Oh yes, of course. Find me at the intermission, old man. I've heard something intriguing about you, and there is a professional opportunity I wanted to get your thoughts on." He turned to Miss Reave. "Miss, I am most anxious to hear your opinions regarding tonight's performance. Until the intermission, then." He picked up her hand once again, kissed it, and flashed a dazzling smile before he bowed and departed through the crowd.

Dr. Whitcraft pulled her by the wrist in the opposite direction. "What an impressive man!" she exclaimed.

After they had found their seats, Miss Reave busily scanned the audience while Dr. Whitcraft stared at the empty stage contemplating tonight's Italian libretto as compared with the French. He had never even known about the difference. He shook his head and looked around the theater.

It was an inspiring building, perfectly designed and acoustically sound for—and then he saw something odd. A few rows over, a woman was staring at him. Staring most intently, as if she had been waiting all evening for him to look in her direction. He couldn't quite place her, although he knew most certainly that he should be able to. When their eyes had met, she broke into the most ecstatic of smiles. He returned the acknowledgement, nodding, searching his mind when it struck him.

Why it was Mrs. Pannade, of course, but he barely recognized her. Usually she appeared without the slightest trace of feminine embellishment, plain and sad—but not this evening! Her face was heavily made up, colored in like an Italian fresco, and she wore an elaborate formal gown just like her peers, but more so. She had certainly not spared any time or expense to make herself more appealing. She sat lodged between two dour society ladies, which only served to highlight her extraordinary transformation. And she was beaming at him.

Well, well, he thought as he smiled at her. The attendance at tonight's social event and the corresponding attention to her appearance were sure signs that his maneuver had worked. How wonderful!

The gaslights dimmed and Dr. Whitcraft turned back to the stage, extremely pleased as the crowd stirred in anticipation.

****

Dr. Whitcraft watched Miss Reave disappear

through the chattering crowd, in search of a girlfriend she had spotted at the beginning of the intermission. He turned and was at once face to face with his lately transformed patient.

"Mrs. Pannade! I say, you are looking well. Good for you!"

Her face glowed. "Yes! How kind you are to notice. It's all thanks to you." She reached over and squeezed him above the elbow.

He tensed and glanced at her hand. "Are…are you enjoying the performance?"

"Oh yes! And *oh*, that naughty Count Ory! Don't you find it coincidental that he recommends *love* as a cure for melancholia?" Her eyes widened at this, and her smile increased wickedly with each nod.

"Yes," he muttered. The entire libretto had been rather a mystery to him given his shaky Italian. "Your husband did not come along this evening?" He gestured at the two ladies glowering in their direction.

Her smile dimmed. "Oh…oh no. I am here with my aunt and her dear friend. You know, this is a new dress. I-I was actually thinking of you when I picked out the fabric." She plucked up the shocking pink organza and proceeded to spin around for his approval.

"Oh, darling, I am so sorry to interrupt." Miss Reave slid in next to him from within the crowd, and cast a quick glance at Mrs. Pannade. "Dr. Marplot is asking for you, and the intermission is almost over."

Dr. Whitcraft shrugged at his patient. "I suppose I must attend to *that*. Mrs. Pannade, how marvelous it's been to see you looking so well. I do hope you enjoy the rest of the performance. I'll see you on Monday, then. Ten sharp."

"Yes, until then." Mrs. Pannade waved, her eagerness deflating as the doctor disappeared into the crowd.

Across the lobby, Dr. Marplot entertained a small gathering of adherents with his insights on the evening's performance thus far.

"That songstress playing La Comtesse Adele! What a magnificent coloratura soprano. Her treble is just sublime! Even better than in Paris—Ah, if it isn't the illustrious Dr. Whitcraft. I was just asking about you." He abandoned his audience and pulled the doctor aside, where the crowd was at its lightest. He ducked down and whispered, "I understand there's a secret you need to share with me."

"What?" Dr. Whitcraft stepped back with a queer look. "I don't follow."

"The word is out, old man. You've had some sort of a discovery in the treatment of hysteria that's got this town buzzing."

"Oh, that is no secret. I'm working on a paper detailing every aspect of the maneuver."

"*The maneuver*? Oh, now you have me intrigued!"

"The Whitcraft Maneuver, actually." He felt himself redden.

"Oh, I see," Dr. Marplot said. "*The Whitcraft Maneuver*. Yes. What exactly is this *Whitcraft Maneuver*, if I may ask?"

"It's a variation of pelvic massage. Frankly, my initial results have proven to be most promising."

"Hmm. You're writing a paper, you say? I'm not sure if you are aware of it, but I work in…in an editorial capacity for *The Lancet*. We must be the first to get a look at your paper when you're finished."

"Of course. I had no idea hysteria interested you. I thought your practice was more of a general one."

"I dabble in it all! I see patients over at The Barts, but I am beginning a small private practice. I'd love the opportunity to offer my patients the very latest discoveries. Anything to give them some relief, you know."

"I couldn't agree more. And, I have to say, I've discovered something that is highly significant."

"As soon as you finish that paper, then. Send it to *The Lancet's* office. Address it to me. I'll see to it that it gets in the right hands."

"Where the devil is Miss Reave? We should be getting to our seats."

Dr. Marplot put his arm around his colleague's shoulder and pulled him back toward the crowd. "Oh, you'll just love the second act. Count Ory is quite the mischief maker!"

****

"What?" Dr. Whitcraft turned round and contemplated the irritated face of Miss Reave.

"You haven't been listening to anything I've just said. I was telling you what Dr. Marplot said about the second half and how we should pay particular attention to the woman playing Isolier. Honestly William, I don't know why I bother."

She continued her scolding, but the opera, the metamorphosis of Mrs. Pannade, even his recent conversation with Dr. Marplot…everything that had been relevant only minutes ago was now forgotten as he turned away from Miss Reave and gazed around the theater for someone else. Someone he had spotted in the lobby as the intermission ended—the stunning Mrs.

Minnock. In an exquisite sapphire-blue gown, she was a vision of feminine perfection, sipping a glass of champagne on the arm of this evening's rakish gallant.

Dr. Whitcraft had gasped at the sight, and nearly pulled Miss Reave's arm out of the socket when he yanked her away from the duo and propelled her through the crowd.

"William!" Miss Reave had demanded. "What on earth?"

"We should return to our seats m-my dear," he had stammered, almost plowing her head first into their aisle.

Now that they were seated, however, he couldn't stop searching the audience. It seemed absurd, but Dr. Whitcraft had never before considered what would happen if he and Mrs. Minnock saw one another in a public place, let alone if Miss Reave was hanging off of his arm like an ornament when it happened. The whole episode had been utterly traumatic.

And that companion! Flaunting her out in public like a prize he had picked up at the Bartholomew Fair. He was probably married, that duplicitous rascal, standing there, sipping his champagne as he leered out at the lobby, so above it all. Imagining them leaving together at the end of the performance—Dr. Whitcraft could only shiver at the thought.

There they were, perched in a loge four levels above the stage, in what must have been the most expensive seats in the house. If he squinted, he thought he could see them chatting and gesturing out at the audience.

Dr. Whitcraft slouched into his seat, suddenly feeling exposed. Miss Reave was oblivious to his torment, and peeked into her bag. He turned resolutely and patted her hand. "I am so happy to be here with you tonight, my darling," he declared, trying to concentrate on his fiancée's face.

"Oh, me too, William. Shh. It's starting again."

The lights dimmed, the curtains opened, and Dr. Whitcraft's attention was completely captivated...by the occupants of the loge four levels above the stage.

Chapter Ten

Dr. Whitcraft set the journal next to the washbasin. This must be met with extreme delicacy, he thought, not certain what to say next. He should have known something was amiss by the way Mrs. Pannade had come dressed for her usual appointment. Rather than her typically dowdy dress, today she wore a curiously revealing ensemble, one that a novice at luring men might have assumed to be provocative, but rather only served to highlight her protruding clavicles and bony upper torso.

Donning his most pleasant smile, he sat next to her, drew breath to speak, but instead Mrs. Pannade blurted, "Please don't be upset with me. I can see that you're upset, but you told me to be honest!" Her eyes pled with him as her gloved-fingers grazed her cheek, darkened today with a stripe of ill-applied rouge.

He held up his hand. "Mrs. Pannade, I am not upset with you. Now, this development is not uncommon, especially in extremely vulnerable patients such as yourself. Why, it's perfectly understandable that you…well that you *believe* you are in love with me. After all, I dote upon you, care for you and so on, but, well, of course you do not love me. You are simply misguided."

The blood left her lips. "Misguided? I assure you that I'm not misguided. Dr. Whitcraft, it has all become so clear to me lately. When I'm alone at night with just my thoughts, I can only think of one thing. You! I have never felt such an intense passion in all my life. You must understand…"

At this, his neutral countenance disintegrated, but he was quick to recover. He cleared his throat, forcing himself to continue with a slow and deliberate string of logic. "I certainly understand how it may *seem* that way to you, Mrs. Pannade, but I assure you, feelings like these are—"

"…and I certainly know I would make a much better wife to you than that dreadful *Miss Reave* you have been running around town with."

"Mrs. Pannade," he gasped. "That comment is completely inappropriate! My private life should not enter into this matter at all. Really!" He tugged at the bottom of his waistcoat, blinking rapidly as he worked to catch his breath and harness his composure. "Now let's just calm down for a minute. You must understand—"

"Frankly, Dr. Whitcraft," Mrs. Pannade added thoughtfully, "I think you are much better off in the hands of that Mrs. Minnock woman rather than with that uppity Miss Reave. At least *Mrs. Minnock* doesn't make any pretense about her business with you."

Dr. Whitcraft's mouth dropped open and he jumped to his feet. "How on earth?" he shrieked. "How could you *possibly* know about…" His voice gave way as he searched her face, feeling his own turn the most macabre shade of crimson. "Madam, that is my private business, not to mention a grievous violation of our doctor-patient relationship. I am…*outraged*! Simply OUTRAGED!"

Mrs. Pannade was undiscouraged. She got to her feet as well, beaming. "Darling, I understand your shock at this unexpected turn in our relationship, and I just know that you are going to come around…and I am happy to wait for you."

"No, no… there is nothing to wait for!" He threw up his arms. "There is *no* relationship!"

Transfixed by his gesticulations, Mrs. Pannade fluttered her eyelids in response.

He dug a handkerchief out of his pocket and dabbed his forehead while attempting to invoke in a more rational tone. "Mrs. Pannade, you are a *married woman* and *my patient.* There is nothing that can ever, *ever* happen between us. For goodness' sake, you must try to clear your head and understand that! And if indeed you have been following me about…well, that nonsense is completely unacceptable and must stop at once!"

"I'll bring you another pie tomorrow at ten a.m., for my treatment. I think that dietary regimen of yours is really very silly, but if you prefer, I'll bring you another roasted capon, instead of the pie. Or perhaps you fancy something else? Hmmm. Oh, don't worry. I'll surprise you. I love you, my darling!" At that, she dove in to steal a kiss, pulled back from the stricken doctor and tousled his hair before parading out of the door.

****

"So, will you help me?" Dr. Whitcraft asked as he drummed his fingers on the pub's battered table.

Dr. Vorago waved his cutlery, his mouth too full to respond. With a gulp, he drew breath for a response, but became distracted by a passing barmaid's tray of eye-catching puddings: a sugar-glazed berry tartlet, a fragrantly spiced gingerbread topped with lemon crème, and a sweetly steaming suet pudding. "I know it's rather a lot to ask." Dr. Whitcraft said, hoping to recapture his friend's attention.

Dr. Vorago turned back to his own joint of roast beef and began sawing at it with renewed fervor. "You know I'd do anything for you, dear sir. I'd be glad to take her off your hands. I guess that'd be quite literal, then wouldn't it. Ha!" He laughed at his own joke, snorting unattractively as he shoveled the remainder of his Yorkshire pudding into his mouth.

After a moment of thorough chewing, he added, "That treatment of yours is driving women to distraction. Do I dare attempt it with her? She may fall in love with me next." He grabbed his napkin and mopped the butter drips from his chin, spreading a thin sheen across his lower face.

Dr. Whitcraft frowned. "Do not confuse the gravity of her symptoms with my treatment, please. It's just rather evident now how extremely ill the poor woman is. I have to say that I feel dreadful about the matter. She's a very decent woman, but I'm no longer in a position to offer her help. I haven't even told you what she did this morning."

"Oh, do tell! Miss? Miss? Bring me another bottle of ale. Does she hear us?"

"Yes, yes, she is nodding at you." Dr. Whitcraft felt a bit nauseated from his colleague's enthusiastic table habits. He wondered how the man could return to a full schedule of patients after such a display.

Dr. Vorago leaned back and patted his belly. "Do tell, doctor. What did she do this morning? Did she bring you another roasted bird?"

"No, I told you, it has gotten much more serious. She broke into my office—I still don't know how she managed that—and climbed my stairs carrying a full breakfast of kippers and eggs! I woke with the woman hovering over me and a full plate of food balanced on my front. She frightened me so terribly, I nearly had a fit!"

"Egad!" Dr. Vorago laughed. "My wife won't like that nonsense when she does that to me." He jammed his fork into the last square of roast beef and stuck it in his mouth. While chewing he added, "How were they, then?"

"How was what?"

"The kippers and eggs. Can the woman cook?"

Dr. Whitcraft stared at his colleague. "I didn't eat them! I wouldn't want to encourage her. I set them aside and demanded she leave at once."

"Oh. That is a pity." Dr. Vorago swallowed and looked off to the side. "So, what, shall I call on her, then?"

"I suppose I'll write her husband and explain the necessity for a change in physicians, then recommend you as the replacement."

"Capital. Oh, thank you, my dear." He grabbed the bottle of ale from the young maid and drank like a man deprived. When he finally set the bottle down, Dr. Vorago gasped for breath and exclaimed, "Shall we have a pudding, then?"

****

Dr. Whitcraft mumbled to himself as he climbed the Reaves' front steps, mentally composing the letter of escape he would pen to Mr. Pannade. But he shook the thought away. The workday was over and now it was time to pay a call on the delightful Miss Reave. Professional matters could wait.

Just as he was about to knock, the gallop of an approaching carriage slowed to a trot. When it stopped, a pair of nicely dressed young men stepped out onto the street, their arms filled with packages wrapped in brown paper. One accepted the parcels from the other, balancing them precariously as his companion disappeared back into the carriage. Moments later, he emerged with an additional lot.

A third man, the driver presumably, came from the opposite side with his own assortment and distributed these amongst the other two men before ascending back to his post. Looking like beasts of burden, the two men turned and proceeded toward the stairs.

"Good Lord, may I assist you gentlemen?" Dr. Whitcraft stepped down and whisked several parcels from atop each pile.

"Oh sir, why thank you, sir," one of them said.

"Would you mind knocking for us, sir?" asked the other.

"Gladly." But he didn't have to. The door swung open and an ecstatic Miss Reave stood glowing with anticipation. She looked right past the doctor.

"Oh! How wonderful! Right this way, I'll show you just where to put it all." She dashed down the hall leaving Dr. Whitcraft holding the door.

As he stepped into the parlor, he set the packages aside and waited while the young men busily stacked and sorted their charges. As per usual, Mrs. Anile was slumped in the corner armchair, very much asleep. Her eye-patch had traveled past her bad eye and was resting squarely in the center of her forehead.

Wasting no time, Miss Reave clawed into a particularly lumpy parcel. "I can't believe that Mr. Varment has completed my order so quickly. The man's a genius! Oh! Oh, will you just look at this! Just look!" She eased a wispy butter-colored habiliment out of its package and glided it past her cheek, groaning in near ecstasy.

As the men continued arranging the packages, Dr. Whitcraft uttered, "My darling, what is all of—"

"Where's the hat?" she asked, remembering suddenly. "There should be a hat that goes with this gown."

One of the young men jumped to his feet and scurried to the couch. "I believe it's in one of these, miss." He pointed at three identical looking square boxes.

"Don't just stand there, find it for me, if you please. I can't wait to see it. William, help him, please."

Dr. Whitcraft walked toward the boxes, unsure of his assignment.

"No need, sir. I've got it." The young man knocked the lid to the side and lifted an oblong feathered hat through the crinkling paper.

Miss Reave shrieked. "Oh! Why it's perfect!" She danced over, took the hat from the bowing man's hands, and placed it on top of her head. Dodging a jumble of purchases, she dashed to the mirror.

Everyone in the room paused, their eyes fixed on the posing Miss Reave as she adjusted and readjusted her new acquisition. Finally, one of the fellows gathered his courage and asked, "Is that all then, miss? Would you like us to stay while you unwrap? We would be happy to assist you, of course."

"Oh…well, hmmm," she said to the mirror. "I don't suppose that will be necessary. William, my dear, would you please be kind enough to see these gentlemen to the door? Thank you, boys. Please give my regards to Mr. Varment."

Dr. Whitcraft gestured to the hall and the men dutifully filed past him.

"William!" she whispered before he had left the room. Her reflection gave him a stern look. "Please tip those men before they leave, and make sure you are generous. I don't want to appear ungrateful." With flattened palms, she removed her new hat by its edges.

In the hall, the deliverymen thanked the doctor. After Dr. Whitcraft returned, she spun around in a sudden burst and contemplated the room.

Dr. Whitcraft shook his head as he stepped through scraps of brown paper and past the sleeping governess. He made his way to Dr. Reave's writing desk and eased open its slim top drawer. He pulled out a small hand mirror and glanced at it before making his way back to Mrs. Anile. Casually, he tucked it just under her nose. He relaxed when the mirror fogged sufficiently.

"Now that they're gone, perhaps you would care to enlighten me. What *is* all this?"

"Well…" She ripped the paper from another package. "After chatting with my friends over luncheon the other day, everyone agreed that I should begin to dress more like a proper doctor's wife." She cast the paper aside and grinned. "Especially when that doctor is swimming in new patients and destined to be famous."

Dr. Whitcraft stifled a small smile. "Well, well. I

see." He tucked the mirror back in its place and then pushed several boxes to the side of an armchair. "I can't imagine the look on your father's face when he sees all of this." He squeezed onto the chair's edge. Envisioning that poor man walking in on this display—it was just dreadful. "This must have cost an absolute *fortune*. I hope you at least prepared him."

Miss Reave had her hands buried deep inside a box and looked up. An impish smile spread across her face. "He won't have anything to say about it at all, my darling." She stood straight now, cocking her head to the side. "I'm surprised Miss Faffle didn't show you, although maybe it hasn't arrived just yet. I had the dressmaker send the bill to *your* office."

In an instant, Dr. Whitcraft was on his feet, huffing and puffing as he frantically reevaluated the contents of the room from the perspective of the man who would be paying for it. "Y-you sent the bill to *my* office?"

"Of course." She stared at him curiously now.

"Well, that's it!" he heard himself shout as he clapped his hands together underneath his chin. "You've ruined me, do you realize that?"

Miss Reave parted her lips as a lilac bonnet dangled from her fingers. "Ruined you?"

"How in the devil can a woman...*a woman*...just march into a shop and j-just...*swindle* the proprietor into squandering what must unquestionably be his *entire* inventory of fabric on a single order and then deliver the spoils of said order to this address? An address to which I have *no attachment*, by the way, and then assign *me* the bill? Why, this is so outrageous as to nearly be a matter for the police!"

Miss Reave cast the hat aside, threw herself on the

couch amongst the packing paper, and folded her arms. "I have to say, I'm surprised, William. I thought you would be pleased. This is all for you, you know. I thought you'd expect your wife to dress like a proper lady."

Perspiration dampened his waistcoat. He shrieked, "Wife? I'm rather certain they don't hold weddings inside the walls of *debtor's prison*, my dear!" He scanned the packages and draping garments, calculating all the while. "What can I do, what can I say to make you return this foolishness back to the opportunistic scoundrel who took advantage of you? If you could just wait until *after* we're married, *after* I know where I stand…I'll draw up a budget and within those reasonable boundaries, I promise to…" His words trailed off seeing the disappointment on her face. What the devil was he doing, anyway?

This *is* what he had wanted: an attractive, socially adept wife to solidify his place administering medicine to London's polite society. Now that they were engaged, shouldn't she expect him to pay for the trappings of that role? Truth be told, in all likelihood he *could* afford such indulgences now that his practice was so busy, even though spending so freely felt contrary to the frugal manner with which he had managed his life thus far. But with his bachelorhood nearing an end, his self-centered view of his finances would have to end as well. His angry words hung in the air between them even as his shoulders dropped in defeat.

Miss Reave stood up and waded through the packages. She reached out and squeezed his arm. "I'm sorry. I suppose I should have asked you first."

"No, no…*I'm* sorry," he whispered, cupping her

chin. "I want you to have it. Have it all. I suppose I'll manage." He winced as he looked past her at the cluttered room.

She let out a gasp and threw her arms around him. "Thank you, William." She spun around giggling at the sight of her new treasures.

****

The Lancet's office was smaller and darker than Dr. Whitcraft expected. Aging treatises burdened the shelves, dusty and cluttered documents lay in crooked stacks on the bureaus. Who would have thought that such a prestigious journal's office would be so haphazardly arranged?

He shifted in his chair as he leered across the desk at Dr. Marplot. He had been under the impression that he would be meeting with the editor, but instead had been augustly greeted by *this* man, who now sat flipping through the pages of the paper he had sent here by post earlier in the month.

"Well," Dr. Marplot said finally, pushing the paper across the desk and looking up. "We can't publish it, old man." He leaned back and studied his colleague's reaction.

"What?"

Dr. Marplot shrugged, staring back down at the paper with a subtle smile.

"What the devil do you mean *we* can't publish it? And why are *you* telling me? You're not the editor. I've asked around. Don't you only work on the *chess* column?" Dr. Whitcraft's voice was thick with suspicion.

"How nice of someone to take notice of my chess column. Do you count yourself as an admirer?" He paused with an arched eyebrow, but softened his voice. "You really just need to calm down. No one said that we will not *eventually* publish your work. You're so oversensitive, Dr. Whitcraft. There is no question of your ability to write a well-crafted, scholarly article. Your peers here at *The Lancet* were all impressed with your pedagogic style, and of course your credentials and reputation are impeccable. It's just that what you are proposing here is rather difficult to believe." He picked up the paper and smacked it on the desk. "A five-step magical machination that induces a paroxysm in *every* woman? We can't just publish something like that until I, for one, see it performed."

"Oh." Dr. Whitcraft leaned back in his chair. "Well, that's different. I'd be happy to arrange a demonstration. We could reserve an operating theater in one of the hospitals. I've had several colleagues who've asked to see it demonstrated. Word is beginning to get around. You can't imagine how many hysteria patients have been begging for an audience with me."

"Really?" Dr. Marplot leaned forward.

"Oh yes. I've turned away at least fifteen women because I simply don't have time in my schedule to accommodate new patients. I barely had the time to come here today, if you want to know the truth. I can't imagine what will happen after my paper is published. When you see it performed, you'll understand its value."

"Of course, most certainly. You know..." He picked up the paper again and thumbed through it. "You never mention in here how you managed to come up with it."

"The maneuver?"

"Yes. It's quite inspired, then isn't it? Where'd you get the idea?"

Dr. Whitcraft looked down at his hands, and cleared his throat. "I've been interested in hysteria for quite some time, and of course saw the need for an improvement in its treatment for my own practice. The difficulty of pelvic massage has been—"

"Yes but, how *exactly* did you discover the five steps? To go about them in that precise way and in that order?"

"Well…" He grasped the arms of his chair and readjusted himself. "Trial and error, I suppose."

"Really? Trial and error?" Dr. Marplot looked directly at him, as if contemplating the countenance of a man bluffing at cards.

Dr. Whitcraft glanced off to the side, his eyes searching for a moment before he turned back to his colleague and began to nod. "Yes. Trial and error." He spoke with the deliberation of one who had recently made up his mind.

"Remarkable." Dr. Marplot's eyes narrowed, but after a moment his expression relaxed, and a gentle smile crept across his face.

"Regardless, I am most anxious to see a demonstration. I'm certain that I… Hey, what the devil? Do you know that woman?" Dr. Marplot gestured at the window, behind Dr. Whitcraft's head.

"What woman?" He spun around, the prickle of fear settling in on his stomach.

"She was just there. That's the third time today that I have spotted that queer looking woman. Once early this morning, and then I could swear I saw her gawking at us when you descended from your cab. Now it appears she's lurking outside the window. Keep watching, I'll wager that she will…look, there."

Dr. Whitcraft's heart sank, as he now saw the unmistakably twitchy blink of Mrs. Pannade just before she ducked back into the bushes.

"Oh my…I don't know what to say." He dropped his head into his hands.

But Dr. Marplot was on his feet and walking to the window. He cranked it open and leaned out. "You there. I say. You in the bushes. What the devil are you up to?"

"No, no. Shh, she will go away, just…" Dr. Whitcraft rose, dreading the forthcoming explanation. He joined his colleague at the window, just in time to see Mrs. Pannade dash behind the building's corner.

"She's an ex-patient of mine, I'm afraid. A hysteric…one of the most troubling cases I've ever encountered, but I've had to pass her off to Dr. Vorago because sh-she seems to have convinced herself that…well, it is rather embarrassing. She has convinced herself that she's in love with me. She believes we are destined to be together or some such nonsense, and follows me around. It's all rather upsetting."

"Really?" Dr. Marplot watched him closely, clearly amused, and turned to gaze out the window again. He craned his neck to get another look at the mystery woman, but gave up and turned back to Dr. Whitcraft.

"You've got women following you around the town? Hiding in bushes trying to get a glimpse of you? Well done, old man."

"No, no—it's nothing like that. I'm engaged to be married. That woman out there is very ill. I can assure you I've done nothing to encourage such shocking behavior."

"Ah yes, Dr. Reave's daughter, that lovely creature. My, my. Who'd guess by looking at you that you have such an effect on the ladies?"

Dr. Whitcraft's blood pressure began to escalate. "Sir, I have not—"

"Kidding, kidding. You are rather *stodgy* for someone so young. Let's sit down and plan out this demonstration of yours, shall we?"

Chapter Eleven

"No, no, Dr. Chimble…you're using too much pressure. The tips. Use only the fingertips. Step two requires a very light touch. There, that's it." Dr. Whitcraft leaned over the man's shoulder.

The patient was a middle-aged widow. Her grey curls spilled over the examining table as she lay flat with her eyes tightly shut. Step two was taking effect, however, because she let loose a long sigh and the wrinkles in her face relaxed.

The other doctors tightened their circle around the table, acknowledging her progress with hushed murmurs.

Dr. Whitcraft counted under his breath while he watched Dr. Chimble's handiwork. "All right, seven, eight, nine…there. Now, commence step three. Yes. Like that, just that way. Dr. Clowclash, step closer, man, you can't see from that angle."

Dr. Clowclash blushed and stepped from the back of the crowd, inserting himself between the two taller fellows in front.

"Are you seeing the way Dr. Chimble is going about the machinations of step three, gentleman? Clockwise. Always clockwise." His eyes followed his colleague's fingertips. "Note the patient's change in pallor. Two more goes, gentlemen, then we commence with step four. Are you able to see, Dr. Marplot?"

"Yes…quite," he answered, entranced.

Dr. Chimble straightened his glasses with his free hand. Nervous perspiration beaded along his forehead.

"Nurse! Dab Dr. Chimble." Dr. Whitcraft gestured to a plump blonde nurse. She scurried over and began madly blotting Dr. Chimble's forehead with a tea cloth.

The patient's breathing had changed. She was producing a singular low sounding gurgle which seemed to emanate from her very core.

"Step four is just a whisper, just a touch and then go immediately into step five." He crouched for a better view, stepping side to side like an anxious wicket-keeper.

"Notice men, take notice how he is putting his *entire* shoulder into step five. Excellent, Dr. Chimble. You must roll the shoulder; feel the roll. Do any of you engage in lawn bowling? It's a similar motion, you see." Dr. Whitcraft made a large sweep of his arm, but most were too entranced by the demonstration to notice the gesture.

Suddenly, the patient arched her back, drew in a full breath, and exhaled.

"Ah, and there we have it." Dr. Whitcraft clapped his hands together with delight. The patient reached her paroxysm with quiet dignity, clearly better for the treatment. "A successful paroxysm in a fraction of the time it had taken in the past. How are you feeling, Mrs. Gillfurt?"

"Could I have a drink of water?" she whispered, making the effort to sit up. She looked surprised, as if just now discovering their presence. "I feel much better, thank you."

"Splendid. Just splendid. Nurse, when the patient

feels steady, could you escort her to the anterior room there and get her a glass of water? Thank you so very much."

As the nurse and patient whispered together, Dr. Whitcraft turned back to his audience, offering a special nod to Dr. Marplot. The stunned doctors stood in breathless silence until one of them began clapping. In an instant, they had all joined in, creating a most appreciative applause.

"Oh, well…" Dr. Whitcraft whispered. He cleared this throat and asked, "Are there any questions?" Several doctors raised their hands. "Yes, you there. Dr. Naffin, I believe it is."

A tall man with a boyish face and a hunched-over frame put down his hand. "You are telling us that this maneuver works on *every* patient, *every* time? Pardon me, sir, but I find that rather unbelievable. I myself have labored for hours on a single patient, and I can't believe that—"

"Forgive me for jumping in, sir, but I promise you, if executed in the precise manner in which Dr. Chimble has just demonstrated, the maneuver will result in a successful paroxysm each and every time. That's the first time he has performed it solo, and just look at his success. Don't you agree, Dr. Chimble?"

Dr. Chimble nodded vigorously, still wiping his hand. "I can't believe how easy it was."

"There you have it. I personally guarantee if Dr. Naffin brings that same patient he had such difficulty with to me, I will perform the maneuver on her, and the paroxysm that had proven so elusive will indeed occur."

The dubious doctor bowed and backed into the

crowd, as if he were already planning to take Dr. Whitcraft up on his offer.

"How many of these, uh, *maneuvers* do you manage in a single work day, Dr. Whitcraft?" a different voice from the back of the group inquired.

He smiled at that question, certain the answer would shock and delight his listeners. "Well my friends, let me begin by saying that I never fully appreciated the epidemic of hysteria gripping the females of our society until I experimented with this maneuver. Before, less than one fourth of my practice were women diagnosed with hysteria, and for those whose symptoms required therapy with pelvic massage, I treated one or two, at the most, per day. But, with the utilization of this maneuver, I have increased my practice—" he held several beats for the maximum dramatic effect then said with a flourish—"nearly tenfold!"

There were whispers and gasps among the doctors.

"I'm actually turning women away, which is why teaching this valuable treatment is so crucial, so more hysteria patients may be served."

"How many patients have you done this to in a *single* day?" An impatient ginger-haired young doctor demanded from the back.

"Ten...sometimes twelve per day, on average. On my most productive day I was able to treat eighteen women, in addition to my other, incidental appointments."

The crowd gasped. Dr. Whitcraft raised his chin just a little higher in the air. He watched the doctors' faces reveal the mental calculation of their possible income adjustment. The room seemed to sparkle as their eyes glittered en masse.

"All right gentlemen, all right." Dr. Marplot stepped past Dr. Whitcraft, upstaging him. "Which among you would care to adjourn with me for a continued discussion of this miraculous new discovery? I believe some libations are in order." His nodding posture and dazzling smile were dialed to their highest setting.

There were enthusiastic calls of approval, but Dr. Whitcraft frowned. Anticipating his maneuver-filled afternoon, he flung open his pocket watch, but looked up just in time to see Dr. Marplot's long arms pulling several colleagues into a huddle. They were whispering and laughing about something or other. Then Dr. Marplot cupped his hand to his mouth and leaned in toward Dr. Naffin's ear. The man threw his head back in appreciative laughter and then glanced at Dr. Whitcraft.

Dr. Whitcraft's face grew hot, and with a most deliberate gait, he joined the others. "Yes...yes of course. A round of libations would most certainly be in order."

****

The doctors crowded around several low tables covered in baskets of bread, plates of cheese, and tankards of foaming ale. Their dark frockcoats wrinkled as they bent forward, chatting astutely to one another under the stifling haze of the pub.

Dr. Whitcraft took his cup of tea from the young barmaid's tray and passed Dr. Vorago his ale. His friend was so engrossed in the pontifications of Dr. Marplot, he hadn't even noticed its arrival.

"Once we at *The Lancet* publish a full, step by step dissection of the maneuver, you will all be able to reproduce exactly what Dr. Chimble has achieved today—a revolutionary method whereby all hysterics may be treated." Dr. Marplot's hand sliced through the air as he spoke.

"Here, here." A rotund chap with a monocle and top hat hoisted his ale over the table, encouraging the others to do the same.

A rather startled-looking young fellow crowded in the center muttered suddenly, "There is one thing that concerns me." Everyone quieted and turned to the man.

"What is that, dear sir…you are Dr. Encraty, are you not?" Dr. Whitcraft asked in his most pedantic tone.

"Yes. I am Dr. Thomas Encraty. I've just finished my apprenticeship with an apothecary, so a lot of this is very new to me." He gripped his ale with both hands and could barely meet Dr. Whitcraft's gaze. "This maneuver. Frankly…uh, excuse me sirs, but I'm almost ashamed for even introducing this notion." He withered low into his chair under the weight of their collective attention. "I believe an issue of some *delicacy* needs to be addressed."

Dr. Marplot spoke up in a clear, booming voice. "We are all professionals here, kind sir. The advancement of our craft depends on candid discourse, so by all means, do not hesitate to voice your concerns. You are among your peers and we are all at your disposal." He reached across the table and patted the boy on the hand, while the other doctors muttered affirmations in kind.

Dr. Encraty smiled appreciatively at Dr. Marplot, and then the others. "Well…this maneuver. If someone could explain to me, what exactly is there to prevent our female patients from attempting to do it to themselves?"

"Shh!" Dr. Naffin glanced around the establishment in a near panic.

"Propriety! We are in a public space, sir!" Dr. Chimble nearly toppled his ale. "How *dare* you *even suggest* such a thing?"

"For all that is good and holy, remember yourself, Dr. Encraty!" Dr. Vorago swung his tankard to his lips, eyes darting at his colleagues.

Murmurs of disapproval abounded.

"Well, couldn't they?" Dr. Encraty persisted. "Why couldn't they just do it to themselves, thereby managing their own treatment and may I add, depriving us of the revenue all the while?"

The doctors gasped and another young man leaned forward with much agitation. "Oh my God, if they could do it to themselves, there's no telling what the effects would be. With no professional to gauge the frequency or duration of such a pursuit, the woman could be driven mad by her own hand."

Before Dr. Whitcraft could address this controversy, Dr. Chimble spoke up with fervor. "No respectable woman would ever dare engage in such scandalous behavior!" He leaned over the table and dropped his voice to a harsh whisper. "Attempting to navigate such a delicate and unpredictable region by one's self... Good gracious. If I had *an inkling* that any patient of mine ever seemed inclined to attempt such a feat, why, I'd not only instruct her about the evils of doing so, but would also caution her guardian—the father or the husband, whatever the case may be—and *demand* she be monitored for any indication of such behavior."

"Yes! Yes, of course!" the doctors agreed most heartily.

Dr. Whitcraft held up his hand, keeping his voice calm and his tone pedantic. "I can assure you, gentlemen, that what Dr. Encraty has proposed is not even physically possible. First of all, the patient is lying on the table and can't see what the administering physician is up to. Unless she were startlingly perceptive regarding their own anatomy—and I have yet to find a patient that is—these women would have no way of knowing how to even go about doing the maneuver."

"That's another problem, then isn't it?" a narrow-faced doctor with curling whiskers blurted, having gained courage from intellectual hullabaloo. "Dr. Marplot, didn't you say that *The Lancet* is planning on publishing a complete explanation of how to do the damn thing? Step by step, I believe you said. Well, I for one could imagine some of my more devilish patients trying to make off with my copy if they knew what it contained."

"No, no!" Dr. Vorago's jowls shimmied as he shook his head. "Are you joking, sir? No *woman* has the slightest interest in picking up an academic journal, and they certainly don't possess the inclination to actually *read* one. Academic journals do not contain gossip or recipes or fanciful romantic stories. I doubt *The Lancet* would publish anything that a female could understand let alone misuse if they were to stumble across it. Am I right Dr. Marplot?"

"Yes...yes of course," he acceded, although he did look concerned.

"But, regardless, gentlemen," Dr. Whitcraft said, "let's say, just for the sake of argument, if they somehow got the notion. You saw it for yourselves. It's simply not possible to...well to *do* to one's self. The limited rotation of the wrist precludes it." He demonstrated by holding his hand above the table, rotating his wrist and then inverting his arm inward. "You see, to turn backwards like that and attempt the clockwise motion that is required for step three...well, it is just not possible."

"But..." All heads turned back to Dr. Encraty.

"But what?" Dr. Chimble demanded.

The young doctor cocked his head with a shrug. "What if the patient were to...what if she were to use *two* hands?"

At that, everyone gasped. Dr. Naffin threw his napkin on the table and Dr. Clowclash's monocle popped away from his face like a champagne cork, bouncing off Dr. Chimble's cane before disappearing under a neighboring table of clergy. Dr. Clowclash apologized to the vicars before crawling on his hands and knees in between their hands and knees in search of the errant eyeglass.

But no one paid much mind to Dr. Clowclash, because they were all distracted by Dr. Vorago. The man had drawn in his breath so sharply at the *two hands* supposition, that he had aspirated his latest gulp of ale, and had begun to acquire the most intriguing shade of violet. Dr. Whitcraft at once pounded on his friend's back, demanding that he *cough, man cough* while another doctor plucked up Vorago's wrist to monitor his pulse.

"Air! Give the man some air!" Dr. Chimble

exclaimed.

A gasping Dr. Vorago jerked his wrist away from his neighbor and waved to his concerned colleagues. After a moment, he dabbed the perspiration from his temples. "Criminy," he croaked.

When everyone was satisfied that Dr. Vorago had fully recovered himself, the men turned back to Dr. Encraty, but it was Dr. Whitcraft who spoke. "Gentlemen, I still believe, even with two hands, the necessary *torque* could not be achieved, thus making the maneuver unfeasible."

Dr. Chimble's face flushed crimson. "God's bodkin man, we're in a public place! Enough of this *two hands* business!" He turned to the sheepish Dr. Encraty, seemingly taking the man's postulation as a personal affront.

"Dr. Encraty, we are talking about *society women* here…not common street harlots from the gutter. The patients in question are, for the most part, from fine families and possess the most unquestionable pedigrees. These are the mothers and wives of the very fabric of our great society. They are upright and virtuous and would never *dare* to consider such…such *scandalous* behavior." He sat up straight in his chair and grabbed his tankard of ale.

"You know," Dr. Clowclash said, having reseated himself and replaced his monocle, "we're all thinking it, so I'm just going to say it out loud. The reason Dr. Encraty here is so lost is because the man trained with an *apothecary* rather than at a legitimate university. Dr. Sangrado, this is just what I was saying to you last week, our profession needs standards. We shouldn't just label someone a *doctor* because they've spent a few months capping pills for one of those drug-peddling charlatans. *I* went to *Oxford* for God's sake...yet we can *both* call ourselves doctors? Shameful, just shameful."

"Oh, that's it!" Dr. Naffin toppled his chair as he jumped to his feet. "How *dare* you, sir! I'll have you know that *I* studied under an apothecary too, you pompous son of a bitch. I pride myself in possessing an utterly unimpeachable knowledge of medicine. *Oxford*? Did your *daddy* buy you in because it certainly wasn't your knowledge of anatomy! Why, I heard only last month that you killed a man right there in your office when you botched a simple bloodletting. Everyone at these tables knows *that,* too!"

Dr. Clowclash rose to his feet, red and growling at his rival. He yanked off his frockcoat, and cast it to the side. Dr. Naffin guffawed in response. He began to strip away his own clothing, pulling at his sleeves and collar with animated vigor.

"This business is going to come to blows," Dr. Vorago whispered to Dr. Whitcraft. They slid their chairs away from the two posturing doctors.

Dr. Marplot had gotten to his feet now too, graciously inserting himself between the two incensed academicians. "Gentlemen, gentlemen, please. We must all remember ourselves. Every man at these tables is qualified to be here, and our profession suffers when we bicker like this. Let's keep to the matter at hand, shall we?"

Reluctantly, Dr. Naffin and Dr. Clowclash relented, each man matching the other's speed and angry grimace as they lowered themselves back into their seats.

"Now, I couldn't agree more with Dr. Chimble," Dr. Marplot continued in a most soothing coo. "We need to give the ladies of our society more credit, so let's not dwell on this distasteful speculation that they will somehow *misuse* the maneuver. We're all here to mark a significant discovery. Let's raise our cups in celebration of such a crucial scientific step forward."

"Here, here," the doctors agreed, settling down once again. With renewed cheer, they murmured and nudged each other with most hearty congratulations.

Chapter Twelve

Mrs. Minnock cupped her chin in her palm watching Dr. Whitcraft search the cabinet.

"I don't want these cups, I want the blue ones." He shut the door and opened another.

"The blue china is up there, on the top shelf," she said. "Why does it make a difference?"

"Because the others dissipate the heat too quickly." He stood on the tips of his toes now, straining to reach. "The blue cups keep the beverage nice and hot, and frankly I just like them better...something about the feel of the handles."

Bemused, she watched him blow the traces of dust out of two Royal Doulton teacups before setting them on the counter. He reached up again and retrieved their corresponding saucers. "Well then, by all means, we should use the blue." She dropped her head and rested it on her folded arms. "I'm very pleased to hear that your demonstration was such a success."

"Well, the demonstration went all right, but afterwards things got a little tricky."

"They would, wouldn't they with a bunch of academics all blustering about, but oh..." She exhaled a long, breathy sigh. "I can't tell you what a difficult day *I've* had." She could hear Dr. Whitcraft fooling around with the copper teakettle.

"I hope you're not going to tell me some brutish

scoundrel got carried away with one of the girls."

"No, no. There was no *scoundrel.* It was a woman." She sat up. "A *wife*, as a matter of fact."

"Oh, good Lord."

"Yes…well, I doubt *the Lord* had anything to do with it. How she made it past the front door, I'll never know."

"What happened?"

"She tackled Arabella, is what happened. The silly girl turned eighteen today and had just been presented with a rather extravagant birthday gift by the woman's husband. Mr. Drumble is very devoted, so the diamond brooch was not exactly unexpected. The wife managed to get Arabella into a rather peculiar grappling hold, all while accusing her of *joining giblets* with her husband in their marital bed when she had gone to see her mother in Surrey."

"Oh dear," Dr. Whitcraft muttered from behind her. "What did the husband do?"

"Not a thing." She shook her head. "He had made himself comfortable on the stairs peeking at the chaos through the railings like a spectator at a circus. It was up to me to quell the passions of the women in his life. According to the other girls, Arabella has been making it a habit of lurking around the Drumbles' flat and taunting his wife when she hangs out the wash." Mrs. Minnock looked up and noticed the empty cup and saucer in front of her. But there was more. Two infusers packed with tealeaves sat at the ready along with napkins, spoons and a small plate crowded with biscuits. Dr. Whitcraft sat down and patted her hand.

"The water should be ready in just a few minutes. Please, continue. You have me in suspense."

She picked up a piece of shortbread and turned it over in her fingers. "Well, you won't believe this part. When Mrs. Drumble tired of squeezing the life out Arabella, she dashed over to her husband and began tearing off her clothes, insisting she would service him on the spot, thereby saving their household the additional expenditure."

"My heavens." Dr. Whitcraft stood again.

"I know." She shook her head again and shut her eyes.

He wrapped his hand in a tea cloth and eased the steaming kettle from the range. "Now that's quite an extreme display for a proper married woman. It almost makes me wonder—" He stopped speaking, and looked lost in thought.

"What?" Mrs. Minnock spun around, cocking her head.

"I was just wondering if the woman might possibly benefit from a diagnostic examination. I hazard to say, perhaps it is even possible that she has—"

"For goodness' sake, not every enraged woman has *hysteria*, Dr. Whitcraft. Is that what you were going to say? Really! Frankly, if my husband drained our household funds so he could buy a silly trinket for his mistress, I'd have been more furious than she was."

"Well, I'm not sure about that," he muttered as he poured hot water into her cup and sat back down.

"I had to dismiss Arabella, of course. What a scene *that* was. I can't run a business if some half-witted girl is going to breech our rules and see clients outside of this house. Not to mention harass their wives." She brought the blue teacup to her lips and blew. She softened her voice. "Thank you for the tea, by the way.

Pampering me this way. It's very kind of you."

He nodded, blowing at his tea.

She set the cup down and stirred lazily with her spoon. "Arabella is the one I blame, much more so than poor Mrs. Drumble. I suppose the moral of this story is not to put faith into ridiculous adolescent girls. They are much too frivolous and silly to be trusted. I need to stick to older, more seasoned women if I am to exist here in peace."

She smiled at Dr. Whitcraft, who looked suddenly stricken as he lifted the cup to his lips.

"Oh do be careful not to burn yourself, doctor," Mrs. Minnock warned.

****

Mrs. Pannade sat at her writing desk, a stack of letters from this morning's post clutched in one hand, a squat glass of her husband's brandy balanced in the other. She took a small sip and winced. The liquid had curiously burned and numbed her lips all at once.

She sighed and set the glass down. The dullness of the morning was unbearable. She cast letter after letter away with a disinterested flick of her wrist. But then her heart leapt. The unmistakably erudite script of her physician, Dr. William Whitcraft, was right there in her hand, addressed to *her,* not to her husband like all the others had been! She dropped the remaining letters, snatched up the paper knife and sliced it open.

Dear Mrs. Pannade,

After numerous unsuccessful attempts to communicate with your husband, I have concluded, most reluctantly, that I have no choice but to bypass his authority and instead plead my case directly to you.

I begin by reiterating that your standing 10 a.m. appointments with me have been TERMINATED; a development of which you are unquestionably aware as I have personally escorted you out of my office each and every day at this same time, an occurrence that has become as regular as the machinations of the heavens. These visits simply must *cease at once!*

Secondly, I have, in fact, discovered that you passed yourself off as my wife and deceived a rather hapless locksmith into duplicating a key for my property...in the middle of the night, no less, while I slept inside unawares*!*

I learned of this plot when presented with a delinquency notice from said locksmith, which incidentally allowed me to change my locks to an entirely new arrangement. I am telling you now, Mrs. Pannade, discard your counterfeit key at once. It will no longer grant access into my home.

Your actions have been utterly shocking. If additional conduct of this nature is attempted or discovered, I will not hesitate *to involve all relevant authorities.*

Finally, so that there shall be no ambiguities between us, I shall enumerate my expectations of you once and for all in writing:

The pursuit of my affections shall end herewith!

There is to be no loitering, lurking, prowling about, spying on or menacing me of any kind.

No gifts shall be delivered, no offers of service submitted.

The attempt to win the favor of my parents shall end henceforth! (I have alerted them of your tactics and treachery, and they will no longer be accepting tokens of affection on my behalf.)

I close this letter with a personal plea. I believe your condition has deteriorated dangerously and beg you to seek treatment elsewhere. I continue to recommend Dr. George Vorago for the position. He is assuredly most capable of rendering cautious and thoughtful care.

Mrs. Pannade, I have never before been driven to banish a patient from my practice, and it truly pains me to do so now. I have deliberated on this issue most thoroughly, and have concluded that I was simply left no other choice.

I wish you only the best, I am,
    Respectfully,
    Dr. William Whitcraft

Mrs. Pannade frowned. She folded the letter in two, pinching the crease crisp before laying it aside. She pulled back the heavy brocade curtain and gazed out, not particularly interested in the view. After a few moments, she thrust her chin forward, scooped up the glass for another go, and commenced sorting the post with renewed vigor.

But the presence of a rather heavy letter gave her pause. A grin spread across her face, and she grabbed the paper knife again and sliced into the envelope, releasing a newly forged iron key that slipped out of its folded invoice and landed on her desk with a heavy clank.

Mrs. Pannade giggled as she inspected her prize, twirling it this way and that. She extended her gloved arm, and fished out its now useless predecessor. She kissed the new key and expertly tucked it in place, relishing the cold metal tingle against her skin.

****

Dr. Whitcraft escorted the day's last patient out of the examining room, and was surprised to see Dr. Marplot seated next to the girl's mother, gazing at him with a careless smile. Perhaps the man had good news about *The Lancet* finally agreeing to publish his paper.

"Are you all right? Is she all right, Dr. Whitcraft?" The mother hurried to their side.

"I am perfectly fine, for goodness' sake, Mama." A few strands of the girl's hair had escaped her elaborate coiffure. She blew at the tickling wisps with a gentle puff. She threw a quick glance back at her doctor, and without realizing it, a most contented smile had settled on her lips.

"How many more treatments, doctor?" The mother adjusted her daughter's capelet over her dress.

"The wedding is, what…in three months? I still believe the symptoms will abate once she's married. Why don't we drop to twice a week until then? Mondays and Wednesdays. Miss Faffle, can you make a note of that, please? Is that all right with the both of you, then?"

"Absolutely. Thank you."

"Yes, thank you."

The mother and daughter departed. Miss Faffle scurried into the examining room, and Dr. Marplot rose with an extended hand. "Good to see you, sir. My apologies for the unannounced visit. May we have a word…in private, if you please?"

"Yes, yes of course." Dr. Whitcraft pulled back from his colleague's grasp and gestured toward his office.

"That patient that just left, you gave her the maneuver just then? Lucrative little situation that is. Too bad she is getting married."

Dr. Whitcraft crossed behind his desk. "The girl has the classic symptoms of hysteria. I am providing her treatment. That is all that matters to me."

"Ah yes. Always the professional. Yes, indeed." Dr. Marplot seated himself most comfortably. "Well, regardless…" He took a breath and stared at his colleague, a twitchy grin beginning at the corner of his lips.

"You look like you have something to share." Dr. Whitcraft tried not to betray his eagerness.

A full grin bloomed on Dr. Marplot's face. He leaned in with his hands on his knees, and announced, "Dr. Whitcraft, *The Lancet* is most eager to publish your paper."

"Well now, how about that!" He smacked his palm on the desk with delight. After all of the tension and anticipation, his maneuver was finally going to pay off.

"Yes. It *is* wonderful for you then, isn't it? Congratulations are most certainly in order. There is one slight hitch in the matter, however." He picked up a pen and twirled it in his fingers. "They insist upon having *my name* attached to it, as well." He raised both

126

brows and shrugged.

"*Your* name?"

"Yes, but you must let me explain."

"Excuse me, sir, but that's the most ludicrous thing I have ever heard. Why on earth would they want *your name* on a paper that *I* wrote? Are you joking with me, sir?"

"Why not at all." He spread his hands like a vicar at the pulpit. "Calm down a moment and I'll explain." He leaned back and took a breath. "So here's the thing. The boys at *The Lancet* were absolutely floored when I described what occurred at that demonstration—a paroxysm in only a few minutes? You should have seen their faces. Frankly, if it weren't for me describing what I saw with my own eyes, not a single one of those fellows would've believed your maneuver was even possible…not to mention that it could be taught so easily to the likes of Dr. Chimble.

"So, when we conferred about your paper, everyone agreed that a scientific milestone of this magnitude should be handled with extra precision, and that amending it to include a perspective of a doctor who saw it performed would provide the necessary credence, you know… the proper point of view."

"So what—"

Dr. Marplot held up a hand. "And because I was there on behalf of the journal, it only made sense that I be the one to do it."

Dr. Whitcraft leaned forward. "What the devil would you even say? I can't have you botch what I've spent hours meticulously crafting. You think you're just going to swoop in and—"

"If you don't want me to be involved, simply say

so. But if you want *The Lancet* to publish it, *someone* needs to contribute a small section about observing the demonstration. If *I* were the one to do it, I'd probably add a few scribbles about what I saw—certainly nothing that would alter the content; I wouldn't dream of it. It's already so well-articulated. But regardless, it would still clearly be *your* paper and *your* maneuver."

Blood rushed through his ears. He despised having his name on a paper with anyone, let alone *this* man. Still, he so very much wanted to get it published, and *The Lancet* was by far the most prestigious journal in London. And what they were asking hardly seemed unreasonable. He sighed and slid his hand through his hair. "I must have the final say, on whatever you contribute."

"Of course. Your formal approval would be required for anything that appears in print."

"I suppose I have no choice, then do I?" he whispered, sinking back into his chair. A dull ache throbbed behind his eyes.

Dr. Marplot reached across the desk for his hand, and gave it a pat. "Good. Then I'll get started on it right away. What an honor it will be for me to have even the slightest association with such an important advancement in science."

"Yes, well that is very kind." Dr. Whitcraft flipped open his pocket watch.

"Dr. Whitcraft?" Miss Faffle peeked into his office. "I'm sorry to interrupt, but Mr. Gamon is here for me. Is there anything else you need?"

"No, thank you, Miss Faffle. Go on then." Her swarthy suitor draped a cape across her shoulders and pulled her toward the front door. Dr. Whitcraft grimaced, and settled his eyes back on his guest.

"You know," Dr. Marplot said, "as I begin to craft my section of the paper, perhaps it would prove helpful for me to have a look at some of your early notes. All of those *trials and errors*. I'd love to get some insight into the process that got you there."

Dr. Whitcraft stared at him for a moment. Finally, he said, "Well...I don't usually make a habit of—my notes are extraordinarily rudimentary, meant only for my eyes." He paused and then shifted in his seat. "They wouldn't mean anything to you."

"I'm sure you must have *something* in your records about the maneuver." He laughed, pointing to the cabinet in the corner.

"Of course. I have a file that covers every aspect of the maneuver...patient records, diagrams, explanation of the theory. Most of that is already in my paper. I suppose if it would be helpful for you to take a look, then have at it."

"I may do that. It was just a thought, really." Dr. Marplot quieted for a moment and glanced around. "You have a pleasant office here. And you live upstairs? I suppose that might change after our article makes you famous."

Our article? He opened his mouth to protest, but startled at the crash of the front door blasting open, followed by a livid Miss Reave. "William? William! You must do something about that deranged woman! She came to my meeting and told me in front of all of my friends that I am to leave you alone. Can you believe the—" She took a breath and froze before offering Dr. Marplot a weak smile. "Excuse me, Dr. Marplot. What a surprise." She glided her hand across her hair.

"A most pleasant surprise, indeed Miss Reave," he replied with a knowing grin as he got to his feet.

"You must forgive my rather brash entrance." She knelt to pick up the bag she had thrown, blushing. "But, I am a bit flummoxed."

Dr. Whitcraft eyed his colleague as he made his way past and into the reception area. He patted Miss Reave on the shoulder. "My poor dear! How terrible for you! Isn't Mrs. Anile with you?"

"Oh…" She walked back to the door and glanced out of the glass, searching. "Ugh, she was right behind me."

Dr. Whitcraft stood behind her, studying the passing crowds for an eye-patch wearing matron. He gave up and turned back to his fiancée. "I'm sure she'll turn up, please, tell me what happened."

She looked from man to man, betraying unexpected delight at having an additional audience member to which she could relate her tale of woe. "I was sitting between Julia and Sarah, of course, at our *Society of Manners* meeting. Julia got up to complain to Mrs. Uppish that Mr. Fustian was telling his filthy jokes again and we could hear every word he said. Before I knew it, that awful *Pannade* woman took Julia's place.

"Before I could tell her to get away from me, *she* began scolding *me*…telling me that I needed to stay away from you, and that if I didn't, she would make a motion to have me expelled from the society, because *I* didn't have any manners. Can you believe it? When Julia came back, they started yelling at each other and it wasn't long before all of the women and some of the men were on their feet, too…shouting the most terrible insults and accusations. Finally, Mrs. Foyce checked the roster and discovered what I had been screaming to anyone who would listen, that Mrs. Pannade wasn't even a member. They finally threw her out onto the street where she belonged, thank goodness."

"Oh my, that is dreadful, just dreadful," Dr. Whitcraft cried. "I cannot apologize enough. I'll go to the police tomorrow morning. I have to believe there is something they can do."

"Is this that woman from the bushes? She's still troubling you and now she's harassing poor Miss Reave? Don't you both lead such *interesting* lives?" Dr. Marplot grinned. "I should spend more time with the both of you."

****

Dr. Whitcraft scanned the headquarters of Sir Robert Peel's new Metropolitan Police Force searching for the sergeant in question. There was so much commotion; men in uniform buzzing amongst ne'er-do-wells and upstanding citizens alike. He became mesmerized by a quarrelling couple: a scullery maid and low kitchen servant judging by their garb, both of whom had black eyes and had just been disarmed of their cutlery by an observant young constable.

"Over there. He's the beefy chap behind the counter," an officer mumbled to Dr. Whitcraft again, without looking up.

He spotted the slouching Sergeant Draffsack at once, posed unattractively behind the counter, picking at his fingernails with his teeth. Dr. Whitcraft approached the man and waited for an acknowledgement. Without receiving one, he began to speak.

"Sir. I was told that you were the man to speak to about an unpleasant quandary in which I now find myself." The doctor described his embarrassing dilemma regarding Mrs. Pannade. By the end of his tale, the sergeant's lips were quivering with laughter.

"I'm not sure I understand. A lovesick woman isn't a police matter." Now that he had stopped laughing, the officer's tone was blatantly patronizing. Dr. Whitcraft took a breath, having anticipated that this conversation would likely be a difficult one.

"Sir, I have thought long and hard about coming here, professionally speaking you know, but I have come to the conclusion that law enforcement must be notified. The patient in question is ill. I have made every reasonable effort to handle the situation myself, giving her repeated warnings to respect my professional boundaries, not to mention those of my fiancée. She has disregarded each and every admonition. I do not wish for you to deal with her harshly because her disease has progressed to a point where she is not fully in control of her actions."

"What's she doing that's so bad?"

"As I previously stated to that other officer, it started with visits to my office in excess of her regular appointments. She would arrive with gifts: first food; roasted fowl, pies and the like. I believe on one occasion she dropped off a trifle. I don't know what else. These were all well and good, but then she persisted with more extravagant gifts, things that she had purchased, culminating with a gold pocket watch and fob—"

"Really?" The sergeant's doughy face brightened as he glanced at the fob hanging from Dr. Whitcraft's waistcoat.

"No, no…not this one. I mean, this one is mine. I returned the watch and fob immediately and instructed her that no such gifts would be accepted. But the gifts and obsessive attention have been easy enough to manage, I suppose, but her behavior has escalated from the excessive to…I hate to say it, but to the rather *disconcerting*.

"She follows me around the town, and has even broken into my home, stirring me out of sleep at the most appalling hours of the night, demanding that I see her. This is all bad enough, but now she has taken to visiting my fiancée at her residence *and* at her social engagements.

"What I am asking is, keeping in mind her fragile constitution, if perhaps you could speak to her, explain that what she is doing is against the law and order her to stop." Dr. Whitcraft took a deep breath.

"That's a problem isn't it, because nothing you're describing is against the law. She can bring you pies and visit your fiancée, or knock on your door at night whenever she pleases. She breaks in, you say? How did she get into your house? Did she break your door, your window?"

"Well, no. I always lock my door, but she had a key made. I've changed my locks, of course."

"A key made? Well, she *is* a resourceful one, isn't she? If she hasn't actually broken anything, then frankly, doctor…" He threw up his hands and shrugged.

"Good God, I have an unstable woman menacing my fiancée, ruining my practice and you are saying there is nothing you can do?"

Sergeant Draffsack looked thoughtful for a

moment. "I suppose I could have one of my men follow her around, see what she is up to, try and catch her in the act of something." He turned and shouted over his shoulder. "Someone tell Constable Duffart to come out here."

"Splendid," Dr. Whitcraft said. Finally he was getting somewhere. "That would be very helpful, indeed."

"While we wait for Constable Duffart to turn up, I wonder if you could help me, doctor. For the last several weeks, I've had this terrible pain in my middle, right here." He grimaced and arched his back, holding his palm flat against his stomach, which hung in a great puddle of substance over his belt. "Oh, yes, there. Just there, ah." He stabbed repeatedly with his index finger to indicate the area of concern.

Dr. Whitcraft sighed. If Mrs. Pannade would leave him in peace, it would all be worth it. He reached over the counter and palpated the officer's middle.

Chapter Thirteen

A diminutive old man in a smart-looking livery and drooping white wig showed Dr. Whitcraft into an empty parlor with a large red couch placed in its center. Excellent, a perfect location to administer the therapy if he deemed it necessary. Now he just needed his patient.

"Excuse me, Mr. Caxon, was it? Will I have the opportunity to meet Mr. Meecher, or will I just be seeing his wife today?"

Mr. Caxon appeared stricken, glancing away from the doctor as if trying to settle on just the right words to answer this question. "You'll have to speak to *Mrs.* Meecher about that, sir."

"I see." Dr. Whitcraft looked around the room and removed his hat.

"Can I offer you anything, sir, while Mrs. Meecher makes her way downstairs? A beverage, perhaps?"

"No, nothing thank—" He didn't have a chance to finish because Mrs. Meecher blew into the room past her servant, traveling within a cloud of faint perfume. "That'll be all, Caxon. I don't want any interruptions, is that clear? Not a sound."

She was a good deal younger than Dr. Whitcraft had expected, and wore a dressing gown made up of many layers of sheer fabric, but did not seem the slightest bit modest in front of her manservant. She grabbed a handful of hair that had fallen across her eyes, and tossed it to the side, watching as Mr. Caxon disappeared from the room.

"Good afternoon, Mrs. Meecher." Dr. Whitcraft set his hat on the pianoforte and offered his hand to the smiling young woman. Her eyes sparkled as she lowered herself on the couch. "Your husband and I have been in correspondence regarding your troublesome condition. I assume you are aware of that."

"Oh yes. Yes I am."

"Apparently I was recommended by a colleague of his."

"Oh, I'm not sure about that." She dragged her hand along the upholstery. She certainly did not seem like the distraught and depressed woman that had been described in her husband's letters.

"Shall we get started?" She scooted back and threw her legs up on the couch, exposing her bare feet and ankles.

"Uh, let's not get ahead of ourselves. Given this is our first meeting, I need to ask you a series of questions to gauge if this therapy is warranted for your case."

Her peculiar expression of eagerness vanished at once. She swung her legs back down and planted them on the floor.

"I have read your husband's letters thoroughly, Mrs. Meecher, and he assures me that the only treatment that has ever helped abate your symptoms has been the administration of pelvic massage. Is that correct?"

"Oh yes. That is the only thing that seems to make any difference. I am so terribly sad. Why don't we just get started?"

"Well, I cannot rely on the work of other

physicians, you see. I must come to a diagnosis myself before I recommend—"

A barely audible knock vibrated the double doors. Mrs. Meecher's already-impatient demeanor inflamed into a passion, and she snapped, "Great ghosts, I asked for some privacy! Caxon I told you—"

"Ma'am, I am very sorry." He put his mouth between the doors, careful not to look inside the room. "Your husband, Mr. Meecher has just arrived." His voice sounded urgent, and very nearly terrified.

"What?" Mrs. Meecher shrieked, jumping up and dashing to the window. "Oh my God!" She spun around, pointing at Dr. Whitcraft. "You've got to get out! He'll kill you if he catches you here!"

He felt the blood drain from his face. "I don't understand, madam. Why would he be upset to see me here? He's the one who wrote to me and inquired about your condition. He insisted upon these arrangements and paid me for several appointments in advance, certainly he—"

"No! He never did any such thing! You fool, it was me! He never knew anything about it! Where's your hat? You had a hat…ah." She grabbed his hat from atop the pianoforte and jerked it down on his head with both hands. She gripped him under his arm and yanked him toward the back of the room. Dr. Whitcraft opened his mouth to protest, but instead watched stunned as she swung open the cupboard door and stuffed him inside.

"Ma'am! This will not do!" Dr. Whitcraft shouted. The door shut, leaving him in complete darkness. He fumbled for the knob and found it, but couldn't escape because the hook and eye at the top of the cupboard's jamb had been engaged. Through the crack, he watched

Mrs. Meecher run toward the window.

"Just stay in there for now," she said through clenched teeth. "I'll fix it so you can leave, but I'm warning you, don't say a word or he's liable to give you a good thrashing. He doesn't approve of strange men being here when he's away."

"Strange men?" Dr. Whitcraft's voice sounded muffled from within the cupboard. "I am not a strange man! I am a physician, Mrs. Meecher and am acting within the utmost standards of my profession. There is nothing untoward about my technique of—"

"Oh, now he's talking to Mr. Caxon," she wailed, leaning against the window sash. "He'll tell him everything...Oh! He's coming up the walk!"

Clutching her chest, she stumbled to the couch and collapsed, flipping herself over in a most awkward pose. But then, she jumped to her feet, and scanned the room before dashing toward the far wall. She yanked one of the dusty volumes from the shelf, turned and leapt through the air like ballerina, robes sailing underneath her as she parachuted back onto the couch. Breathing heavily, she flipped open the book and rested it on her lap.

"Mrs. Meecher? Mrs. Meecher?" Dr. Whitcraft stood on his toes; he poked a finger through the crack, trying to loosen the hook.

She whipped her head around and hissed, "Oh, will you stay quiet!"

"Stay quiet?" He put his lips to the crack. "Madam, I insist you let me out this instant! I am certain your husband will understand that even now you're having an hysterical episode. This is exactly why he contacted me, Mrs. Meecher!"

The parlor doors swung open and a looming, well-dressed but disheveled figure appeared in the doorway, his teeth bared. "Where is he?"

Mrs. Meecher cocked her neck unnaturally. "My darling, I wasn't expecting you."

Mr. Meecher huffed and puffed from the doorway like an enraged Canadian goose. "It's clear you weren't expecting *me*! What the hell *were* you expecting?"

She shrugged, trembling now, and pretended to commence reading her book.

Mr. Meecher stormed past his wife toward the far door leading to the back hallway. In a moment, he returned to the parlor. "Where is he? Where have you put him? Did he go out this way, because if he did, Caxon will stop him."

"Who?"

"You think I'm a fool, don't you? Caxon told me another one of those charlatans has come and I—" Mr. Meecher stopped speaking, letting the silence fall over the room.

The wooden floor creaked underneath each step as he approached her.

"He's in this room, then, isn't he?" he whispered, turning from his frightened wife to the back of the room. Dr. Whitcraft silently shrank deeper into the cupboard.

Mr. Meecher crept toward the cupboard door like a cat burglar on tiptoe. Dr. Whitcraft groaned at his approach, straightening his glasses while trying to breathe. Certainly this predicament could be diffused with logic, he told himself.

Mrs. Meecher let out a cry when her husband reached for the handle, but he paused, noticing the engaged hook and eye. Licking his lips, he growled with renewed certainty, and released it with the flick of his forefinger and thumb.

All the air seemed to leave the room when the door swung open, exposing a rigid Dr. Whitcraft. Attempting to maintain a façade of self-righteous certainty, the doctor croaked, "Well, good afternoon Mr. Meecher. I am Dr. William Whitcraft. I must admit, sir, this is an awkward encounter, but I assure you that my purpose here is one of purely the most professional—"

The blow was instant. Dr. Whitcraft collapsed backwards into the cupboard like an umbrella snapped shut. The good doctor's hat, however, remained exactly where his head had been, hovering frozen as if it too had been struck dumb by the clenched fist still waving with rage.

Mrs. Meecher shrieked.

Mr. Meecher shouted, "Get up, get up you...you proprietor of lies! Have you had your hands on her? Stand up and answer like a man!"

At that instant, an earsplitting shriek came from the parlor's doorway, followed by a pale-blue flash of fabric and lace.

"What have you done?" the voice screeched. Mr. Meecher was blown aside by the blur sailing into the cupboard. It proceeded to pepper the doctor's face with kisses.

Stunned, Mr. Meecher looked first at his wife and then at Mr. Caxon, who had since entered the room. "Caxon, who is this woman?"

"I haven't the faintest notion, sir. She's been lingering out on the stoop, but got past me when the commotion began. I assumed she was waiting for the doctor to finish his business."

Dr. Whitcraft managed to sit up and feel for his spectacles, which were crumpled to the left side of his face. "Mrs. Pannade. Really."

"Don't trouble yourself, my darling," she purred into his ear. She whipped around and screamed, "What the hell have you done to him?" Her manner was beyond any normal feminine tenor, and her eyes seemed to spin with an otherworldly possession.

This disturbing display gave even the livid Mr. Meecher pause. He stepped away, unfolding his fist into a flattened palm, as if hoping to relegate this unpleasant sight back in to the cupboard from which it came. "I don't know what this is," he muttered to no one in particular.

Just then, Constable Duffart passed through the double doors, looking more perplexed than anyone. "Uh, excuse me," he said to the crowd. "I have reason to believe that an individual of interest to the law has taken shelter in this house."

At that, Mrs. Pannade dropped all parts of Dr. Whitcraft, jumped to her feet, and made a mad dash for the open back hall door.

As the officer jumped forward in pursuit of his claim, he caught his large black boot on the leg of the couch. His tumble was not simple, but rather a complicated dance of many phases. Every observer in the room was certain that he would manage to catch himself and recover, but alas, they were to be disappointed. He sailed over the couch, crashed through a mahogany side table, and ricocheted off of the highboy, toppling its cornice. His flailing arm took out a silver service for twelve, which had been prominently displayed on a wall shelf. Forward momentum carried him down, down until he slid along the hardwood before landing under the pianoforte. And there he lay like a blue whale blowing and beached, helpless save for his confused moan.

Everyone was aghast.

"Someone get a doctor!" Mrs. Meecher screamed, frozen in her place.

At that, all heads turned to the cupboard, where Dr. Whitcraft remained. He placed his hands on the floor and crawled out into the chaos of the room, righting himself silently. He straightened, gave the bottom of his waistcoat an authoritative tug, and brushed the dust off of his frockcoat. His right eye had swollen into a magenta wink, but nevertheless he cleared his throat, strode across the room, and commenced an examination of his newest patient.

****

Dr. Whitcraft had nearly mastered the art of perceiving the world with only one eye. Walking presented a challenge, and descending the stairs seemed nearly impossible, but regardless, he had a full schedule today and a responsibility to his suffering patients. He pondered the viability of doing the maneuver in his lessened condition when he heard the distinctive soft sound of a woman's sobs coming from downstairs. He stopped and listened, fearful that Mrs. Pannade might be waiting to accost him in the reception area.

He crept down the remaining stairs, wondering if another officer had been assigned to follow her now that Constable Duffart had broken his clavicle. Bracing himself for a confrontation, he cracked open the door and was instead much relieved to discover a distraught

Miss Faffle heaving great sobs atop her desk.

"Miss Faffle?" he whispered. "My heavens. Is there anything wrong?"

She lifted her head, revealing a face streaked with tears. "Oh, doctor." She stood up and threw her arms around him, burying her face in his shoulder.

Dr. Whitcraft stood stiff as she clung to him, his remaining eye wide and searching. "Miss Faffle, I'm sure—"

"Oh Dr. Whitcraft! I have…I…have…ruined my…life," she gasped in spurts, becoming more agitated with each syllable.

He wanted to writhe out of her grasp and escape back up his stairs, but chivalry dictated otherwise. He straightened himself, gripped her by the upper arms and peeled her away from his chest. "Now I am certain that you have not ruined your life. What nonsense are you spouting?"

"He t-told me he would *marry* me. He promised he would."

Dr. Whitcraft cringed. The thought of Miss Faffle's love life was horrific enough, but, oh good Lord, had there been some intrigue with that filthy greengrocer? Had that dreadful man gone and debauched this poor girl?

"All right then. It's all right. Let's have a seat." He led her to one of the chairs, shaking his head, angry at himself. He was the only legitimate male figure left in this girl's life, and should have thought to warn her about the dark nature of men—especially *that* man.

He swung his pocket watch into his palm. In less than five minutes, this room would be filled with hysterical women, and his assistant was draped over a chair in the depths of despondency. He had palpitations at the very thought of it.

She looked up at him with watery brown eyes. "He told me he would marry me, but now… I heard there's another girl. Oh, he promised me!"

"Well, that is just, just dreadful. I wish there was something I could do." He glanced at the front door.

She sobbed in response to his kind words, dropping her face into her hands and bobbing up and down while the distressed doctor watched in silence. Then, all at once, she sat up. "You! You could go talk to him. Tell him how much I love him, and, even if there's someone else, I don't care. I'll be his wife. Please, my mother will throw me out if she discovers."

Dr. Whitcraft felt as if his blood were being drained from his body. Now was he to be a mender of broken hearts? What on earth could he possibly say to that terrible man? Give him a lecture about the nature of polite society, and his responsibilities to this young woman with whom he had apparently taken liberties?

As his first patient climbed the stairs, he would have promised Miss Faffle the moon and the stars if it would make her take her place behind her desk.

"Yes. Of course, I'll speak to him. I'd be happy to."

"Oh, thank you. Thank you!" She leaped up and threw her arms around his shoulders, squeezing him with the force of an executioner's noose.

"Good morning, Dr. Whitcraft. I'm right on time. I hope I'm not interrupting anything," the fur-draped woman drawled. She made herself comfortable taxing one of his chairs.

"Good morning, Mrs. Princod. Just a little office

business. I'll, uh, be right with you, then." He pulled Miss Faffle back to her desk and whispered, "Now, I can't promise anything, you know. I don't want you to get your hopes up."

"Oh yes. Thank you, doctor, I understand." She wiped the tears from her cheeks, took a determined breath and picked up his schedule for the day.

Relieved, he turned to Mrs. Princod. "Shall we?"

****

The restaurant was full, the tablecloths starched, silver-domed trolleys rattled by, and the tinkling crystal goblets punctuated the muted and appropriate conversation.

"What would the lady care for this evening?" a balding middle-aged waiter asked Miss Reave.

She squirmed in her chair and wore a superior grin on her lips. "I will have the fricandeau à l'oseille, if you please."

"An excellent choice." The waiter took the bill of fare from her hands. With an air of indifference only seen in restaurants such as this, he turned to Dr. Whitcraft. "And you, sir?"

"The game bird, roasted if you please. And please bring us a bottle of white wine. I'll trust your selection."

"Ah yes." The waiter's bland manner abruptly changed into one of grateful deference. Apparently the gesture with the wine meant a great deal to the man. He just hoped it wouldn't cost him the day's wages.

He reached across the table and grasped Miss Reave's hand. How lovely she looked this evening, in the candlelight. She flashed him a fervent smile, but spun back round to continue her study of the other patrons.

"Mr. Grannows ordered the lobster, can you see? I'm sure that's the most expensive thing they have here. How he can possibly afford that on his solicitor's salary, I don't know. His wife is so shabbily dressed, maybe he saves money on her clothes. Oh, I can't wait to tell Sarah that you took me here."

"Well, I'm just glad to be here with you tonight. I'm actually going to break my streak and have a glass of wine. What do you think about that? Oh, it has been such a week."

"Your eye is looking better, poor dear." She leaned across the table and reached under his glasses, touching the tender shaded skin beneath his eye. "I should kiss it and make it better."

He reached for her hand, and slid it down across his lips. After a small kiss, she pulled her hand away, blushing.

He took a breath, and sighed. "I haven't even told you about today's drama."

"Not that horrible woman. William you can't—"

"No, no," he said, wincing. "Good Lord, let's not even breathe her name here, please." The very mention of his ex-patient made him glance around the room, certain she was observing them from behind a potted plant. "No, it was Miss Faffle. Oh, she was in a dreadful state."

"What was the matter with her?" Miss Reave asked, looking at her fork.

"Well, it's inappropriate even to discuss this with you, but it seems her beau," he paused and dropped his voice to a whisper. "Apparently he has taken some liberties with her."

"Really?" Miss Reave looked up at once, but after a moment's reflection, she wrinkled her nose. "With Miss Faffle? How did you find out?"

"Oh, you should have seen her. She was utterly distraught this morning and told me so. And now the man has become hesitant about marriage."

"She told you? Oh, the silly fool."

"She seems to be under the impression that I can talk to him. Get him to reconsider."

"Oh, you should do no such thing. You need to get rid of her, William. Turn her out!"

"Well, my goodness," he whispered.

"William, you're a physician. People trust you! You can't have some tainted young woman sitting there in your office representing you. It won't be long before the whole town knows of her exploits. What will your society women think, then? They certainly won't want *her* escorting them into your examination room."

Dr. Whitcraft was at a loss. He had never considered that aspect of the problem.

"They don't travel in the same circles. I can't believe word would get out."

"Oh, it does. You wouldn't believe how fast. Papa had to dismiss my first governess when I was a baby. She got mixed up in some intrigue with an Irish man, and everyone found out about it and Papa was humiliated. I'm telling you, this could dampen all of the excitement surrounding your work, and I for one can't sit back and let your misplaced feelings of compassion for this girl ruin your practice."

The waiter approached, carrying a dusty bottle of wine. Miss Reave widened her eyes with a slight nod, a sure signal that the discussion of this topic must cease at once. The waiter did not notice, and began a rather dramatic performance of uncorking the wine.

When he poured, Miss Reave drawled, "Sir, I seem to have misplaced my fork. Isn't that silly? Could you bring me another?" Her smile was sugary-sweet.

"Oh, why of course, Miss," he replied, charmed.

He bowed at the pair and then ducked by Dr. Whitcraft's side. "Sir, a *Mrs. Anile* in the back of the restaurant is asking that I bring the money you are holding for her. She is in a bit of a jam."

Dr. Whitcraft glanced at Miss Reave. "Is the woman at cards?"

"Yes, sir," he whispered. "She's had a bad run at Faro and now owes a rather surprising sum to our scullion."

Dr. Whitcraft sighed and reached for his wallet, removing two half-pound notes. He handed them to the waiter, who bowed again before scurrying away.

****

The waiter hastened through the restaurant, sailing down two steps to the lower dining room toward the small table all the way in the back. He approached his most peculiar customer of the evening, hoping she would finally be ready to order. Only the feathered tip of her elaborate hat could be seen from behind the large, opened bill of fare, as if an exotic bird were nesting at this table for one.

"Are you ready to order, madam?"

Mrs. Pannade peeked out, not at the waiter, but at some distraction across the room. "Look at how she throws her head back like that. She's just *so* affected," she seethed.

The waiter wrinkled his brow. "I can come back

if…"

"No. I'll take a bottle of wine. Whatever that short man with the spectacles over there ordered. And bring me the plovers' eggs in aspic jelly. Yes, that will be lovely."

"Very good, madam." The waiter reached for the bill of fare, but she whisked it out of his grasp.

"No, no…I'll keep it. In case I want to order something else." She offered a prim smile and shadowed her face behind it, continuing her surveillance.

The waiter glanced over his shoulder at the couple, who appeared to be the object of this woman's attention, and suddenly remembered the fork. He smiled and hastened toward the kitchen.

Chapter Fourteen

The back door slipped out of Mrs. Minnock's hand, bounced up and clattered back into its jamb.

"Oh, I'd forgotten how peaceful it is out here," Dr. Whitcraft said. The lush ivy crawled over the wrought-iron fence and a single linden grew tall from the center of the tiny courtyard. It spread like a leafy parasol, protection against all of the noises and pollution of London.

"Why don't we come out here more often?" he asked.

"I don't know, really." She sat on the bench and watched how he balanced himself on the wooden swing hanging from the linden. "Are you going to tell me that you *actually went* and spoke to that man?"

"Oh, I did indeed." He sighed, swaying lightly.

She shook her head, making a tsk, tsk sound. "Oh, Dr. Whitcraft, that was so ill-advised."

"But I had to do *something*, Mrs. Minnock. Miss Faffle's mother discovered the intrigue and has cast her out like dirty dishwater. She can't continue staying with her friend forever. I had to at least try."

"What the devil was there to even say to the man?"

"I don't know, I don't know. I'd rehearsed a speech in my office about chivalry and the honor of young ladies...I wanted to assure him about Miss Faffle's character, something like that." The branches sagged as he planted his feet.

"Tell me what happened." She stretched her arms out behind her, waiting in earnest for what was sure to be a compelling story.

Dr. Whitcraft's frown turned under. "The man's shop was more dreadful than I ever could've imagined. I've walked past it dozens of times, but frankly the window looked so cloudy, I've always suspected I should find my produce elsewhere. I don't suppose you've ever been in there?"

She shook her head, a similar look of revulsion on her face.

"Wise. Very wise. When I opened the door, I was blasted by a sweet fermenting fruit odor...just awful. And the dust! It covered absolutely everything. Even the cobwebs hanging from the ceiling beams were lined with dust. It was shocking how filthy it all was. And the disarray! Melons and peppers bunched together with no order or reason. I'm telling you, for a greengrocery, it was a depressing place. I can't imagine what Miss Faffle was thinking. She had to have gone in there, but..." He waved a hand, as if trying to wave away the vision of it all.

"So I found him, of course, in the back, behind the counter sorting through a bin of bananas, with his fuzzy black arms. He was in the midst of battling with a decrepit old woman. You should've heard how he grumbled at her, but I didn't follow their conversation because of what happened next."

Mrs. Minnock widened her eyes. "Well?"

"Well, the shop was set up like a maze, so I could barely make my way." He paused and pinched up his frockcoat. "Look! His asparagus painted me with these disgusting green streaks. And this is new! Right there, can you see?"

She pursed her lips. "I can get one of the girls to wash that out for you."

He waved his hand again. "I wanted to tell you about the disaster."

"*Disaster*? Oh, Dr. Whitcraft," she giggled. "Please, continue, by all means."

"Well, I walked toward the man, and must have stepped on a clump of wet peelings or something, because my feet just flew out from under me." He reenacted the motion with a whisk of his feet underneath the swing. "I grabbed at a bin to catch myself and in an instant it was pandemonium."

Mrs. Minnock let loose a laugh, but the doctor continued unabated.

"Oh, the pears, the pears! They were everywhere—green and yellow, loose and rolling in every direction. And the flies; I can't leave out that horrific detail! They ascended from God knows where buzzing all around me. I was on my hands and knees, mind you, trying to sort out the madness, grabbing this pear and that, all while that awful man shouted at me to put them back.*"*

"So I did my best to replace his pears, which was nearly impossible because the vessel they had been in was absolutely inadequate to manage the load—only half of them would have been *too much* as far as I was concerned, but regardless. That old lady stormed past me swearing oaths, toppling even more fruit on top of the pears. After I replaced the pears, I finally gathered my courage and approached him."

"What did you say?"

"I didn't say anything, I didn't have the chance. I

must have stuffed one of the pears in my pocket, and he accused me right then of being a thief. He said, *I can see that pear bulging out of your pocket, you simple-minded fop.*

Mrs. Minnock's face grew rigid at that.

"Do you think I'm a fop?" he asked.

"What? No...no," she answered. "I don't think I would have chosen that word at all." She dropped her head low again, hoping to hide her amusement under the shadows of the linden. "So, what did you do?"

"I was completely taken aback, not so much by the fop comment, although that was completely uncalled for. I worried he actually thought I'd tried to steal his pear, so I gave it back to him at once, explained the situation, and advised him not to stack his merchandise so precariously in the future."

"I'm sure he was very receptive to that."

"No! He wasn't. Not in the least. He told me to get out...and I hadn't even had a chance to mention that his filthy floor nearly cost me my life, but that doesn't matter, I suppose. So I left, like a coward, without saying the slightest thing to him about the matter at hand." Dr. Whitcraft's shoulders dropped as he twisted helplessly on the swing. "What am I going to do about Miss Faffle?"

She sighed. "I'm afraid it's more complicated than you realize."

"What do you mean?"

"Your Mr. Gamon, the greengrocer. Unfortunately, I'm familiar with him. He is not just a scoundrel, debauching your young lady for the fun of it. He has another endeavor besides his grocery, one that is not quite so genteel."

Dr. Whitcraft quit swaying and waited for her to speak.

"Mr. Gamon is under the employ of one of my, oh, how would you say it? Competitors, I suppose, although I don't like to be associated with her. Frances Harridan. I doubt if you are familiar with her."

"I've never heard of her."

"I didn't think so. She has an entirely different philosophy about her business practices than I do...preferring *quantity* over quality. She employs a revolving collection of girls, and to meet the demand for new faces, she has several strategies. There are the innocent girls from the country who arrive in London without knowing a soul. They are penniless, you know. She befriends them, invites them to stay with her. Before they know it, they're in her debt because she charges exorbitant fees for every last little thing, even making them rent their clothes from her. Soon they discover that the only way to pay her back is by seeing gentleman callers."

"She also employs men like Mr. Gamon, who get a bounty for every unfortunate girl they deliver up. Apparently, he set his sights on Miss Faffle, knowing that if he took her maidenhood she would be thrown out of her house, which, of course, she has been. Then, she would most likely lose her position with you. When that happened, she would become desperate enough to be employed by that loathsome woman. This can be an ugly business."

"That man, that terrible man," he breathed. "You're telling me he was planning to do that to her the entire time?"

"Yes, I'm afraid. Terrible business, that. You going

there on her behalf was not only futile, but perhaps even dangerous."

They were silent for a moment.

"Well, I certainly can't dismiss her now that I know that," he whispered, almost to himself.

She smiled at him, although he didn't notice. She stood up, walked to the swing and knelt, placing a hand on his knee.

"Your girls?"

"Their clothes are their own and they can come and go as they like. I never understood the advantage of having unhappy, desperate souls in one's employ. Everyone here stays because they want to. Unless, of course, some man decides to sweep one of them off of her feet and take her away. It's been known to happen."

Chapter Fifteen

"Look! That would be the *guest* bedroom. We'd have a guest bedroom, can you imagine? My darling friends could come and stay when you're at the hospital overnight. Oh, look at that window…" Miss Reave darted across the room. "What a marvelous view of the street. And look!" She grabbed the blue-patterned curtain and wrapped it around herself like an Indian sari. "Isn't this the most sumptuous fabric? Do you think these come with the house?" She didn't wait for an answer but tossed the curtain to the side and dashed to the mantel. She ran her fingers over its elaborately carved wood and sighed.

Dr. Whitcraft strolled across the empty room to the window to have a look for himself. It offered a perfect view of Mrs. Anile, who stood on the pavement cross-examining a costermonger, pointing at the man with a bunch of carrots.

"I don't know," he said over his shoulder. "I'm sure this townhouse is very expensive. And it's rather large for the two of us, don't you think?" He turned around.

She had dropped her arms to her sides, and bit her bottom lip. She looked around the room. "Yes, yes…I suppose it is large. Certainly more so than that ridiculous flat you are living in now." She crossed the room and picked up the curtain again, kneading it through her fingers. Her pout had melted into a look of reflection.

"But, William..." She dropped the curtain and sidled toward him. "We'll need all this space, someday." She tilted her chin low, stifling a grin. "It won't always be just the two of us, you know." She picked up his hand and flattened it against her sternum. Like a paintbrush, she glided it over her chest and down to her middle. Her eyes were sparkling as she pressed his hand into her belly. He could feel the smooth lines of her corset underneath her dress.

His lips parted to speak, but could only draw in a short breath.

"And this house is so close to Papa," she whispered, holding his hand in place.

Dr. Whitcraft was spellbound. He slid his hand down and around, and clutched her by the hip, pulling her close. He breathed on her neck and she giggled. He giggled back, and kissed under her chin, planning to make his way to her lips, but paused.

Over her shoulder, he saw that Mrs. Anile had entered the hallway. He pulled away at once, startled, conjuring excuses for his lapse, but they were unnecessary. Mrs. Anile had not noticed the embrace—her eye had the view of the opposite room.

Miss Reave retreated as Mrs. Anile walked past. The matron dug in her bag and produced a remarkably long carrot. She yanked it from her mouth with a loud snap, and crunched while considering the hardwood.

"What do you think, Mrs. Anile?" he said, breathing again.

She nodded half-heartedly, and walked toward the stairs.

He turned to the window again, trying his best to hide from the both of them that negotiations were already underway for him to buy it. It was so expensive, much more than he ever dreamed of spending, but the house was perfect in every way. He just had to work out a payment schedule with his creditors and come up with the substantial down payment. And he wanted it to be a surprise, a perfect wedding present for his lovely new bride.

He turned back to Miss Reave, and attempted a skeptical tone. "We'll have to see. Perhaps I'll look into it."

"Oh you will? Oh how wonderful! Let's go upstairs and see the bedroom."

He watched her go, dashing up the stairs like an excited schoolgirl. He followed, but stopped to run his hand along the mantel. He took a deep breath as he surveyed the empty room. It was rather an ideal place to begin their life together, wasn't it?

****

After leaving the house, they'd lingered over a late dinner, and then wandered about trying to locate Mrs. Anile. Miss Reave finally spied her inside an ill-lit alehouse, playing cards with two farriers and a cobbler. On the way to collect her, Dr. Whitcraft remembered that he needed to make a quick stop at his office, which was only around the corner.

"I won't be a minute," he assured Miss Reave. He unlocked his front door and stepped into the abandoned reception area.

"If we leave her there any longer, she is going to be positively flushed."

"I know, I know, but your father will never forgive

me if I don't return his treatise. I promised to have it back yesterday, and I simply can't make the man—" He stopped speaking when he noticed a line of light glowing from underneath the examining room door. His eyes widened, and he signaled for Miss Reave to be silent and take notice. She did at once, and hastened to his side.

"Is it a burglar? Are you being burgled?" she whispered in his ear.

"Probably some miscreant looking for laudanum or morphine. Happens all the time in London," he whispered back.

His heart beat faster as he crept toward the door, but thought better of it and stopped. Maybe he should arm himself before daring to intercede with these types. He glanced around the office, at a loss. The only possibility appeared to be the empty hat stand, but it looked rather large and unwieldy. Still, it offered the best promise to intimidate even the most loathsome and drug-addled criminal.

He adjusted his glasses and awkwardly picked it up, shocked by the difficulty of managing such a heavy object. Now that he had it within his hands, he was quick to realize his mistake. It was a terrible weapon, but because his bride-to-be looked on with much interest, he had no choice but to commit to his selection.

"Stand back, Miss Reave," he grunted, struggling under its unbelievable weight and tendency to topple. "Uh, could you…get, get the door for me…I'll strike him down with this…but you need to get the door." He staggered; trying to keep his feet set properly to act as counterbalances. Good Lord what type of wood was this, he wondered.

Miss Reave did as she was told and tiptoed to the door. She reached for its knob, but the door swung open wide, revealing a petrified Miss Faffle in her nightclothes.

Miss Faffle screamed.

Miss Reave screamed.

Dr. Whitcraft gasped and the hat stand toppled backwards, flipping over his shoulder and cartwheeling across Miss Faffle's empty desk. It came to rest protruding out of several splintered wooden floorboards in the corner.

Everyone froze, blinking and gauging the situation, before bedlam returned and everyone began shouting at once.

"William! What is this woman doing here?"

"Miss Faffle, Good Lord, you nearly scared us to death."

"Oh doctor, I'm so sorry!"

"I thought you were going to *dismiss* her!"

"What on earth are you doing here, Miss Faffle?"

"You're going to dismiss me?"

"William, this won't do, not in a proper doctor's office."

"I don't have anywhere to go!" Miss Faffle screamed before throwing herself to the floor and clinging to Dr. Whitcraft's trouser legs.

"All right, all right…just a moment, both of you women!" He spread his hands open. "Miss Reave, please." Noting the outrage on his fiancée's face, he softened his voice. "Why don't you go into my office, or better yet, go up to my room, there. I'll meet you upstairs. Let us have a moment, if you would be so kind."

Miss Reave frowned at the pitiful Miss Faffle, a puddle of flowing nightclothes and tears, and gave an exasperated sigh before disappearing through the office door.

Dr. Whitcraft offered his hand to the shattered girl, helping her up and steering her toward a chair. She sniffed between seizing gulps of air. He fished his handkerchief out of his pocket, handed it to her, and pulled a chair close, sitting in silence.

After a moment, he spoke. "My dear Miss Faffle, I have no intention of turning you out. I think your mother has acted disgracefully, and I will not do the same."

She looked up from her handkerchief, shocked. It was as if he had breathed the very hope of life back into her. She jumped from her chair and threw her arms around him, squeezing as hard as she could.

Dr. Whitcraft reached over her shoulders and straightened his glasses, knocked askew by her embrace. After a moment, with the girl showing no signs of releasing him, he patted her awkwardly on the back.

"Uh, so…how long have you been staying—?"

She pulled back and spoke without taking a breath. "My friend couldn't keep me any longer. It's been two weeks. I've had nowhere else to go. I have a blanket and I keep my nightclothes in the bottom of my desk drawer."

Dr. Whitcraft shook his head. That rogue, Mr. Gamon. He had never shared with Miss Faffle what he had learned about that scoundrel, knowing that hearing such news would drive the fragile girl to distraction.

"Do you sleep on the table, then?" he asked, trying to picture what exactly had been going on in his examining room while he had been asleep upstairs.

"Oh no, I would never do that. I sleep on the floor, in the corner."

It all made sense now. For the last two weeks, she'd been turning up before he even made it downstairs.

"Miss Faffle, if you please, if there are any more unfortunate turns in your life, I am begging you to let me know. I simply cannot handle these types of shocks." He stood up. "As far as I'm concerned, if it does not interfere with this practice, you may stay in the examining room for the foreseeable future…until other arrangements can be made, of course."

"But Miss Reave…she thinks I should be turned out."

"This is my practice, Miss Faffle, not hers. Do not trouble yourself with Miss Reave's opinions." He walked past the hat stand sticking out of the floor like a javelin. He shook his head at the sight of it, and vowed to see to it in the morning.

As he crossed his office, he wondered how exactly to explain to the unsympathetic Miss Reave that Miss Faffle was now his unofficial and non-paying tenant. He braced himself as he climbed the stairs.

When he opened his bedroom door, she nearly tackled him on the spot. And she wasn't red-faced and fuming. She was thrilled.

"You didn't tell me about this?" She hung on him and waved something in her hand.

"What? What is that?" He pulled it from her fingers and saw that it was the invitation he had received a few days ago to a conference in Paris, one specifically dealing with the mysteries of hysteria. He sighed. He hadn't planned on telling her about that. Not yet, anyway.

"Paris! We'll be going to Paris! I can't wait! It's such an honor that they asked you to go."

"Just a moment, just a moment." He held out his hand to stop her. "It's not an honor. Dr. Vorago got one too, and for all I know, every physician in London was invited as well."

"Oh." She pulled herself away. "Well, still…Paris! I've always wanted to—"

"Calm down and sit, if you would." He steered her to a chair and took a breath. "Now, even though I'd love to go, I just don't see how I could possibly manage it. The time away from my patients, not to mention the expense. It would be crippling. And if indeed I am considering spending such a staggering sum on that *house,* well…" He hoped reminding her of the house would quell her disappointment, and gauging by the sparkle in her eyes, he had been correct. "But my darling, if I could go, I dare not bring you along. You know your father would never allow it."

She stared down at her hands. "What about Mrs. Anile? Or one of my friends, or their mothers could come along to chaperone?"

He sat on the edge his bed. "Even if I could afford to bring a chaperone for you, I still don't think it would be proper. We need to wait until after we are married for that sort of thing." He reached over and patted her knee. "I don't even know if *I'm* going, so let's not worry about it just now, all right?"

Miss Reave looked disheartened, but didn't argue.

She had to know that he was right.

"Well, there is something else." Her tone had changed from dejected to mischievous as she gestured to the piece of paper lying on his pillow. "You should be glad I'm not the jealous type."

Dr. Whitcraft leaned over and snatched it up.

"Good Lord," he whispered.

The flowery rounds of the feminine script could not have contrasted more with the string of lascivious entreaties penned in this astonishingly inappropriate letter. It was signed with a flourish by none other than his ex-patient, Mrs. Pannade. He looked up into the smirking face of Miss Reave. "Dear God, tell me you didn't read this."

"Of course I did."

"Oh my." He swallowed hard and looked back down at the letter, shaking his head. Could Miss Reave even *understand* such shocking references and suggestions? The thought made him shudder. "I just do not know what to say," he whispered, bringing his hand to his temple. "How in the devil did she get in here again?"

"*Again?*"

****

Mrs. Minnock's study was shadowy and quiet; the ticking grandfather clock in the hall counted each passing second, loudly enough to be heard over the nervous drumming of Dr. Whitcraft's fingers. He jumped to his feet and paced the small room, traveling to the shaded window and back, trying his best not to hover.

"You know, I really appreciate you looking at this. You could have said no, you know. And I can't think of anybody who has as much knowledge about business as you have. It just gives me tremendous peace of mind to have someone else's eyes on this. Yes. Tremendous peace of mind." He sat back down across from the desk. "Is it too dim in here? Would you like me to get you another candle, oh my, but it is so late, I'm so sorry. You probably want to sleep."

"For goodness' sake, Dr. Whitcraft, I can't concentrate on your books while you are babbling so. Take another sip of your tea. Won't you even consider having a brandy and water? It will do you worlds of good, you know." Mrs. Minnock pulled her robe back up over her shoulders as she flipped to the next page of his ledger.

"No, no. I mustn't. That wine I had a few weeks back ruined all my data. I still feel guilty." He took a breath, determined to stay quiet, although the sight of her poring over his books made him slide side to side in his chair.

He had spent the earlier part of this evening adding and re-adding the columns of numbers, trying to decide upon the prudence of making such a substantial financial investment. At his wit's end, he had packed up his books and brought the whole lot to his usual appointment with Mrs. Minnock.

Finally, he couldn't contain himself. "What do you think? Should I even consider buying that damned house?"

"Well…" She looked up and leaned back in her chair. "I think this looks remarkable. Your practice is thriving, doctor. You should be very pleased."

"Of course I'm pleased…but can I afford it?"

"I don't think there's any question that you can

afford both the new house and your current building, but it will require you to keep up this pace. If your practice should drop off for some reason, or if you no longer want to stay so busy…you should think seriously if you want to live under that kind of pressure, to make payments so large. You must be exhausted even now."

He waved his hand. "That's of no concern. But what about next year, and the year after that? One can only imagine how expensive being married is going to be. Miss Reave's father has set a standard for a rather permissive lifestyle, I'm afraid. She could wreck me if I'm not careful."

She frowned at this, but remained silent.

"Still, I can't very well go into marriage letting her perceive me as a pinchpenny, either."

Mrs. Minnock shrugged and reached for her glass of brandy.

"The furniture she will demand, the household amenities she will require. I've recently discovered that her clothing allowance for a single month is more than I spend on myself in an entire year." The doctor shook his head just thinking about it.

"Do not begrudge an eighteen-year-old girl her dresses, Dr. Whitcraft. They are the tools of her trade." She set the glass back down on her desk. "You, on the other hand, have always been satisfied with a rather austere lifestyle, haven't you?"

"Yes, of course. I've usually just reinvested any profits I make right back into my practice. Keeping a physician's office modern and adequately stocked is very expensive. But I'm no ascetic. I do allow myself a few personal indulgences now and again."

"Like what?"

"As far as I'm concerned, any medical book, journal, or treatise is fair game for purchase and nonnegotiable. When I began this career, I vowed to keep my scientific knowledge up to date, and it's not cheap, I tell you."

"Research tools are not exactly a personal indulgence."

"What? Well, they are for me." He paused, and looked away. Lowering his voice he added, "And then, of course, there's the not inconsequential cost of frequenting *your* corridors."

She smiled, picking up the glass again and pointing at his ledger. "Ah yes. I saw that noted under the *personal medical expense* column. I assumed that's what the EM stood for."

He felt himself redden and glanced down at his lap, exposing a smile. That expense was also nonnegotiable. He looked back up with renewed urgency. "Oh, and I didn't mention, a colleague of mine, Dr. Vorago—he's planning on attending a conference about hysteria in Paris, and he's badgering me to go along, as well."

"Oh, Paris! I think you should go, doctor. I think it would do you good to get away."

"Actually, I'm desperately keen to attend, but could I afford to go *and* make that ridiculous down payment?"

"At this point, Dr. Whitcraft, I believe you could afford whatever strikes your fancy."

"You know, I've never left England."

"Well then, you should go. Most definitely. I wish I could go with you."

"Wouldn't that be pleasant? Well, who's to say?" He leaned forward and squinted at his upside-down ledgers. "I was considering letting my flat, after I move that is, but with Miss Faffle in such a quandary, I suppose I'll let her use it, at least until her situation resolves itself somehow."

She twirled the golden liquid around her glass. "You are chivalrous, then aren't you, Dr. Whitcraft?"

Just then, a scream echoed throughout the house. They looked at each other. Mrs. Minnock jumped up from her desk and hurried around him, the long panels of her robe billowing behind her.

"What is it?" she yelled at the girls standing in the parlor.

One of the girls running down the stairs screeched, "It's Brigitte! Her man, he is dead!"

"What? Oh my…"

Dr. Whitcraft dashed around Mrs. Minnock and up the stairs.

"Show me! Where are they?"

"In there."

He pushed through a crowd of girls into a tiny bedroom, and saw the voluptuous Brigitte on her knees weeping on the floor. Her arms were crossed, barely covering her breasts. An elderly man lay prone atop the bed, naked save for the tightly bound corset encircling his middle.

"Mrs. Minnock," Dr. Whitcraft exclaimed over his shoulder, "help me turn him over!"

They flipped the man and saw his white-whiskered face had contorted into an expression of profound concentration. His lips were just now turning blue.

Dr. Whitcraft gasped, "Oh dear Lord!" He smacked the gentleman's unchanging face and shouted, "Dr. Forspent?"

"Is he dead?" Brigitte wailed from her place on the floor.

The doctor held his ear to his mentor's mouth and felt his neck for a pulse. "No...no, thank God." He tugged at the corset, but the hooks, the eyes, the ties—it was a mystery. "Mrs. Minnock! Help me get this ridiculous thing off him."

She jumped on the bed and clawed at the satin undergarment.

"Dr. Forspent!" He slapped the man's face as the livid blue rose onto his cheeks. Upon prying the elderly doctor's mouth open, he saw that his top gums were bare. "Oh, never mind with that. Roll him on his side, hurry!"

Mrs. Minnock did as requested. Dr. Whitcraft dropped off the bed and onto his knees. He reached into his patient's mouth and slid his hand in and down, as far as space would allow. And then his fingertips grazed the obstruction.

"Ah, there it is..." he whispered, perspiration beading on his forehead. He wiggled it and eased it up, feeling the suction loosen as it gave way. Gently, gently he coaxed it out further still.

"I believe...yes...I've got it!" A set of dripping wet porcelain false teeth appeared, clasped in the tips of his crossed fingers.

Dr. Whitcraft tossed them aside, dropped his body in exhaustion, but rose again quickly to examine his dear professor. He was still unconscious, but his face had begun to regain its normal pallor as the breath of life was once again restored and flowing easily. Dr. Whitcraft dropped his head onto the bed for a moment and then looked back up into the amazed face of Mrs.

Minnock.

"H-he's my professor. Oh my…"

"Is everything all right in here?" Another gentleman stuck his head inside the room. He wore an impeccably tailored double-breasted frockcoat layered atop a buff-colored, high-buttoned waistcoat with an ascot fixed in place over his ruffled shirt collar. By all appearances, this gentleman was ready to attend the most civilized of affairs, except there was not a stitch of clothing covering his lower effects.

Irritated by the interruption, Dr. Whitcraft snapped, "Everything is fine, so please go back to your…*Mr. Wedfellow*?"

"Oh, Dr. Whitcraft! Well, how pleasant." Mr. Wedfellow's eyes were wandering and red as he swayed in the doorway. The distinctive juniper indication of gin lightly drifted into the room.

"Don't worry, Corrine," Mr. Wedfellow called into the hallway. "There's a doctor in with the unfortunate man. I'm sure the old fellow's in good hands then, isn't he?" He nodded at the scene with much approval and returned to the hall.

Brigitte got to her feet, still crying. "He told me…he told me to do those things," she muttered at Mrs. Minnock, stealing an occasional glance at her client.

"It's all right." Mrs. Minnock patted her on the shoulder. "Go put your clothes on, then."

"But he's wearing my corset."

"Then, go find another."

Brigitte left the room sniffing. Dr. Whitcraft pulled a blanket over his patient and reached up to the man's neck for a final check of his pulse. Satisfied, he walked to Mrs. Minnock.

She grasped his elbow. "Are you sure he'll be all right?"

"Yes. Just let him lay there. He'll come around." They both stared at the unconscious professor. "He looks so old, doesn't he?" Dr. Whitcraft whispered.

"He'll be so proud of you, when he wakes up and finds out what happened." She reached around the doctor's waist.

He stared at Dr. Forspent, imagining the man's eyes popping open, confused at first but then filling with recognition as he focused on the unexpected presence of his favorite protégé. Frowning, Dr. Whitcraft flipped open his pocket watch.

"I should be going, probably. Yes. And there's no need to mention, uh…my presence here this evening, I think."

"You don't want him to know you saved him?"

"No! Good Lord, no and please don't tell him. If he sees me here, the poor man will be overcome with embarrassment. And frankly, so will I! Just tell him there was a doctor here who helped him. He may not even ask." He turned to leave the room, then paused. In the most secretive of voices, he whispered, "Please tell Brigitte, should there be any future…endeavors between the two, make sure the man removes his teeth, you know, *before*." He pulled back, grimacing at the vision he had just conjured.

She grasped his cheeks, tipping his face toward her own. "Thank you," she whispered and then kissed him. "Oh wait. Don't you want to take your ledgers with you?"

"Oh. No, I'll come get them tomorrow. I don't feel

like collecting them now. Maybe you could go over them again, in the morning, you know, just double-check for me…before I speak to the creditors. Just to make certain."

"I'll be happy to. You know, doctor, you could always stay here."

"Oh no. I couldn't possibly sleep. I need some exercise, something to calm my nerves. Walking home will do wonders for me. I need to get myself back into order, after such excitement."

"But it is so late…"

"There's no better time. No one will bother me."

Chapter Sixteen

The night air had cooled and felt crisp in his lungs as he walked through the Covent Garden back toward Berkeley Square. The stars shimmered high above London, a most pleasing scene, the perfect antidote for the recent excitement of the evening.

It occurred to him that he didn't have his walking stick should he need to protect himself against potential mischief, but the streets seemed strangely empty on this night, and the walk home was not a long one.

He enjoyed a leisurely pace gazing at the shuttered shop fronts while contemplating the exhilarating direction his life would be taking over the next few months. The purchase of the new house, the conference in Paris, the imminent publishing of his article in *The Lancet*; there was so much to look forward to.

He passed a few shadowy figures warming themselves over a rubbish-bin fire. Glancing sideways at the pitiful characters, Dr. Whitcraft turned down a side street to escape their observation. He pulled his frockcoat tighter around his person and increased the pace of his stride. The moon disappeared beneath the high floating clouds depriving the entire scene of illumination, save for the dim streetlights.

Perhaps it was his imagination, but he thought he heard a muffled clattering somewhere behind him. He glanced over his shoulder. There was nothing, of course. His mind was playing tricks, but nevertheless he again increased the velocity of his steps.

All at once, a force propelled him from behind and slammed him into a shop front. At any moment, he expected to hear the menacing voices of the perpetrators demanding his money and pocket watch.

"Just take it! It's in my pocket there. Take it all! Please," he gasped, waiting for the sharp pierce of a knife blade at his throat. Oh how foolish he had been to walk home at this time of night! He should have just stayed with Mrs. Minnock.

But it was not a knife that the doctor felt. It was the curious sensation of warm breath on the back of his neck coupled with a deliberately roaming set of hands.

"No, not in my trousers. My wallet is in my *waistcoat*…in the pocket, there." His breath fogged the window as he waved to his right side, afraid that digging it out might be misconstrued. They might think he was reaching for a weapon, after all.

"It's not in my trousers, I tell you," he repeated frantically now that the criminal's hands had migrated onto his hips. Something was indeed queer about this act of delinquency, and when he turned to confront the malefactor, a hand plunged into the front of his trousers like a terrier after a rabbit.

At that most startling sensation, Dr. Whitcraft emitted a girlish shriek, instinctually holding his attacker's arm stiff as he wrestled the devil down and away—preserving himself, as well as his very nearly tarnished honor.

He found himself on the ground and up against a wall, his trousers badly ripped. His attacker lay in a tangled huddle beside him. When the criminal turned over, the moon appeared from behind the clouds and illuminated the wild-eyed face of Mrs. Pannade. She breathed heavily as she jumped over top him.

"Dr. Whitcraft! Don't be afraid. Oh, have I frightened you, doctor? I assumed you knew it was me all the while." She grinned wickedly and glanced down at his lap.

"Mrs. Pannade," he panted, unable to form a single coherent thought.

"I cannot abide you going to see *that woman* when you could have *me,* at any hour, at any place you wish and for *free.*" She brought her face startlingly close to his, her gloved-hand stroking his cheek, the other in position to make another go at his trousers.

"Mrs. Pannade! Get hold of yourself, for God's sake!" He slid out from under her, flattening himself against the building. Coquettish behavior was a well-known symptom of hysteria, but he had never imagined that it could strike in such a profound way. He would have to record a detailed account of this episode when he managed to get home, for posterity if nothing else. Perhaps this incident would prove to be the catalyst for yet another article in *The Lancet.*

"Mrs. Pannade, y-you must take a deep breath. You are in the throes of an hysterical episode, and must try to get your wits about you. You are a married woman and I am going to be married. Harness these impulses and remember yourself! Good Lord! And you simply can't go around *accosting people in the street*!"

"There has been no other way to get an audience with you." She placed her hands on her hips. "You've banned me from your office and forbidden me even to speak with you. What other choice do I have? And since you mentioned your abhorrent fiancée, I must tell you that she has engaged in the most shocking behavior."

"*She* has engaged in shocking behavior?" he shouted, and then paused. In spite of the delicate situation in which he now found himself, Dr. Whitcraft's attention had indeed been captured. He took a breath and slid himself further away, pulling his ripped trousers together as much as possible. "Mrs. Pannade, if there is something about Miss Reave you wish to share with me—"

"She's disgracing you, running around London holding hands with *him; that other doctor*. I saw it with my own eyes when I followed her to his flat and—"

"What *other* doctor?"

"That awful, pompous *Dr. Marplot*."

Dr. Whitcraft gasped, and a look of utter adoration settled across her features. "So you see?" she drawled, "you must cast that foolish young minx aside and take *me* instead, oh my darling! I would never disgrace you like that! What a most wonderful life we could have together." At that, she threw herself atop him once more, peppering his face with kisses and caressing his torso with long and lingering strokes.

"You there! Stop that at once!"

Mrs. Pannade spun round at the sound of the distant voice, climbing off of the doctor and jumping to her feet. She squinted at the bobbing lantern approaching from up the alley. At once, she dashed in the opposite direction, amazingly fast for a corseted woman in heeled boots sprinting across the slick and darkened cobblestones.

"Wait! Wait! Come back here this instant!" Dr.

Whitcraft called after her, feeling the panic rising in his chest as he too saw the silhouette of a uniformed man approaching directly. Dread flooded his heart, and his voice cracked as he called, "Uh, good evening to you, sir."

"All right, then. On your feet and place your hands where I can see them." The officer was close enough now for Dr. Whitcraft to see the bemused expression on his face. "Not a very appropriate place for such a passionate romp, is it then?"

"What? Good Lord it was nothing of the sort. I am a physician and…that was a deeply, deeply troubled patient—a *female* patient. I was attacked in the darkness." He knew how shrill his voice must have sounded as he rose to his feet. "The woman in question is known to the police. If you just let me explain, I'm certain your superiors have a record of my complaint." Now that he was standing, his trousers slipped, and he reached to catch them.

"Keep your hands where I can see them, there. Now explain what you mean about this patient."

At that, his trousers gave way, settling around his ankles in a heap, leaving the doctor's small clothes exposed and his knees chilled by the night air.

"Well, well. This *attacker* of yours…what was she after exactly?"

****

Miss Faffle stood trembling in the doorway, mesmerized by the unexpected presence of the policeman. She pulled her blanket even tighter over her nightclothes and held the lantern to the side so she could unlock the door. Had the rumors about her and Mr. Gamon led the police to her door?

"Miss, I am sorry to bother you at this hour. Do you know this man? He claims he is a doctor." The officer grasped the frockcoat of his most agitated captive and pushed him forward for her inspection.

Miss Faffle exhaled, noticing her boss for the first time. "Yes. He is Dr. William Whitcraft. Oh doctor, your trousers are—"

"And he lives here?"

"He owns this building. I work for him."

"You see?" Dr. Whitcraft sighed, holding his trousers shut with both hands. "Now that she has identified me, may I please go in to my home and see to the repair of my clothing?"

"Yes, but you'll need to answer some questions."

"Miss Faffle, would you kindly explain to the officer the nature of our problems with Mrs. Pannade while I change my clothes. She accosted me in the street." He stepped past her and disappeared into his office.

She brought her hand to her face at the news. "Oh my. How dreadful."

"Miss Faffle is it? I'm Constable Fettle. Sorry to disturb you."

"Oh no. I wasn't asleep yet." She stepped aside, and gestured for him to come in. "*I* sleep in that room there, and the doctor lives upstairs and that is where *he* sleeps." She was desperate not to allow the officer to misconstrue the situation and add to her already scandalous reputation.

"Now tell me, what did the doctor say? You know about this woman who accosted him on the street?"

"Oh dear, yes. She's one of his patients—was a patient, I'm afraid, but yes. She's gone mad, you see.

Follows him everywhere…his fiancée as well. She's very disturbed."

"The fiancée or the patient?"

"The patient. Yes. Her name is Mrs. Pannade. Would you care for something? Perhaps some tea?"

"Oh, I would love some tea." He dropped himself into a chair. "You say his fiancée also follows him everywhere?"

"What? No, no…just Mrs. Pannade. She's the ex-patient."

"I see."

"Would you care for some lemon with your tea?" she asked.

"No, but I wouldn't mind a couple lumps of sugar, if it's not too much trouble."

"Oh, it's no trouble at all. Will you have some biscuits, as well?" She walked into Dr. Whitcraft's office and crossed to the bottom of the stairs.

"I don't want to put you out, but yes, that would be lovely. I never turn down a biscuit. No, indeed." He patted his rather rotund belly. "You know it's getting very cold out there this evening. I wouldn't dream of strutting around London with shredded trousers, like your boss there." The officer chuckled and Miss Faffle's eyes grew large as she laughed, too.

"He doesn't usually do that."

"Oh who knows with these doctors, reading all that nonsense about suffering and dead people, it's all so ghastly. It's a wonder they don't all go mad."

"Oh, I know." Miss Faffle nodded at him. She cupped her hands around her mouth and called up the stairs, "Dr. Whitcraft? Constable Fettle would like some tea. He'll take it with two lumps of sugar…" She turned back to the smiling constable. "Is that right? Two lumps?"

The officer nodded.

"Yes, he wants two lumps of sugar, and a plate of biscuits."

****

Dr. Whitcraft could hear Miss Faffle and that police officer chatting even though it had to be in the small hours of the morning. Upon Miss Faffle's request for tea service, he had gritted his teeth, boiled the water, put together a spread suitable for his majesty himself and then carried the whole lot downstairs on a tray.

As the officer daintily selected a biscuit while balancing a teacup on his thigh, Dr. Whitcraft answered the man's questions about Mrs. Pannade. After a suitable cross-examination, the officer was finally satisfied. But rather than leaving, he elected to stay and have another cup of tea. It was not long before he began expounding on a variety of topics, including the merits of exercise, the role of the police in a civilized society, and the probable existence of an afterlife.

Miss Faffle had been enthralled by the discussion of such radically disparate topics, but the doctor had been ready to tear out his hair. When he couldn't stand it any more, he got to his feet and announced his retirement for the evening.

After the day's traumatic series of events, he wanted nothing more than to be left in peace. But an hour later, it still sounded like they were having a garden party downstairs laughing and chatting amongst the clanking of cups and dishes; it was all rather gauche.

He sighed as he pulled the blankets under his chin.

Mrs. Pannade's face remained fresh in his mind—her evil suppositions regarding the honor of Miss Reave still lingering. Unquestionably, however, he must dismiss the accusations outright. Logic dictated so, for heaven's sake. Perhaps she had misinterpreted something she saw, or more likely, she concocted the entire story in a pathetic attempt to get him to abandon the pursuit of Miss Reave altogether. The poor, misguided woman. Perhaps tomorrow he would call on Dr. Vorago and demand he keep a firmer leash on his patient.

He flipped on his side, bunching the covers underneath his head, as Constable Fettle's belly-laughs drifted around his bedroom from below. He imagined the exquisite face of Miss Reave, the poor darling. How proud he was to have a woman like that agree to be his wife. He should spoil her, and if he couldn't take her to Paris, at least he could surprise her with a new house.

That settled it. He would put the cash down on the house first thing tomorrow, and be done with it. He would move his office upstairs into this room, and make the old office into another examining room, thereby doubling his productivity. It would be exhausting, but he could manage. Then Miss Faffle could stay in the other room upstairs. Yes. That would be a perfect arrangement.

The excitement of his plans gave way to exhaustion, and as he lost himself amongst his drowsy thoughts, his eyes snapped open at the sound of Constable Fettle—was he singing now?

Indeed he was, having just begun a highly ornamented rendition of *The Last Rose of Summer* in a not terribly offensive tenor. Dr. Whitcraft sighed and shut his eyes again, letting the wavering melody lull him into a deep and much needed sleep.

Chapter Seventeen

Dr. Whitcraft's Hansom cab trotted to a halt in front of The Barts. Dr. Marplot dashed up to the door and eagerly helped his colleague onto the street.

"So glad you've come today, doctor, so very glad." He studied him and offered a sudden embrace. "And you're right on time, as well."

"I appreciate the invitation." Dr. Whitcraft cleared his throat and threw his shoulders back as they approached the front door.

When Dr. Marplot had invited him to spend a Saturday morning touring St. Bartholomew's Hospital, he initially declined. Under most circumstances, he would have jumped at the chance to mingle with other doctors at such a prestigious hospital, one that he rarely had the opportunity to visit. But he suspected that spending any amount of time with that blustering windbag in a professional setting would only prove to be irritating at best.

That was until Dr. Marplot had alluded to the possibility that the two may be able to assist in a *surgery*. Dr. Whitcraft had witnessed scores of surgeries over the years, but had never actually had a chance to participate in one because physicians and surgeons held separate licenses, and almost never worked in concert. The chance to get his hands inside a living person, delving into the blood, bones and gore of it all…well, it was too good to pass up. Tolerating Dr. Marplot for a few hours seemed a small price to pay.

But there was another motive for accepting the man's invitation. Perhaps a few pointed questions could reveal if there was any substance to Mrs. Pannade's distasteful accusations about Miss Reave. But as it happened, an interrogation was unnecessary.

"I had the distinct pleasure of escorting the future Mrs. Whitcraft and her chaperone back to her father's home a few evenings ago," Dr. Marplot said as they strolled through the hallways. "What a delightful young lady. I'm sure she told you."

"No, actually she didn't," Dr. Whitcraft murmured, the muscles in his neck tightening.

"Oh, well…she must not have wanted you to hear how disappointed I was that you weren't by her side at last week's *Society of Manners* meeting."

"What the devil were *you* doing there?" After he'd said it, Dr. Whitcraft wished that he had blunted his accusatory tone.

"I've heard of their great works for years and decided to attend a meeting myself, and I'm so glad I did! I found the zeal of that assemblage positively invigorating. Those people are really on a mission. I joined immediately and am actually toying with the idea of running for toastmaster. You have to be elected, of course. They drummed the last fellow out, you know, after the exposure of a rather unsavory ruse the man had cooked up, but I'm not privy to the details. Toastmaster! Me? Not that I have the time. Miss Reave thought it an excellent idea. What do you think?"

Dr. Whitcraft shrugged, noticing how the hospital workers stepped out of their way and whispered deferentially as they passed.

"Enough of this chit-chat." Dr. Marplot stopped in front of a surgical theater and flipped open his pocket watch. "We've got a leg to sever!"

He swept past two dressers standing at attention to assist, as well as an older, less interested nurse.

Dr. Whitcraft followed closely, forgetting all about Miss Reave and the *Society of Manners* as he glanced around the cavernous sky-lit room, unable to hide his delight. "How wonderful," he whispered.

"I know."

"Where is the surgeon?"

"Oh, you mean Mr. Looby? He's left it up to us, old man."

"Left it up to us? What do you mean?"

"Why just what I said. Amputations are pretty straight forward then, aren't they?"

"Shouldn't the man at least be here? I mean we aren't licensed for this sort of business."

"Oh, who needs a license? We know more than any surgeon any day! We're the ones who went to school, after all. Why not use it? Anyway, Mr. Looby isn't even in the building. He's gone deer stalking in Wiltshire. He begged me to take over. Have you ever met Mr. Looby? Positively a ghoul. We're better off without the man. Let's have a look at our fellow, then."

The patient in question was Mr. George Twitchel, who lay unconscious and at the ready, tightly strapped to a table and naked under his drapes. The ghastly disease-ridden wound on his right leg was uncovered and exposed to the air, and a tourniquet had been applied just above the area of concern.

"How much did he consume, Mr. Smittlish?" Dr.

Marplot asked the taller of the two assistants.

"Mr. Twitchel has had a good deal of laudanum and an entire bottle of spirits, sir. Quite an accomplishment given he's an officer in the temperance society."

Everyone gave a reserved laugh as they huddled around the comatose man.

"Let me tell you about our boy, then Dr. Whitcraft." Dr. Marplot gestured at the patient. "He came to us several weeks ago, and as you can see our treatments have proven to be most unsuccessful; that ulcer there has run rampant."

"Oh, yes. It's appalling," Dr. Whitcraft whispered, pulling the drape back further still. "What caused the original injury, do you know?"

"The old boy has insisted he fell off his horse and impaled his leg on a fence post, but…" He glanced at the assistants, and leaned toward Dr. Whitcraft. "There's a rumor going around that his mistress gave him a good gouge with his decorative sword." He straightened and shrugged. "We are all capable of a little misadventure now and again. Regardless, we've all settled on it. The leg must go."

"Undoubtedly," Dr. Whitcraft agreed.

"Aha." Dr. Marplot selected a large saw from a tray of half-dozen similarly purposed instruments all resting on a wheeled cart adjacent to the table. "I prefer this one." He waved it over the patient, casting a dancing flash across the room.

Dr. Whitcraft studied the assortment of tools. "Which knife will you use for the incision, Dr. Marplot?"

"You mean, which knife will *you* use?" He nudged

him.

"Are you certain that you want *me* to do it?"

"Of course…you came all this way. Have at it, old man."

Dr. Whitcraft gave a tug at the tourniquet and then scanned the faces of the dressers as he picked up an astoundingly large knife and held it over the patient. Perceiving no objections, he licked his lips and laid the blade flat against the upper thigh, estimating the best place for the incision. He swallowed hard. "All right, then. Is everyone ready?"

Dr. Marplot waved his saw. "Ready, doctor!"

Dr. Whitcraft couldn't stifle his enthusiasm as he pantomimed a stroke in the air before making a fast, deep slice in the man's thigh. The skin broke apart easily into a wide gape.

"Nicely done. Tighten the tourniquet, Mr. Smittlish." Dr. Marplot hurriedly traded places with Dr. Whitcraft. He put the instrument in place and began sawing at once, but still managed to preserve his neatly styled hair and imperturbable countenance. "You know…I meant to tell you," he panted, "I-I've nearly finished….m-my section of our paper."

"That's wonderful." Dr. Whitcraft watched the business at hand over his spectacles.

"Indeed…should…should…have it ready in a day or so."

"That's splendid. The sooner the better as far as I'm concerned." Dr. Whitcraft arched himself over the table on the tips of his toes for a better view. "I've decided to expand my practice and will be buying a house, so my article being published just now would be perfect timing."

"Expanding your practice, eh? Whew. That femur is tricky…you want to give it a go? My arm is about finished." His shoulders dropped in exhaustion.

"Oh, why yes. Please." Dr. Whitcraft exchanged places with him again and took hold of the saw, but the table began suddenly to sway.

"Oh dear, he's coming round, isn't he?" Dr. Whitcraft noticed the patient had begun to moan and roll his head side to side. "I'll try to hurry it up, then."

Mr. Twitchel's eyes snapped open. After an initial moment of confusion, he lifted his head, shrieked and threw himself against his bindings in a wild panic. The dressers dashed over, each using their entire weight to hold Mr. Twitchel in place. Dr. Whitcraft quickened the pace of his labors. Dr. Marplot leaned over reassuringly. "Don't worry, old fellow," he shouted, "we're just about there."

"One more should do it," Dr. Whitcraft gasped. "Ah, there we are."

"Well done!" Dr. Marplot swooped his lower leg off of the table and proudly carried it toward Dr. Whitcraft, like a midwife presenting a newborn to its mother. The patient's eyes rolled and his mouth opened wide as he dropped back lifelessly on to the table.

"Merciful thing, that." Dr. Marplot gestured at the patient with his chin.

"Quite," Dr. Whitcraft agreed, breathing heavily as he cast the saw aside and turned his attention to the oozing arteries.

"Why, what a perfect reef knot. Well done, Dr. Whitcraft."

"How kind of you. I'm out of practice."

"Nonsense! Would you care to examine this leg

with me, doctor? It has an extraordinary buildup of necrosis that I believe is very rare on the living—"

"Of course. I'm surprised you asked."

"Nurse, come along now," Dr. Marplot called in a silly singsong as he walked the leg to a waiting table off to the side. "Let's tidy this up. Mr. Smittlish and Mr. Flepper, you too, boys…"

"Oh, you know, don't say anything about that house business." Dr. Whitcraft grabbed a lancet and hurriedly caught up to his colleague. "It will be a wedding present for Miss Reave. I want it to be a surprise."

"Isn't that the most charming thing I have ever heard?" The leg landed on the examining table with a heavy thud.

They stood in place, thoughtfully staring down at the table whilst holding their lancets like two revelers contemplating the Christmas goose. After a moment, it was Dr. Whitcraft who said, "Let's carve into this bugger, then shall we?"

"After you, sir."

"No, no. I wouldn't dream of it. After you."

"Don't mind if I do." Dr. Marplot ducked toward the table and skillfully began a most thorough dissection. "Where is it? The house I mean."

"I've gotten rather lucky. It's just a few doors down from where her father lives."

"Is it now? In St. James Square? I'm very familiar with that area, but oh, it is expensive."

"It certainly is. You know, Dr. Marplot, I must say that this has been a real treat. I spend so much time at The London Hospital, I barely ever come here, and I surely never dreamed I would get a crack at cutting off a man's leg. How delightful!"

"After our article comes out, you'll be up to your elbows in hysterical women. Even more than you are now, that is. Likely no more amputations for you."

"What a shame."

"Well, you can't have everything."

****

Dr. Marplot cast the tails of his morning coat aside with a dramatic sweep of his hand and sat down in front of the pianoforte. "What would anyone like to hear?"

"Oh my! Mozart? Do you know any Mozart?" a female guest inquired.

A coy smile spread across his face and he arched his brow. "Do I?" With that, he straightened into the upright posture of a concert musician, picked up his hands, held them loose over the ivory keys and proceeded to fill the parlor with the richest, most lush version of Mozart's A Major Sonata that Dr. Whitcraft had ever heard. The women swooned, and guests mingling in the other rooms came rushing in to see which of the party guests had proven to be so talented.

Mrs. Anile, however, made her way through the revelers in the opposite direction, sliding against the parlor wall toward the exit whilst monitoring the splashing drinks in each hand.

Dr. Vorago appeared and patted Dr. Whitcraft on the shoulder. The two watched the impromptu recital in awe.

"No sheet music, can you believe it?" Dr. Vorago whispered. "Marplot's got the whole business committed to memory."

"It's quite something, isn't it?"

"Quite."

Miss Reave stood across the room, tucked in amongst a group of admiring ladies, all captivated by the extraordinary performance at hand.

Dr. Marplot had chosen a selection from the second movement and was having a heyday with the piece's interpretation, playing it at varying speeds and in a swirling sort of manner. He would offer the crowd a placid smile as his fingers bounced along the keys, his mane feathering in time with the beats. But on the very next phrase, his fervor would slow and his fingers would droop and brood over the notes. His face would darken in kind, tormented by artistic malaise. Everyone was completely captivated.

Weeks ago, Dr. Whitcraft would have found such a display from this man to be outrageously over the top, and frankly, it was difficult not to do so now. But after working so closely with him regarding the article and just days ago in the surgery, he felt ashamed that he had let himself be led astray by such base feelings. The man was a gifted artist. What was wrong with entertaining friends and colleagues on an occasion like this?

When he began Alla Turca, the sonata's final movement, Dr. Marplot manipulated the keys with such speed and dexterity that he had the entire crowd perched on their toes in silent suspense. He played faster and faster still. The crowd gasped and clutched at one another when he leapt to his feet, toppling the bench as he barreled on toward the finish. After a series of flourishes, and one final pound of the pianoforte, the man's arms lifted away from the keys and cut through the air. He exhaled in exhaustion, doubling over the instrument as if he could barely stand.

Everyone erupted in ecstatic applause.

Dr. Vorago wailed and slapped Dr. Whitcraft on the back. Dr. Whitcraft clapped too, sidling through the crowd toward the enraptured Miss Reave.

"Oh did you see him? Did you see?" she gushed.

"Yes. Indeed. It was marvelous. Uh, darling, I hate to say it, but we should be going, I have a full schedule of patients tomorrow and I simply can't—"

"What? Oh no! No, he's just finished playing and I haven't had a chance to speak to even half of my friends yet. Oh you're such a spoilsport!" She flicked the stylish little bag hanging from her wrist and struck Dr. Whitcraft squarely in the lower arm.

"Ouch! Good Lord, what do you have in there? I'm nearly injured!" He rubbed his arm.

Miss Reave appeared stricken, blinking as she steadied her swinging bag. "It's nothing. Just a few—"

"Did I hear right?" Dr. Marplot appeared, breathing heavily. He inserted himself between Dr. Whitcraft and Miss Reave. "You have to leave so soon?"

"What a wonderful performance, dear sir. You are a gifted musician," Dr. Whitcraft said.

"Oh no, I'm *so* out of practice." He dabbed at his dry forehead with a handkerchief.

Dr. Whitcraft patted him on the shoulder. "I have such a busy schedule tomorrow, I hate to leave, but we must."

"Oh, well of course you do, but wait here a moment. I've got something you need to see, before you go." He disappeared from the room and hurried back with his hand buried in a satchel. He produced a folded packet of papers and tossed it at Dr. Whitcraft with a bemused smirk. "There it is, old man. I'll need your final approval before I give it to the editor."

"Ah." Dr. Whitcraft brightened at once. He straightened his glasses and flipped over the cover page.

Dr. Marplot turned to Miss Reave. "I think it is brilliant, just brilliant. The kind of thing that can really propel one into fame. I wouldn't be at all surprised if it caught the fancy of The Royal Society."

"Oh, how wonderful!" she said, glancing from man to man.

Dr. Whitcraft looked up, his eyes sparkling. Being inducted into the Royal Society was a dream for any English scientist, a possibility he never dared to imagine. He continued reading, relieved to see that the majority of the paper was still exactly how he'd written it. There were additions now and again, but they only enhanced the paper's merits.

Their combined efforts, taken as a whole, were truly startling—an excessively clear pedagogical analysis of the maneuver, an elegant diagnostic paradigm, along with a simple, straight-forward explanation of the five steps, usable for any doctor, anywhere in the world.

He finished reading and looked up into Dr. Marplot's smiling face. "Well? What did I tell you? Do I have your blessing for them to print it?"

He couldn't conceal the grin beginning at the corner of his mouth. "I suppose it is ready. I would ask that my name be listed first, of course."

"Why of course. I wouldn't have it any other way!"

"When do you think it will come out?"

"Who knows with these things? A few weeks…a month. It depends on the other material the editors have."

Satisfied, Dr. Whitcraft turned to Miss Reave. "Well, then, my dear. We do have to go…"

She turned her bottom lip under and glared at Dr. Whitcraft before glancing apologetically at Dr. Marplot.

"I tell you what." Dr. Marplot arched a brow as if he were hatching a plan. "I'll be here for at least another hour. Why don't I see to it that Miss Reave and Mrs. Anile get home safely? If that would be acceptable to Miss Reave, of course."

Her dismal expression reanimated at once. "Oh, yes! Yes, that would be perfect. I hate to leave a dinner party so early. Are you sure you don't mind, Dr. Marplot?"

"Of course not." He bowed as if he were her manservant. "You're just a few streets away, aren't you?"

"Yes, she is." Dr. Whitcraft said, his tone more grave than he meant it to be. As he considered the two of them colluding together, he studied their faces, attempting to detect if anything untoward were being betrayed by either of them. There was nothing, of course, and he immediately felt ashamed for thinking such a thing.

"Are you sure, Dr. Marplot? Escorting Mrs. Anile can get a bit complex…depending upon her willingness and general state, you know." Dr. Whitcraft turned to Miss Reave. "Where is she, then?"

At that, all three searched the faces of the crowded party.

Dr. Vorago wandered over, tapping Dr. Whitcraft on the shoulder. "If you're talking about Mrs. Anile, she's trying to find a fourth among the footmen for a game of All-Fours. I was just coming to warn you."

"Oh, good Lord."

"Oh, for goodness' sake, I'll go and stop her." Miss Reave said. "Darling, I'm certain that Dr. Marplot can handle her. If she's trying to get a game together, then she's not all that far gone, so please don't worry."

Dr. Whitcraft sighed, enjoying the way her eyes sparkled as she tried to persuade him. "Well then, I suppose it's settled. Go and find her, before she gets herself into trouble." He turned to Dr. Marplot. "Please don't keep her past ten. Her father will never forgive me if she is out past ten." He held out his hand.

Dr. Marplot shook it heartily, and then embraced him. "I'm so glad you are pleased with the paper. I am, too. Most pleased. I just know that your life will never be the same after it is published."

Dr. Whitcraft grinned. He hoped so.

****

Dr. Whitcraft rushed around his office, trying to account for every last detail. He clapped his hands together and took a final look around, barely able to contain his excitement. "Miss Faffle, you have the list of my patients, yes? Dr. Scamble should turn up later this morning to collect it. I tried to make satisfactory notes on each of them, just in case. I included basic backgrounds, medical histories and such, so just point that out… "

"I'll tell him, sir." She used her foot to push his large trunk across the battered floor.

"Oh, don't trouble yourself. I'm sure one of the carriage men will get it for me."

"Will the weather in Paris be like it is here?" she asked.

He grinned. "I don't know, but I believe I've

packed attire suitable for any condition." But the question reignited his anxiety. Did he indeed have everything? He glanced at his trunk and wondered.

Having never left England, he supposed watching the green isle of his birth disappear when they crossed the English Channel would likely be a life-changing experience. But what a wonderful change it should prove to be. The exposure to so much knowledge, to entirely different cultures, and new ways of thinking about medicine, he could only imagine how different his perspective of the world would be when he returned.

He glanced out the window and saw a large and rather rickety carriage appear up the street, and moments later he could make out the familiar face of Dr. Vorago beaming at him from inside its window. Within moments, the carriage had parked and two young men were lifting his trunk and carting it down the stairs. He watched them go, and his heart raced with anticipation.

"All right, Miss Faffle. This is it, I suppose." He took a final account of his office and turned to her.

Her eyes filled with tears as she clasped her arms around her middle. "Oh, doctor."

"It'll only be a few weeks, Miss Faffle," he whispered.

She nodded, blinking her tears away and replacing them with a shy smile.

"Well then…" He took a long and satisfying breath. With a most satisfied air and erect posture, he swung open his front door, stepped over the threshold, and was at once swept off his feet by a fleeting dark blur which left him crooked and sprawled in the doorway.

He sat up, blinking at the panels of emerald green silk and black lace. He followed it up, and up further still, past the gaping bodice atop the featureless chest, over the bony angles of the clavicles working like blades in time with the excited respirations of...Mrs. Pannade. With an untamed urgency etched upon her face, she held a rather slim, pointed and peculiarly bejeweled dagger in her right hand.

Dr. Whitcraft screamed, his eyes fixed upon the weapon, and Miss Faffle's shriek harmonized in kind, the disturbance causing Dr. Vorago and several other inhabitants of the carriage to begin shouting and blundering about.

Mrs. Pannade, however, looked around dumbly, baffled by the unexpected reactions from her audience. "Why, Dr. Whitcraft," she lowered her weapon, "what on earth is the matter?"

"Stay back, woman!" he shrieked, kicking himself back into his office. "What, will you *slay* me now?"

"Slay you? I brought this for you...for your protection!"

"Mrs. Pannade, God-a-mercy, we have discussed this over and over," Dr. Vorago bellowed as he lurched up the steps and threw himself over her, disarming his patient quite easily. "I was very specific about you NOT coming here." He puffed and perspired as he examined the ostentatious dagger in his hands. "What the devil is the meaning of this?"

Dr. Whitcraft got to his feet, still reeling. "Why on earth would you come here *armed*?"

Mrs. Pannade shook herself loose from Dr. Vorago. "To give you some means to defend yourself... from the highwaymen, of course. Don't you read the papers?"

"Highwaymen?" Dr. Whitcraft said.

"Yes. They are attacking carriages on all routes out of London. I thought you'd be pleased. My husband bought it last summer when he played Polonius. The actors had to supply their own murder weapons. I thought you might need it." She put her hands on her hips. "At least someone was thinking about your safety!"

"You're mad!" Dr. Vorago said. "Everyone knows Polonius was killed with a *sword*."

"Everyone but my husband," she added, bitterly.

Dr. Vorago turned the dagger over his hands. "If these jewels are real, then this thing may be very valuable." He nudged Dr. Whitcraft. "Don't these look like rubies?"

"Oh. Why they're not real, are they Mrs. Pannade?" Dr. Whitcraft asked as he brushed off his trousers.

She looked thoughtful. "I don't know, really. I wouldn't put it past my husband to spend a small fortune on a prop for the stage."

"If they are real, the only thing the highwaymen may actually be interested in is this dagger," Dr. Vorago said, snorting.

"Are there actually highwaymen?" Dr. Whitcraft had worried about a storm sinking their paddle-steamer, about the long and difficult conditions on the road, about being accosted in Paris, but he had never thought about being robbed and left for dead by English highwaymen.

"Well, the fellows in the carriage assured me, they are well prepared. They have drilled for such an unpleasant eventuality, and have a plan."

Mrs. Pannade threw herself around Dr. Whitcraft. "Oh, my dear, darling. Promise you'll come home safe, and please, if nothing else…take at least one meal at A la Petite Chaise. Ask for the poulet roti. I just know you'll love it! I'm absolutely certain—"

Dr. Vorago pulled his patient away from Dr. Whitcraft. "Mrs. Pannade, please…"

Concerned for the citizens of London in their absence, Dr. Whitcraft pulled Dr. Vorago close. "I hope you have arranged for another physician to watch her while we're gone."

"Ah yes." He nodded. "I've arranged for Dr. Marplot to take over."

Mrs. Pannade nodded as well, narrowing her eyes. "I will keep an eye on him for you, my dear."

Chapter Eighteen

Physicians and scientists from every walk of life had come from all over Europe to attend the conference in Paris, each basking in the excitement of being in the very midst of all modern thought on hysteria.

The conference proved even more stimulating than Dr. Whitcraft had hoped. He couldn't remember the last time he felt so intellectually exhilarated. He'd barely any time to take in the sights of Paris, as his days were filled running from lecture to lecture, symposium to symposium, trying to take in as much academic theory as possible.

Dr. Vorago, on the other hand, had taken his opportunity in Paris to become intimately familiar with the local indulgences, disappearing from the conference after the first day. As far as Dr. Whitcraft could tell, the man only seemed to return to their quarters for an occasional change of clothing or sleepy intermission. The last time Dr. Whitcraft had seen his friend was when he'd discovered the man's fully dressed and unconscious body slumped in the lavatory, splashed with what appeared to be *marchand de vin sauce*.

Feeling like he may have been missing out, Dr. Whitcraft promised himself a break from his academic rigors, if nothing else, to find out what Dr. Vorago had been up to. And he was especially anxious to tell him about the controversy he had witnessed in a standing-room-only lecture hall that afternoon.

Two illustrious physicians, a Frenchmen and an Italian respectively, had presented their papers on the mysterious origin of hysteria. The majority of attendees still accepted the Frenchman's perspective, which advocated the age-old belief that hysteria originates from a disturbance of the uterus.

But the Italian insisted that hysteria was not a disease of the uterus at all, but rather a collection of symptoms somehow located in and controlled by the brain. Of course, it followed from this reasoning that if a uterus was not required to cause hysteria, then *men* could also be affected and diagnosed with the disease. This particularly iconoclastic section of the Italian physician's paper had caused a wave of disapproving murmurs among the audience.

One gentleman became so outraged by this postulation, he stood up and shook his fist at his colleague on stage, letting loose a tirade of what Dr. Whitcraft had presumed to be profanity-laced Italian.

When others in the audience jumped up to defend the presenter, the man became so infuriated that he picked up his chair and tossed it at the stage before stomping out of the lecture hall. The Italian speaker, watching unimpressed as the man made his exit, speculated to the audience that his accuser likely had hysteria himself, thus accounting for his profoundly inappropriate outburst.

Dr. Whitcraft hoped next year's discussion about his maneuver would generate this much enthusiasm and controversy. He'd squirmed in his seat just thinking about it.

On the conference's final day, Dr. Whitcraft

stumbled upon a sparsely attended lecture given by a balding young Frenchman named Dr. Guillaume Duchenne, regarding the use of electricity in the treatment of hysteria. Given that he had already considered that concept, and scorched his own arm in the process, he looked forward to hearing about this man's experience.

He sat in the small room; finding himself among only a handful of other physicians listening to the heavily-accented man discuss his theories. At the end, the other doctors streamed out, but Dr. Whitcraft stayed behind and approached the presenter as he tucked away his notes. He was really no more than a youth.

Dr. Whitcraft held out his hand. "Sir, I am intrigued. I believe that you are quite possibly on to something here."

The young man looked at him in wonder. "You are the only one. Frankly, I think I've wasted my time even coming to this conference. Women's issues leave me a bit cold."

"Really? I thought what you said about electricity to be very compelling."

"It wouldn't be limited to hysteria treatments, of course. Electricity could apply to many areas of interest, the reanimation of cells, perhaps. But these hysteria fellows...so single minded! And I'm not sure I agree with these men about the nature of hysteria. It has always seemed to me that they are classifying any unpleasant symptom shown by a distressed female to be indicative of hysteria, thereby dismissing her."

"Regardless, I am fascinated by what you just proposed up there. I wrote a paper on the possible medical applications for electricity myself. It was published about six months ago. It's funny, I've nearly forgotten about it, because I've moved on to this hysteria business."

"I've read everything on the subject. I'm sure...what is your name?"

"Dr. William Whitcraft. I'm in from London."

"Ah," the young man's face lit up. "What an amazing coincidence running in to you! I work under two other doctors at the university. They are very well-known, well respected gentlemen. They are admirers of your paper..."

"They are?" Dr. Whitcraft was giddy. "How nice to hear!"

"Would you care to join me for dinner? I would love to hear about your work."

"Why I'd be delighted to, actually." He followed the young man out of the stuffy little room and into the Parisian twilight.

Chapter Nineteen

Dr. Whitcraft woke early, completely energized about being back home after an exhausting trip abroad. It would take weeks to go over his notes and digest everything he had learned in Paris, but now, crossing his tiny office toward the first patients since his return, he felt reflective.

He wouldn't be a bachelor much longer. It was difficult not to become sentimental about the time he spent living in this building while he had built his practice. Ah, but on to bigger and better things. He opened the door. The wan Miss Faffle looked up from her desk. He smiled warmly. "Why good morning, Miss Faffle! How wonderful it is to see you! I feel like I've been gone for a year."

Miss Faffle looked at him with wide, frightened eyes. "Good morning, doctor," she whispered, unsettled somehow, like her chair had become prickly. "When did you get in? I waited up for you last evening."

"Oh, it was so late. I don't even know what time it was."

"I see. Uh…" She looked at her hands, like she was searching for something else to say. Finally, she uttered, "H-how was your trip?" Her question was barely audible.

Dr. Whitcraft strolled past her. "Splendid. Just splendid."

She jumped to her feet and rushed after him. "Uh, doctor, there are some matters—issues. I need to speak to you."

"Of course, of course." He flipped open his pocket watch. "How many appointments do I have scheduled after Mrs. Princod and Mrs. Chankings?"

"That's just it. You don't have anything scheduled for the day. Not any more."

When he turned to face her, she winced as if expecting to be struck. He was in such a good mood he couldn't help snicker at the girl's fragility.

"What do you mean? I've had those women scheduled for months now."

"Yes. But when you were gone, they—and some of the others—well, they elected to seek treatment elsewhere." Tears had filled her eyes and her lips were quivering.

"Miss Faffle, take a breath. Everything is all right. Now, what the devil are you talking about?"

She gripped the sides of her dress and took a breath. "After that journal came out, and it has been in the newspapers too, of course. Everyone has been talking about it." She brought her hands to her ears, like she expected a gunshot. "Everyone has been very excited about…*The Marplot Maneuver*."

Dr. Whitcraft cocked his head and echoed, "The *Marplot* Maneuver?"

She nodded.

It was as if Miss Faffle had been speaking a language with which he wasn't entirely familiar. He stared, watching as she clasped her arms around her head, while the meaning of her words began to take hold of his heart.

"What?" he whispered.

"*The Marplot Maneuver!*" she repeated, as if he had actually needed to hear it spoken again.

He inhaled a long, strident breath before his voice broke into a shrill cry, "What are you talking about?"

Miss Faffle just shook her head, tears falling now. "On my desk. It's in the journal and the newspapers—the newspapers have written something about Dr. Marplot almost every day since you've been gone."

He ran past her, his heart fluttering dangerously within his chest. He grabbed at the pile of newspapers. He only had to flip through a few sheets before he saw it.

Revolutionary New Treatment for Hysteria
Dr. Edward Marplot Makes the Most Important
Discovery of our Day

She puffed and wiped tears from her cheeks as Dr. Whitcraft collapsed into a chair, dumbfounded. "I don't understand. Why have they printed this?" he whispered, crumbling the paper in his hands.

"It's that journal, Dr. Whitcraft." She dashed to her desk, digging under the newspapers to produce a two-week-old copy of *The Lancet*. She glanced at it before holding it out, like she was giving a straight razor to a suicidal man.

He snapped it away and at once saw that virtually the entire issue was a celebration of Dr. Edward Marplot and his miraculous new treatment for hysteria.

"Is my name mentioned at all...at all?" He clawed through its pages, recognizing his own prose in print.

"Y-yes. At the end...it mentions you."

He flipped to the end and gazed mouth agape at the last page. "*His research assistant?*" He jumped to his feet and searched the devastated face of Miss Faffle.

Then it occurred to him. Of course it was *his* maneuver, and he could prove it! He had scores of evidence in his cabinet—notes, diagrams, explanations, patient records. He threw himself into his office. Maybe if he hurried, he could take the lot down to *The Lancet* and be there when they began business, proving to them all how he was a victim of that evil man's treachery.

He cackled like a man possessed. He flung his cabinet open, easily flipping through the familiar papers, one by one—but then his stomach lurched. He spun around, trying to manage the building panic as he searched the top of his desk. Surely he hadn't left it out, mislaid it, somehow.

"Miss Faffle," he said in a quivering, breathless plea. "Miss Faffle, he wasn't here, was he? You never would have let him in here…"

"No! No, of course not!" she cried from the doorway.

"My papers…my records on the maneuver. I don't understand where—" He spun around and the deathly-white pallor of Miss Faffle's face betrayed something. Something worse.

"H-he wasn't here. But…" her arms were draped over her head again, bracing for his reaction.

"But what?"

"*She* was. *She* came and took some—"

"WHO?"

"*Miss Reave!* She said *he* needed them to finish the paper. I didn't know what…"

But the throbbing in his ears made perception of any further information impossible. The thunderstruck doctor disintegrated on the spot, feet sliding out from under him as he landed on to his floor, dissolved into an indiscrete collection of humors and misery at the foot of his cabinet. It was too much to comprehend.

Catherine.

After a few moments, his head snapped up. "My patients…my patients. I don't understand."

Miss Faffle had slid to the floor as well, and was propped in the doorway. "Dr. Marplot told them that *he* could do the maneuver since *he* had invented it, and that *he* was the famous one. He told most of them that you had *moved* to Paris, and wouldn't be coming back. I tried to call on them, sir, but they wouldn't listen to me."

Dr. Whitcraft jumped to his feet, leaped over the body of Miss Faffle and sprinted full-speed out his front door.

"Doctor!" she called from the floor. "Doctor?"

****

"*Where is he*?" he shouted at the surprised looking matron behind the desk.

"Ah, you must be Dr. William Whitcraft."

"Yes, I must be! Where the devil is that *charlatan*? That *fraud*!"

"Oh dear. Dr. Marplot told us to expect you. He said you might be a little excited. Have you had a difficult trip, then?" she asked, her face wrinkled in concern.

His body trembled, his fists opening and closing in rage. "Take me to him this *instant*!"

"Oh, he is not here. I'll give him a message, if you like."

Women of various ages were seated in the small space. A few held books in their laps, and one was knitting a long red scarf that twisted into a puddle on the floor. Most frowned at him suspiciously.

"These patients are obviously waiting for him. Wait…*Mrs. Princod*?"

Mrs. Princod's hat was tipped over her face in an obvious attempt at disguising herself from her enraged former doctor. At the sound of her name, however, she looked into his eyes with self-righteous indignation and announced, "Dr. Whitcraft, I am here to receive the *Marplot* Maneuver, if you must know."

"Dr. Marplot will be back, of course," the woman at the desk interrupted. "He was called to the hospital. He'll be back this afternoon if you'd care to—"

He turned and darted out the door, knowing that if he ran, he could be at The Barts in fifteen minutes. But he stopped short. A terrible thought occurred to him, and remembering it felt like an icy claw tightening around his heart. He would go to the hospital, but he had to make another stop first.

****

"My check…I need to have my check back. I've run into some, some financial complexities." He was sweating and disheveled, having just sprinted across town to the estate agent's office.

London was just waking up when he had dashed though its streets. Shopkeepers had leaned out of their doors to watch him in wonder. Calling street-hawkers went silent as he had sped past. A frightened barrow boy leaped out of his way. The movement flung his cargo of fish all over the street, but to Dr. Whitcraft, it was all a blur. All he could envision was that empty house in St. James Square, gaping and open, like a giant mouth ready to swallow him alive.

In his haste, he barely heard a voice calling to him. When he slowed for a passing carriage, Dr. Scamble rushed over.

"Good to see you," he panted. "How was your trip? Did you hear about Dr. Marplot's good fortune? The news has been absolutely everywhere."

Dr. Whitcraft grunted in reply. As the traffic cleared, he catapulted himself into the street once again. But Dr. Scamble was undeterred, and trotted alongside. "Weren't you up to something similar? Too bad he got there before you did."

At that, Dr. Whitcraft made a sudden turn and quite accidentally knocked his friend into the curb, causing him to lose his footing and land in the gutter with a dull thump. He would apologize later, he thought, nearly toppling the handcart of a costermonger as he doubled his speed and left his friend splattered and struggling in the mud.

When he had reached the estate agent's office, he had stayed outside for a time, gasping for breath and composing himself the best that he could. Now, he stood rigidly in front of the old man's desk, trying to keep from betraying his desperation.

"Well, normally, you'd be out of luck. Once you make a deposit on a house, you don't usually get it back, but in the case of this property, there has been a stop to the whole process." The old man looked quizzically over his spectacles. "I'm surprised someone didn't contact you about this."

"I've been out of town." A stop to the whole process? Thank God. Maybe now he wouldn't be ruined, owning a house he couldn't bloody afford now that his practice had been obliterated thanks to that, that cloven-footed imposter.

"Out of town. Yes. I see." The old man opened a file and pulled out an envelope. "There you are, sir."

Dr. Whitcraft's body sagged as he took the envelope, the exact one he had delivered here so many weeks ago. It had been opened, but his check remained inside, uncashed. Thank God!

"Thank you so much. I can just take this, then, and the deal is off?"

"I am rather relieved you are so understanding," the man said. "Yes, the deal is off. When the other offer came in, the seller was delighted, and just went ahead—"

"*Other* offer?"

"Yes. The gentleman agreed to just buy the house outright…and for more than the asking price. Apparently the chap has access to boatloads of family money, or some such thing. He'd been wanting a house like that for quite some time. I'll tell you, property in that part of London does create quite the stir."

"Wait a minute." Dr. Whitcraft's ears began to buzz. "Wh-who was it that put in this *other* offer?"

"Hmm." The old man went back to rifling through the clutter on his desk. He looked under one sheet of paper and then another until he finally seized a particular page. He skimmed the script with a thin, bluish finger, and stabbed at one line in particular. "Yes…oh look. Another doctor, like yourself. A *Dr. Edward Marplot*. Maybe you know the fellow?"

It was as if he had been struck by a sledgehammer, the blow taking the breath right out of his lungs, leaving him palsied and wheezing. His uncashed check wafted gently to the floor, while he staggered and grabbed at his throat, the blood rising red up his face like a thermometer plunged in hot water.

"My boy? Angels in heaven! This man's been stricken! Someone get a doctor!"

****

As Dr. Whitcraft sprinted down the long and crowded hospital hallway, he growled the name Marplot, but received only opened-mouth stares in response. He dove into an empty surgical theater and out again, nearly tripping over a trio of wheel-chaired unfortunates. He hurdled past them like a champion of track and field, ignoring the shouts of the hospital workers as he indiscriminately canvassed the hall, opening doors and then slamming them shut. There was no method to his search, other than a personal vow to scour every ward, every office, every engaged surgical suite for the man who had ruined his life.

He flung open yet another non-descript door, and there, as if by divine providence, stood the object of his passion. The tall, well-made form of Dr. Edward Marplot casually struck a pose against the room's back counter while he chatted with a pretty young nurse.

Dr. Marplot turned at the sound of the opening door, and took note of the doctor's appearance with an arched eyebrow and a quick, gentle smile. "Ah, Dr. Whitcraft."

Dr. Whitcraft remained in place, snarling as his hands clenched into fists.

The nurse's pleasant expression darkened at the sight, and she began walking backwards, feeling for the door. Finding it, she disappeared with the swiftness of a specter. The two doctors were alone in a large and cluttered examining room.

"Judging by your rather flustered appearance, Dr. Whitcraft, perhaps you would like to sit down and talk about this like the two rational and learned creatures that we are." He sounded chipper and calm, like he was chatting up an old woman at the post office.

Dr. Whitcraft stepped in, but stopped, throwing a quick glance at the shelves next to the door, estimating which of the articles within his reach could be used to kill.

"Listen my friend, you think this has been some terrible plan on my part to arrange your undoing, but that is where you are wrong. It has merely been a series of unfortunate misinterpretations by a variety of people, none of which has the slightest thing to do with me...other than my getting the credit for work which you surely believe to be your own."

At that, Dr. Whitcraft grabbed an empty porcelain basin and cast it full force at the man's head, but Dr. Marplot had anticipated the launch and ducked. The basin smacked the floor with a hollow clank, and he rose back up with a look of surprise and thrill on his face.

"Well, whoever would have guessed you had such a temper, Dr. Whitcraft? And such good aim, too."

It was as if a dam had broken. Propelled by a strength he had never known, Dr. William Whitcraft leaped forward into a running dive and tackled his oppressor, knocking him into the long side of an examining table, sending both men and the table toppling onto the floor with a thundering crash.

Briefly, Dr. Whitcraft had the upper hand and landed a rather solid blow, but the slippery Dr. Marplot wriggled out of his grasp. His escape was thwarted, however, when Dr. Whitcraft managed to grab both ends of his fluttering ascot, jerking him backwards like a jockey pulling on the reins of his horse. "There you go, *old man*. How do you like it?" The image of himself at the gallows for this man's murder was at present judged to be well worth it.

"You're mad!" Dr. Marplot sputtered, clawing at his throat. He squirmed and kicked, grasping for anything that might disable his attacker. As luck would have it, a wooden leg that had been resting in wait on the now toppled table, rolled loose among the fray; his hand had just glided across it.

Dr. Marplot seized the limb. In a single burst of strength, he pivoted his body and smashed the weapon directly into the eighth, ninth and tenth left ribs of his opponent. Dr. Whitcraft collapsed to the floor, windless and writhing.

"Stay back or I'll give you another whack," Dr. Marplot warned, getting to his knees and waving the upside-down leg in the air like a bat. His crumpled ascot slid to the floor when he got to his feet, and his hair hung limply over his eyes. "You just need to listen to me," he breathed, trying to measure his tone. "We can write another article…another. I'll make sure you get the credit."

"Have you no shame!" Dr. Whitcraft wheezed, turning over but unable to stand. His left side felt like fire, and exhaustion had settled down on every part of his body. "Wh-why couldn't you just keep my bloody name on it?" he gasped. "Why did you have to take my *patients*…and my *house*, Why?"

Hearing these words, Dr. Marplot relaxed his weapon a little. He seemed to stand taller, arching his back to display his full height while deliberating over these very relevant questions. A complex series of expressions flashed across his face while he stood there, his fingers loosening and tightening over the leg. Finally, he arched both brows. "Why not?" and a fast smile crossed his lips.

As if lightning had stricken him, Dr. Whitcraft jumped to his feet and once again tackled Dr. Marplot, the momentum knocking the leg out of his hands, where it sailed well out of play.

The two grappled with one another for a time, first rolling into the collapsed table, then away from it, one flipping on top of the other and then back again, grunting and struggling all the while. Dr. Marplot managed to land a blow to Dr. Whitcraft's lower jaw, but Dr. Whitcraft replied by grabbing a handful of the other's hair and pulling his head up and down like a marionette.

Dr. Marplot tore himself away, twisted around, and shoved Dr. Whitcraft into the shelves against the back wall. A middle shelf split and showered splintered wood and metal instruments over him. He scooped up each item and threw it as Dr. Marplot crawled toward the exit.

In search of more missiles, Dr. Whitcraft's hand found its way to a jar of leeches. Undeterred by the obvious unpleasantness of doing so, he plunged his hand into the jar and hurled leech after leech at Dr. Marplot, grinning malevolently as each hit its mark.

"You are unhinged! Demented! Do you know that? You're a demented person," Dr. Marplot called, but was silenced when a particularly fat ball of leeches smacked him squarely in the mouth.

One of the doors swung wide just then.

"Oh my darling, what in the world? What's happened?"

At once, Dr. Whitcraft recognized the voice. Buried within a mound of broken wood and medical clutter, he tossed a splinted board away from his face and saw Miss Reave embrace his rival.

He could only manage a soft, plaintive groan.

Miss Reave turned at the sound. She squinted at the spectacled eyes watching her from underneath the debris and gasped. She clutched her chest, looking from one man to the other.

Dr. Whitcraft tried to stand, but in doing so, dislodged the top shelf, and a large clay vessel that had been precariously balanced during the fray finally gave way, landing directly on the doctor's head and knocking him into a fast unconsciousness.

****

Voices were coming from somewhere. Dr. Whitcraft reached up to touch his forehead and winced. It throbbed terribly. Someone had tied a bandage around his head like a crown. His entire body ached like he had been beaten. Wait a minute, he thought vaguely, he *had* been beaten. He opened his eyes, but shut them seeing the fuzzy forms of two nurses standing outside the hospital ward door.

"No, I can't because Dr. Marplot says we need to watch that man. He's a danger to everyone in this hospital. That's why they put him in here I suppose. Did you hear about how he attacked the poor doctor and what he did to that examination room? It'll take days to clean that up."

"I saw it and I'm shocked. Why would anyone

want to attack the doctor like that?"

"No one knows."

"Who is he, anyway? Does anyone, know?"

"No. No one knows that, either. Dr. Marplot says the police will sort it out. He's probably some kind of fiend, going after famous doctors like Dr. Marplot."

"Well, as soon as the police get here, they'll take care of it."

"Don't you think he is handsome?"

"Who? *That* man?"

"No, no. Dr. Marplot!"

"Oh yes, of course. That black eye makes him even more mysterious and dashing." She giggled as she walked off, leaving the other nurse alone to return to her desk.

Panic filled his already over-taxed system. What would happen when the police came? There was no doubt he had assaulted that vile conniver, but in all likelihood, the police would never accept his defense that the wretch had deserved it.

Oh, and the horror of seeing Miss Reave! He moaned, remembering how she had looked with her arms wrapped around that…that… But he couldn't let matters of the heart get the better of him now. No, what he must do now is scientifically analyze this situation, take an inventory of this room and the possibilities it contained and then consider each and every diagnosis for this most appalling predicament.

He was the patient now, dressed in a flimsy gown without his glasses, lying in a hospital ward. It appeared that the majority of the other beds here were empty, except on either side of him. The man on his right was in all likelihood dead. He was rigid, and staring blankly into the ether. What luck!

The man on his left, however, was awake and stirring. If he squinted, Dr. Whitcraft could see that he recently had a rather large gash on his face mended. Judging by the atrocious scar, however, the surgeon had been woefully unskilled. What a pity, he thought, looking past his feet. His clothes had been neatly piled on the chair at the foot of his bed. Thank God, his glasses were sitting there, too.

He scanned the room. It possessed a single door, but escape that way seemed unlikely and ill-advised. But there was a large window opposite the door and he could reach it if he could manage to climb up to its ledge, although he had no way of knowing if he was still on the ground floor. But he couldn't very well escape while the nurse sat at her desk. He had to get her out of this room, if only for a moment.

She would certainly leave if she needed to summon a doctor. Dr. Whitcraft had never been ill enough to convulse, but he had seen multitudes of patients over the years that had, enough times that he thought he could probably present a very convincing imitation. Decision made, he glanced at his ward-mates, took a deep breath and plunged himself into his performance.

The nurse, hearing something amiss, looked up from her desk and gasped, horrified to see her patient tormented by such a dramatic fit. She arose and hurried out into the corridor.

He threw off his coverings and jumped up. On his way to the door, he scooped up the closest chair and jammed it securely underneath the door's latch.

"Hey!" the man with the gash exclaimed, sitting up.

Dr. Whitcraft nodded to him as he hurried past, the cold floor stinging his bare feet with each step. Where the devil did they put his shoes, he wondered as he threw on his glasses. But there wasn't any time to search, and he struggled to pull his trousers up underneath his gown.

"What's going on? Open that door!" the man with the scar demanded indignantly.

"It's quite all right, good sir. I am a physician."

Someone was pounding on the door. Clearly it wouldn't be long before they burst through. He threw his waistcoat over the gown, grabbed another chair, and hurried toward the window, but paused, and turned to his unfortunate neighbor.

"I realize it is not likely that you are in a position to do anything about it, but the surgeon who has tended to your face has done a remarkably poor job with its repair. If it were me, I would go at once to The London Hospital, right over there on Whitechapel Road, and seek the treatment of a Mr. Prinking. He is an excellent chap, educated in Edinburgh if memory serves, and will most certainly restore you. Oh!"

The door bowed and seemed ready to burst off its frame as a collection of shouting men slammed against it. The doctor abandoned his consultation and scurried to the window. Stepping on the chair, he climbed to the ledge and saw that, thank heavens, he was indeed on the ground floor. The sash slid open with minimal effort. Dr. Whitcraft tossed his legs over the sill, gave a final nod to his astonished neighbor, and escaped like a thief into the streets of London.

Chapter Twenty

Dr. Whitcraft's back was flat against a cold marble façade and his knees were tucked against his chest as he sat on the bare ground. Branches clawed at his face and tore at his bandage. His bare feet were nicked and bleeding from the short sprint from the hospital courtyard.

With the disinterested populace scurrying to and fro, who would have thought that a battered and barefoot man running down the street with a hospital gown tucked into his trousers and a bandage encircling his head would generate so little attention.

Regardless, the prospect of creating a spectacle in the busy mid-day streets made him duck into the first spot that offered cover, which had turned out to be the dense mulberry bushes adorning this anonymous public building. From there, he would plan his next move.

Dizzy, probably from the head injury, it was difficult to get his thoughts in order. He watched the citizenry hurrying past, each soul unaware that their lower halves were being observed from within.

He wondered if the police would be waiting for him when he managed to get home. There was certainly no reason to believe that Dr. Marplot, that loathsome Mephistopheles, would not have joyfully given them his name. Why wouldn't he? Why not have him arrested for the wanton destruction of St.

Bartholomew's property not to mention the assault on his eminence, the discoverer of the famous *Marplot Maneuver*? It was all so perfect! The man had orchestrated the ruination of his life; why not end the whole business by sending him to the pillory, subject to the scorn of the entire city of London.

He was queasy and put his head in his hands. He wanted to go home and collapse in his own bed. Maybe after some sleep he could figure everything out.

Dr. Whitcraft awoke disoriented, but still snuggly tucked within the bushes. He had lost consciousness, and was unsure exactly how much time had passed. It seemed to be dusk now, or was that only the fog settling down on the city and obscuring the afternoon sun. Regardless, his entire body ached, and he couldn't think anymore. He just wanted to go home.

He patted the pocket of his waistcoat, but wasn't at all surprised to find it empty. In his rush to leave the office this morning, he had left without his wallet.

The walk would be too long without any shoes, and the lack of money would certainly be a sticking point in any negotiation for transportation, but perhaps he could at least try. The carriages hurry by. His interest piqued when he saw an ornamented, yet shabbily maintained covered sedan chair held up on either side by two men wearing tattered uniforms. And it was empty.

In all his days in London, he had never ridden in one of those contraptions, but had seen them buzzing around, here and there. With the streets clogged by carriages and Hansom cabs, sometimes the only way to get somewhere quickly was in a sedan chair because they could dodge through the throngs and navigate tiny streets that were impassible by other, larger vehicles.

As fate would have it, the lackadaisical pair and their jaunty conveyance were directly in front of him now.

"Excuse me, gentlemen." He crawled out of the bushes.

Both men seemed unfazed by his sudden appearance. "Y'or in us way," the taller of the two said.

"I would like to engage your service. I don't have any money on me, for I have been the victim of numerous crimes, but I offer you my personal word as a physician that I have money at my home, and if you take me there, I will gladly pay double whatever your normal—"

"Enough," the shorter one said, bored. "Where do y'want ter go?"

"Berkeley Square, Bruton Street, Number 2, if you please. I know it's not that far, but I can't very well walk there." He gestured to his naked feet.

And with well-rehearsed fluidity, they lowered the sedan chair to the ground; the taller of the two released the grip on his poles and walked around to the front of the booth. He unlatched the door and pulled it open. As he stepped aside, the man made a sweeping motion with his long, thin arm, and in a voice laden with sarcasm declared, "*Entre-vous.*"

"Why, thank you." Dr. Whitcraft stood straighter, smoothed out his filthy waistcoat and climbed in.

"As you see, it's been rather a troubling day."

The door swung shut, sparing the conveyers any further details of his excessive misfortune.

The dull operative latched the door and silently resumed his place at the back. Dr. Whitcraft slid his fingers along the handholds, feeling vulnerable inside this box. It was covered in layers of grime and smelled of sweat and onions. The flabby, checkered seat cushion had been worn limp from the backsides of countless prior passengers; and the windows were so distorted and scratched, one could barely see through them at all. The surroundings did little to inspire his confidence as he ascended, and he suddenly remembered the face of a young gentleman he had treated at the hospital several years ago. Hadn't he been tossed out of one of these things like a rag-doll and broken his wrist?

But there was no time to reconsider. His two drivers rushed into the street like a team of horses spooked by a gunshot. Slammed forward, and then back again, he found himself crumpled on the compartment's sticky floor, grasping at anything to steady himself. Up and down, jiggled and juggled this way and that; the ache in his cranium turned into fire.

He managed to climb back to his perch, gripping the seat edges as he squinted through the scratched windows. If they had been clear, the passing scenery would have been nothing but a bouncing blur. Oh, how much longer, he wondered, savoring a sudden pause while his drivers waited on traffic.

The trip re-commenced, jarring loose his grasp and tossing him back to the floor. The faster they went, the more helpless he became. He felt like a pair of dice being tossed about in a giant hand, only to tumble out and roll head over heels before finally expiring on the pavement. And then, mercifully, the sedan chair stopped moving.

He climbed up from the floor and could just make out the rough impression of his townhouse, looking so much like it always had in the dusky pollution of

London; he wanted to weep with thanks upon seeing it.

He felt himself lowered back to earth. One of them opened the door and he staggered out onto the street. It took him a moment to speak. "Gentlemen, thank you. Please wait here. I will be back with your fee straightaway. How much... Oh, I'll bring it all," he mumbled, ascending his steps, grateful to see Miss Faffle through the glass, sitting behind her desk as if nothing at all had happened. When he opened the door, she looked up, startled.

"Miss Faffle, please see to it that those gentlemen out front are paid. Oh, you cannot imagine how happy I am to be home." With that, three policemen filed out of his office, chatting to one another before turning silent and taking note of the strangely dressed individual presenting himself in the reception area.

In a singular line of motion, as if it took no thought at all, Dr. Whitcraft was suddenly being transported away, out the door, back down his front steps, past the uniformed troglodytes who had brought him here, and up the street. He wasn't aware of how fast he was running, or even that he *was* running. A survival instinct had taken over his being that was so base, so primitive, he was unable to access it with his rational brain and harness it's power for his own control.

Miss Faffle had run to the door as he disappeared through the traffic and crowds, closer and closer to the horizon.

"Doctor? Doctor! It's all right," she called.

Constable Fettle joined her on the stoop. "He's far gone, that one. Poor devil. If he comes back, tell him no one's going to arrest him. We've got to figure out a way to arrest that dreadful bully, Dr. Marplot. You let me work on it."

****

"Thank God you're back!"

"Oh you won't believe it!"

"We've been waiting—"

"Corrine sent Lilly to find you."

The girls were talking all at once. Mrs. Minnock's head still felt fuzzy from the champagne she had consumed at the theater. "What is all this?" She slipped her arm from her companion's grasp.

"He's locked himself in your room," one of them sputtered.

"He finished all your brandy."

"Yes, and then he went into Corrine's room and found *her* bottle."

"He's wearing a hospital gown under his clothes, and has a bandage on his head."

"Who? What are you all talking about?" Mrs. Minnock looked from one frightened face to another.

Corrine pulled her aside, and whispered, "Why it's *Dr. Whitcraft*."

"What?" Mrs. Minnock breathed, certain she had misunderstood the distraught girl.

"Yes! Dr. Whitcraft! He arrived here in an absolute state, injured and looking for you. I told him that you were out for the evening, but he wouldn't leave and now he's gone mad and shut himself in your room. He isn't answering anyone." Corrine's forehead wrinkled with dread.

Mrs. Minnock pursed her lips for a moment and looked back at her date. This evening's gentleman was a grumpy old fool from parliament. Gauging from his frown, he was not impressed with the unexpected

225

excitement. He flipped open his pocket watch and glanced at it.

She stepped back toward him. "Geoffrey, my dear, would you mind terribly if I sent you off with another one of the ladies? An unpleasant situation has arisen that demands my attention."

The man's frown remained unchanged, but he made a "humph" sound before casting a disinterested glance at the other ladies. He turned his mouth under and looked back at her, radiating displeasure.

Mrs. Minnock thought for a moment before saying, "All right then. How about *two?* Any *two* girls?"

His mouth twitched a bit and he turned back to the girls, considering the notion with a raised eyebrow. After a moment, he spoke. "Well, that is different."

He scanned each of their lovely personages now with intense deliberation, like a man who had finished his meal and been presented with an assortment of sweets on a tray.

"I think I'll take…hmm. Why don't I take that piece over there. The little one with the auburn hair. Yes. And which one of them did you say was from Marseilles?" Three ladies pointed to a girl with long dark hair standing on the stairs. "Yes, I'll try that one. And I'll not pay a penny above my normal price."

"Yes, of course." Mrs. Minnock made no attempt to hide her disgust as Missy and Michelle made their way to either side of the gentleman, and escorted him up the stairs. She sighed and took Corrine by the arm, pulling her toward the hall. "How long has he been in there?"

"I don't know. At least a few hours. You cannot imagine the state he is in."

They arrived at the door to her room, but the lock had indeed been engaged. She knocked softly. "Dr. Whitcraft? This is Mrs. Minnock. You are in my room, and I need you to let me in…this instant. Do you hear?"

There was a slight scraping from the interior, and perhaps too the sound of labored breathing, but it was difficult to make out anything else.

"Dr. Whitcraft?" She knocked again, but there was nothing. She turned to the girls who had gathered behind her. "Sally, would you be a dear and go fetch the key ring from the top middle drawer in my desk?"

A young girl wearing too much rouge dashed off. Mrs. Minnock put her mouth right next to the door, managing to keep her tone constant and calm. "This won't do, doctor. Whatever is troubling you, I'm sure there's a solution."

Sally returned with a jingling ring of keys. Mrs. Minnock sorted through them, finding just the one.

"Ladies, please leave us." She unlocked her door with a sharp click. The door swung open, but the ladies stood in place, each holding her breath as they rose to their tiptoes with choreographed synchronicity. What they saw was appalling.

Dr. Whitcraft lay facedown on the floor, his arms flung out to the sides, his naked legs white and exposed, his trousers collected in a bunch around his ankles. He sported a rumpled and torn hospital gown where his waistcoat should have been, and had a ragged bandage loosely encircling his head like an unwound turban. An uncorked and nearly empty bottle of brandy lay just beyond the grasp of his right hand.

A variety of gasps escaped the audience of girls.

"Oh my goodness, Corrine, help me!" Mrs.

Minnock rushed in and dropped to his side. She shook him. "William! William?"

She rolled the doctor over and was shocked to see his eyes open and blinking behind his glasses. He had a ridiculous smile plastered on his lips.

"Mah darling," he crooned upon seeing her. The alcohol content in his breath made her eyes water, and she pulled away and turned her head. "Corrine, get on his other side and help me. Can you stand, William?"

He cackled as he attempted to sit up, squinting at her. "Can I stand? Sssssstand? You know what I *can't* sssstand?" His words were thick, his movements slow and his bruised face distorted with emotion. "I can't ssstand that awful, aud-audacioussss teller of lies."

"Let's put him on the bed." Mrs. Minnock struggled to lift one side of his dead weight while Corrine puffed and heaved with the other.

"Yes, l-let's put him on the bed," he echoed while the cluster of enthralled girls watched from the doorway, a most receptive audience.

After several steps, he seemed to become cognizant that it was Mrs. Minnock's lovely form that he leaned against. A wry smile spread across his face. He rolled his head toward her and began nibbling at her neck, all the while cooing, "Mahhh dahhhhling." His legs gave way and he dropped to the floor with a thud.

"Oh!" Corrine yelled, appalled at the unnatural position in which he now lay, the top half of his body folded over the bottom, the way a manservant might fold a suit to fit it into a valise.

"Stand him back up! We've almost made it," Mrs. Minnock managed to say, perspiration adding a pleasing glow to her already flushed face.

For a moment, they all believed him to have fallen into unconsciousness because his eyes were shut and he had ceased moving. But as they hoisted him onto his feet once again, his eyes snapped open. "I won't stand for it, I tell you. I'll not—" He stopped speaking and seemed puzzled now that he had managed to focus on the exhausted Mrs. Minnock.

"What the devil are you doing here?" he inquired.

"Drop him," she said, and down he went, on the bed.

"All right. Out! Everyone out this minute."

The girls recognized their mistresses' tone, and promptly evacuated the scene.

Mrs. Minnock sat on her bed, feeling it shake while he jerked himself into a comfortable position. She kicked off her shoes and noticed his soiled waistcoat draped across her dressing-table, next to the empty decanter toppled on its side.

She reached behind herself and skimmed her fingers over the doctor's bandage and through his disheveled hair, but her voice was stern. "What a sorry display, William. Would you care to tell me what this is about?"

She waited for an answer, but turned to see that it was pointless. His body was drained of all animation, other than the deep, guttural snores emanating from his open mouth. She sighed, rising and making her way to the foot of her bed where she paused for a moment and contemplated each bruise, tear and bloody smear on his clothing. With the lightest touch, she slid the doctor's bunched trousers over his battered feet and smacked the garment with her hand as she held it in the air, waving the dust cloud away. She folded them once, then twice and set them on her side table. Next, she eased off his glasses with her fingertips, and placed them next to his trousers.

Considering the man in her bed once again, she lifted his bandage away from his forehead. She winced at the ugly gash that it hid, and bit her lip as she dropped next to him on the bed. He didn't move when she held his hand.

Clearly, she would have to wait several hours to find out what in the world had happened to cause this most extraordinary transformation of her stodgiest client.

****

Mrs. Minnock was the very picture of gentle encouragement as Dr. Whitcraft confessed every excruciating detail of what had caused him to regress into such a pitiful state. His recitation of events would periodically slow to a trickle and then stop, at which time he'd rise from her bed and reveal a most unhealthy complexion. Then he'd dash out of the room and stagger back a few minutes later, his ashen face now flushed, his filthy hospital gown hanging over his body, the partially unwound bandage dangling in a strip from his head; the doctor looked like a wretched and abused patient as he dropped back down beside her and continued his pathetic tale.

After a half an hour of this cycle, he concluded by describing how he had come there to find her, and became distraught at her absence, thus proceeding to drink every drop of her brandy straight out of the decanter. From that point on, he could remember nothing.

Having purged himself of his tale, as well as a

great many of the impurities from the night before, he lay motionless, sprawled flat like an empty shell atop her blankets, utterly drained and staring into the ceiling.

She wasn't sure if he was conscious as she lay next to him, letting the astonishing details of his story hang in the air like smoke from an explosion. Finally, she spoke. "William, that has to be the most unbelievable thing I have ever heard. What kind of a man would do such things...to *you* of all people? And I thought I'd heard everything."

The doctor groaned in reply, and tossed his arm over his face, wincing at the pain he had reignited in his forehead.

After some time, she asked, "Weren't there other professionals, other doctors who knew that it was *your* maneuver? Why didn't anyone speak up on your behalf?"

He was silent for a moment. Finally he said, "Dr. Vorago knew it was mine, of course, but he was with me in Paris, and probably still doesn't know about all this. And the others...that fiend listed me as a *research assistant* in the article. Maybe they assumed we were working together, I don't know. Who knows what he's been telling people?"

"What if you contacted the editors of *The Lancet* and told them about his treachery? Surely they would print a retraction."

He put his head in his hands. "You know, I thought the same thing, when I first heard. I wanted to run over there with all of my notes, my work, prove that it was mine, but while I was gone..." He choked on the words. "Miss Reave. Apparently, she came to my office when I was gone and collected everything. Every last reference to the maneuver is missing from my cabinet."

Mrs. Minnock's frown turned into a wide-eyed look of rage, but she said nothing.

He shrugged. "They know him at *The Lancet*, anyway, and would probably believe *him* over anything that I might say."

She was quiet. After a moment she whispered, "I suppose you're right."

They lay there in silence and stared at the ceiling. Mrs. Minnock, though, wrinkled her forehead and chewed her lip. "William, I hesitate even to tell you this, but in deciding how to handle that wretch…well, I believe it is important that you know *all* the facts."

He turned to her with the face of a man being led in front of a firing squad. "Oh, oh no. Not more—"

"While you were in Paris, Dr. Marplot…well, he came *here*. He sauntered into our parlor there, introduced himself to everyone and asked to see me. When I approached the man, he looked me up and down in the most lascivious of ways and said…well, he told me that *you* had referred him, to me specifically, and asked to engage my services."

At that, Dr. Whitcraft leapt off the bed, spun about the room, and shrieked as he dropped to his knees.

"William! Get hold of yourself!" She jumped up as well. "He didn't! Do you understand? He didn't…*I didn't!* It's all right!"

It took over ten minutes of repeated assurances before she was able to convince him that indeed nothing had happened. When he calmed down enough to formulate a sentence, he wheezed through his hands, "How could he possibly know about you? I never breathed a word to anyone."

"Oh William, there are no secrets in this town. You'd be shocked if you knew. I'm sure all he did was ask around." She rose from his side and began to pace, her arms folded across her chest. "You know, when he mentioned your name, it was very odd, come to think of it. He called you the creator of the...I believe he said *the illustrious three-step Whitcraft Maneuver*, which I found odd...very odd."

"Three step?" he murmured from the floor, his face still covered by his hands.

"Yes. I didn't correct him," she whispered, almost to herself, but then added, "oh, but Lilly did. She giggled about the *five* steps. Oh William, William." She brought her hand to her face and suddenly looked concerned. She knelt beside him again. "Did he ever ask you how you came up with the maneuver?"

He squinted at her. "I... What?"

"Think, William! He must have asked you about your process...how you developed the maneuver."

"Yes, he did, actually," he said, coming around. "On several occasions."

"What did you say?"

"Well what could I say? I certainly couldn't tell him I learned it from you! So I made up some nonsense about trial and error."

"Don't you see?" she said. "That son-of-a-bitch figured out that you'd probably learned the maneuver from me, and came here to confirm his suspicions. That's why he tried to get me to correct him about the number of steps, so he could be certain that you couldn't defend yourself against his treachery."

He stood up, took a few steps and flopped down on the bed. "Brandy."

Mrs. Minnock got to her feet as well, and sighed at the defeated man on her bed. "I'm afraid your stock is gone and you drank all of mine."

"Get more."

She hated to abet the already-compromised doctor, but what else was there to do to provide the man some comfort? She walked into the hallway and spoke in a hush to the girls lurking by the door.

When she returned, he was sitting up, legs swung over the bed, looking determined.

"William? Are you all right? Are you going to be ill again?" She rushed over and at once contemplated the curious look of decisiveness in his eyes.

"No. I'm simply going to kill him. That's really the only thing to do, then isn't it?"

"Oh, now let's not be absurd."

"I'll challenge him to a duel. Or better yet, I'll shoot him right through the skull as he lays there in bed." His eyes were unnaturally wide as he spoke.

"That's ridiculous." She put her hand on his arm. "Have you ever even fired a weapon?"

His face sagged at that, and then the doctor threw up his hands and deflated back toward despondency. After a moment, he turned to her and asked with pleading eyes, "If he told you I sent him, why…why *didn't* you?"

She took a breath and patted his hand. "Well, now. There are two reasons for that. I knew when he strutted into our parlor that he was not to be trusted. Something about his eyes. And he was so pompous and full of himself. I never deal with men like that."

"Yes," he said, eyes searching the floor, "I can see. What was the other reason?"

Mrs. Minnock grasped his chin and lifted his face so that his gaze would meet her own. "William, I have been at this business for a long time. Too long, frankly. And in that time I can count on one hand the number of truly decent men that I have come across. You don't treat me like a plaything...you treat me like a human being, and you never, ever would have *recommended* me to anyone, especially to someone like that. Never! I just knew you never would've done that."

Dr. Whitcraft sighed deeply, leaned over and withered in her lap. She steered his body back down on the bed just as Lilly opened the door.

"Ah, look, William. Here's our brandy. Two glasses, Lilly dear. Pour two, if you please."

Lilly did as she was told. Mrs. Minnock left the doctor's side to collect the glasses. She took them and gestured with her chin for the girl to leave.

"Here is your brandy," she whispered, sitting back on the bed.

But he didn't take it. Instead he turned to her with tragically miserable eyes blinking wet behind his glasses. "I'm so glad you knew. God knows, I would never have done that."

Chapter Twenty-One

"Ahh, look who is awake." Mrs. Minnock smiled as she set down a tray at the foot of her bed. Dr. Whitcraft lay silent, eyes open, staring at the ceiling.

"I sent Lilly to pick up some of your clothes and a pair of shoes from Miss Faffle, who was beside herself wondering what became of you, by the way. They are over there on my dressing table. She assured Lilly that Constable Fettle has the crisis well in hand, and has talked his superiors out of charging you with the assault of… Well, of course you know who. And apparently Mrs. Pannade has been hovering around your office as well, but I suppose you don't want to hear anything about that, do you?" She paused and studied him lying there unchanged and lifeless.

"Today you are going to eat something, clean up, get dressed, and leave this room. That's the plan," she said with what she hoped would be a contagious optimism. He had been in a stupor for the last several days, too depressed and embarrassed to leave.

"Look, I made you soft-boiled eggs and toast. I haven't done that since my husband was alive, so count yourself among the privileged few who can elicit such a domestic response."

He sighed and continued blinking at the ceiling. Undeterred, she went over to the window and drew up the shade, causing golden morning light to flood the room. He winced and threw the sheet over his head. At least she had gotten a reaction out of him. Mrs. Minnock picked up a piece of his toast and gnawed on it.

"You know, I've been thinking. I think you should let the bloody bastard have the maneuver. Let him have *all* of it."

He threw the sheet off of his head. "What? What the devil do you mean *let him have it*? Let him have all the credit that should be mine? I should just, just…let him take away my patients, too, I suppose. My livelihood, m-my house, not to mention my fiancée. And you? *Even you*?" His face had turned dark and he glared at her.

"Oh come now," she said with the firmness of a school marm. "First of all, that thing you call the Whitcraft Maneuver was never actually yours, as that bastard so cleverly discovered. It was *mine*. Where's *my* name in your precious journal? Where's my husband's name? I like the sound of *The Minnock Maneuver*."

"Oh, don't be absurd. You both couldn't have dreamed of its importance to science."

"No, of course not, but if it wasn't for me showing you the damn thing, you wouldn't be lying there right now. None of this would have happened, and that ungrateful, capricious, spoiled young woman would have ended up as your wife. You should consider yourself lucky that *he* got her instead of you!"

She put her hand on her hip and paused. She had meant to get him out of his stupor, but perhaps not like this. She eased her tone, and began again. "So here's my plan. Let him have the damn maneuver. Let him have all the glories, but let him have the responsibilities, hazards and liabilities along with them, too. You yourself said it could be dangerous if performed inappropriately."

Dr. Whitcraft's glare melted into a look of intrigue. "What are you getting at?"

"How about this? Suppose women start dropping dead, and there is some speculation that it's because of that bloody maneuver. I bet his practice would likely suffer as a result."

"No one is going to drop dead...except maybe me."

She picked up a piece of toast and handed it to him. "Sometimes it only matters what people think. So much so that it isn't long before what people think eventually becomes the truth."

He chewed as he reflected on her words. "I am not sure if I follow you."

She climbed over and tucked herself beside him. "All doctors lose patients, yes?"

"Yes, of course. We see dozens of them die, especially in hospital, but what does that have to—"

"Dr. Marplot works at The Barts, yes?"

"Yes, in addition to his practice, but again, I'm not sure what you're driving at. The only patients who received the maneuver are wealthy women from our private practices. Hospitals are filled with every malady that—"

"Yes, yes...hospitals are horrible places, I know. But what if, someone of importance, someone who people trusted on matters like these, what if this person perhaps concluded that one of Dr. Marplot's patients *died* because of this maneuver?"

"Who the devil would do that? I don't think you

understand. It's not going to kill anyone!"

She shook her head. "You're not listening. It doesn't have to. We just need someone who could help us spread the word, if you will, that your Dr. Marplot and *his* maneuver killed someone. Are you familiar with Dr. Edward Boodler?"

His eyebrows rose. "Of course I'm familiar with him. He's the bloody coroner. Do you seriously want me go to his office, introduce myself and then bribe him or something, get him to falsify some inquests to frame th-that imposter, that—"

"No," she said. "You don't have to do a thing. But, I believe I might have some influence in this matter." She looked at him with a searing gaze whose import was unmistakable and not to be trifled with.

Dr. Whitcraft opened his mouth to speak, but appeared to think better of it.

"What we need is a name. We need to find the name of some unfortunate soul, a female, to whom he attended during the time when he was performing the maneuver. It is irrelevant how she died. It is irrelevant even if she got the damn maneuver. Those are unimportant details. Just get a name. If you can get more than one, do it."

****

"It's there, right up those steps," Dr. Whitcraft muttered, pointing toward his front door.

"Well, well. What a charming building, William. It's exactly how you described it." Mrs. Minnock brushed her hand past his and climbed up the stairs in front of him.

As soon as they appeared on the stoop, Miss Faffle looked up from her desk and gasped. She nearly tripped over her feet sprinting toward the door.

"Oh! Oh, doctor!" She flung open the door. "Thank goodness, thank goodness."

"Oh…oh my yes. Why thank you, Miss Faffle. Everything is quite all right." He took a deep breath. "Mrs. Minnock, this is my assistant, Miss Faffle. Miss Faffle, if you please, this is Mrs. Minnock. She is…she's a dear friend of mine."

Miss Faffle glanced at Mrs. Minnock and nodded before spinning back to her boss. "I was so worried, Dr. Whitcraft! I didn't know where to find you. Constable Fettle and I have been…" She paused and drew a hand to her mouth as she stared aghast at his forehead. "Oh! Are you injured?"

The gash on his hairline was visible now that he had removed his filthy bandage. "It's nothing." He passed his hand along the raised wound, flinching underneath his own touch.

Miss Faffle inched closer. "Did Dr. Marplot do that to you?" she whispered with much gravity.

He opened his mouth to reply, but only managed to shake his head.

Perhaps sensing his imminent return to despondency, Mrs. Minnock jumped in. "Miss Faffle, my dear, would it be too much trouble for you to run an errand on behalf of your boss? There's some information he needs to collect. William, why don't you go into your office and have a seat while I explain to Miss Faffle what we are after."

He felt dizzy and very much befuddled as he looked into the nervous face of Miss Faffle and then into the serene countenance of Mrs. Minnock. He marveled at the contrast. That woman had it all under control, he thought, feeling himself surrender to her strategies. "Yes, I would love to sit down in my office."

"Good for you, William. Go on then." Mrs. Minnock gave his shoulder a gentle push and then turned back to Miss Faffle. In the gentlest of all voices she explained, "I'll need you to run down to St. Bartholomew's, dear. In Smithfield. Are you familiar with it?"

****

Dr. Whitcraft was resting his head on his arms when Mrs. Minnock slipped in to his office. She ran her hands along the faces of his books, scanning their titles with a bemused smile, turning and nodding at the stacks of journals on his desk, taking it all in.

"You know, this office looks exactly how I pictured it…papers, books, all crowded together like this. I suppose you know just where everything is, too, don't you?"

"How do you know that Miss Reave is a…I think you called her a spoiled, capricious young woman?"

Her smile vanished as she sat down in the chair in front of his desk. "I wondered when you would ask." They sat in silence for a moment, looking at one another.

"Whatever there is to tell me, feel free. It certainly doesn't matter now." He looked down at his hands.

"I suppose it doesn't. Actually I don't know her, but I know her father, though I doubt he remembers me. Did I ever tell you how I got my house?"

"No."

"Well, it was after my husband had died, of course. I loved him dearly, but you know that. He was the most romantic man, sailing off to exotic places and then

241

coming home to tell me about his adventures—worlds I could only dream about, you know? I was so young, William. I had never left England." She paused and turned toward the window. "When the man died he left me with nothing. Not a farthing. And I was from a good family, too, not unlike your darling Miss Reave.

"My parents were gone and all their money went to male relatives I had never met, so asking for assistance was out of the question. Things looked bad for me, very desperate indeed. I eventually found my way to that house on Upper Newman Street that you are so familiar with."

Dr. Whitcraft stared at her, never having dreamed of asking how it had come to pass that she should be endeavoring in her current profession. Now that he knew, it seemed that some intangible veil had been lifted, and for the first time he saw the vulnerable soul inside of this very strong woman. He was positively intrigued.

"I was perhaps the luckiest woman in London, because without realizing it, I fell into the hands of Mrs. Anne Pettish, one of the rare breed of London procuresses. Rare because she was *honest*. She took me in, listened to my woes without judgment, without attempting to make me beholden to her through debt or anything else. She didn't force me to do anything I didn't want to do. I stayed with her in that house until I had a new sense of the next chapter of my life. Certainly nothing I had ever imagined, but not all that bad, either. This really does relate to Miss Reave, I promise.

"Mrs. Pettish had managed her affairs quite well, and had been rather prosperous. Eventually, when she retired and left London, she gave me the house. Just *gave* it to me. It doesn't cost me anything to live there…but that's neither here nor there. One of her most loyal gallants was none other than *Dr. John Reave*."

Dr. Whitcraft's eyes grew large. "Really? What do you know about that?"

"From what I hear, I'm sure your Miss Reave would be amazed to know she took her first steps in our front parlor there, right by the fireplace. Her mother was dead and there was some kind of nonsense with her governess, so he brought her on his visits to Mrs. Pettish."

Dr. Whitcraft shook his head. How he wished he could share this lovely piece of information with The London Society of Manners. Perhaps that collection of self-important hypocrites would toss her out if they knew.

"Toddling around our parlor there is all fine and adorable, but as she grew up she gave that poor man fits. Mrs. Pettish and he spent hours devising ways to handle that girl. William, she has been a coquettish, spoiled brat her entire life. But by far her most grievous transgression has been…how shall I say it—the girl has a penchant for taking things that do not belong to her. Frankly, I'm amazed you never noticed. Poor Dr. Reave has found everything from money, trinkets, cutlery, and God knows what else in their house. He's bribed half of London attempting to keep her antics quiet."

He sank deep into his chair, remembering those instances where small items had turned up missing. A lost fork, earrings from a friend, even Miss Faffle's locket that her father had given her. When that had gone missing, they had ransacked the entire office looking for it. Had Miss Reave made off with it?

"I-I can't imagine. Why wouldn't you tell me something like this?" He felt angry, but he wasn't sure with whom.

"What business is it of mine who you marry? And you were in love with her, of course. Maybe you still are. No one wants to hear something like that about the woman they are in love with. Who knows, maybe she grew up and quit doing it. What do I know anyway?"

He sat in silence for a time, studying the face of Mrs. Minnock, so familiar and so honest. He reached across the desk for her hand. "You know a great many things."

She patted his hand, but looked grim. "I promise you. Do not despair the loss of that silly girl. You deserve much better."

He smiled, but his face settled back into an expression of preoccupied worry. "Well. Given that your expertise knows no bounds, perhaps you can help me with this." He held up a slip of paper that had been sitting in the middle of his desk. She leaned in to read it over.

"Judge Ingler. Hmm." She looked out the window again, still holding the summons ordering Dr. William Whitcraft to appear in criminal court to answer to the charge of the destruction of St. Bartholomew's property.

"This isn't a surprise then, is it?" She picked up his pen, dipped it into the inkpot, and wrote two names on the bottom of the summons.

Mister Edward Jarkman, Solicitor
Mister Arthur Kelter, Barrister

"Go to Mr. Jarkman's office whenever you feel up to it. Tell him you want to hire Mr. Kelter as your barrister. Don't let him pick any other. I believe they're both located near the courthouse. You don't have to tell either of them I sent you, but you may need to pay up front. Mr. Kelter's rather a fanatic on that subject, I'm afraid. He'll do the job for you."

****

"Unbelievable! Just shocking, really! Dr. Whitcraft, I'm absolutely floored after hearing that!" Mr. Kelter leaned against the edge of his desk, waving the summons as he spoke.

"Yes, I can imagine that you must be, hearing about that *awful* man for the first time."

Mr. Kelter got to his feet and began to pace. "*Eighteen* women in a single work day? *A single day!* In addition to other patients as well? And that was before the article was published? My goodness, how much do you charge per maneuver?"

Dr. Whitcraft squinted at this man. "What? My fee isn't the point."

"Of course it's the point; why it's at the very heart of the matter. It all boils down to provocation then, doesn't it? That man deprived you of your ability to make a living, which is why you committed the acts in question."

"That wasn't the only reason."

"So, you're telling me that patients afflicted with hysteria require this treatment *every* day? Oh, the calculations are astonishing! The remunerations, good God, man! Now, you only have one examining room. What if you had several? How many women could you see in a day, then? Scores! Positively scores! Oh, look!

I've got gooseflesh just thinking of the billable hours! Look at my arm! My God, your practice is a treasure trove! No wonder you were going to buy that house!"

Dr. Whitcraft drew breath to speak, but Mr. Kelter sputtered on. "Can the maneuver be taught to assistants? Could you open a clinic? Of course all of that would eat into your profits, but still! Still, without any of that, going the way you were. If I'm lucky, *lucky* mind you, I can see maybe three clients in one day—if any of those damn solicitors send me clients, that is— and then who knows if those dodgers are even going to pay me! Why, most of the time I spend in court is trying to get *those ungrateful bastards* to pay what they owe. And do you know how much *that* costs? I don't want to tell you how much I pay for this building…probably not half of what your current place in Berkeley Square goes for, though! How anyone can anyone afford to do business in this city I'll never know."

"What about Judge Ingler! Am I liable to be sent to jail?"

"Jail? Oh, no. No." He looked down at the summons, and shrugged. "They aren't charging you with assault. It's just a property issue. Given that you are a professional man, no record of trouble, upstanding citizen, you know…not to mention you were substantially provoked by a devious fellow professional. The worst of it will be the reading of the charges in court. That's bound to be embarrassing for you, I'm afraid. If his Majesty's public prosecutor wants to take you to task, it could get ugly. But jail? Certainly not. I'll arrange it with the judge. In all likelihood you'll just have to pay for the damage, maybe a small fine…and let's face it, you've got plenty of money then, haven't you. How many years did you spend at school? I could kick myself for not getting into doctoring, but I never had the stomach for it. Think of it, eighteen billable clients in one day. Solvent ones at that! Good for you, man!"

Dr. Whitcraft stared at this man. What on earth had Mrs. Minnock been thinking when she sent him here?

Chapter Twenty-Two

Dr. Whitcraft escorted the woozy Mr. Larking out of the examining room. The man's incision had finally stopped bleeding, but lavender semi-circles now darkened underneath his eyes, like ink soaking through thick paper.

"That's it, Mr. Larking. Right this way."

Mr. Larking gazed around the office as if unsure which door was the exit. But a slight muddle was normal after such a thorough bloodletting.

"Why don't you have a seat in here while you keep pressure on that arm. Mr. Larking?" Dr. Whitcraft knelt and inched closer to his face. "Mr. Larking, can you hear me, sir?"

After a moment Mr. Larking nodded.

"Capital." Dr. Whitcraft stood back up.

Miss Faffle appeared outside on the steps and threw open the front door. She rushed past the nearly translucent Mr. Larking and stopped in front of the doctor. "I hope this is what you wanted, sir," she exclaimed, gulping a breath of air. Her thin fingers produced a crumpled piece of paper from the pocket of her dress. "They told me it took the entire week to go through all the records, but I think this is what Mrs. Minnock asked for. No men…no children."

"Yes. Only the women, if you please, Miss Faffle." He walked them both back to her desk.

"Well, there was a Mrs. Shardborn," she read. "She expired due to advanced tuberculosis, in hospital last month."

"Tuberculosis, hmmm. All right. What else?"

"Then there was a Miss Drizzen. She died in hospital also, of unknown causes."

"All right. Miss Drizzen. Anyone else?"

"Oh, and then there was Mrs. Fussock," she said, her forehead wrinkling as she bit her lip.

"Mrs. Fussock? Is that *our* Mrs. Fussock?" He snatched the paper out of her hands and studied it, appalled.

"Yes, I believe so. What a shame! Her husband was quite wealthy if I recall. He always paid two weeks in advance."

His eyes narrowed. "That rogue stole her from me!"

"I can't believe she's dead," she muttered.

"She was one of the first women I performed the maneuver on." He put his hand to his temple, remembering how her symptoms had almost completely abated after the treatments, giving him so much hope and excitement. "How on earth did she die? It doesn't say here. She was older, but not ill if I recall."

"Hit by a carriage in the street, straight after leaving Dr. Marplot's office. That's what the woman in the hospital told me."

"What?" Dr. Whitcraft sank in her chair, his heart skipping a beat. "Are you telling me that he gave that woman the maneuver and the moment she left, she was struck by a carriage and *killed*?"

"Yes. Isn't that terrible?"

"Oh yes…terrible." A small grin tickled his mouth.

****

"I've got it!" Dr. Whitcraft proclaimed with a flourish as Mrs. Minnock opened her front door. Without giving her a chance to speak, he clasped her arms and kissed her on the lips.

"My goodness." Stepping back, she laughed, "A kiss in the doorway? Anyone could have seen such a display, doctor. You are a changed man."

He grabbed her wrist and led her through the entryway into the parlor. When they were both settled comfortably on the couch, and after a quick glance around for potential eavesdroppers, Dr. Whitcraft leaned in and whispered, "Mrs. Edna Fussock. That's the name. I've got two others, but I think that one's the ticket. Mrs. Fussock, a former patient of mine, mind you, left his office after getting the maneuver, and was flattened by a carriage straight away. So if you could get that Boodler fellow to conclude that the maneuver was simply too powerful for the likes of weary old Mrs. Fussock, leaving her disoriented and vulnerable to misadventure, well, that would be just, just…I mean the poor woman should have been supervised! Foreseeable carnage, I'm afraid, clearly due to his negligence as a physician. Good Lord, it might even be true! Wouldn't that be a lucky break?" He clasped his hands in delight.

"Not for Mrs. Fussock, I'm afraid." She raised a brow.

His smile diminished appropriately. "Yes. Yes of course, poor woman."

"Now that we have a name, things should get rolling rather quickly, I believe." Her blue eyes glowed with confidence. "All you have to do now, William, is sit back and watch." She smiled and patted his knee.

Dr. Whitcraft was overcome. He grabbed her up in his arms while fixing the most passionate of kisses on her lovely lips.

"Doctor!" A familiar voice sounded from within the corridor. "How wonderful to see you!"

Dr. Whitcraft looked up, and was at once seized with panic. Mrs. Pannade had just emerged from one of the back rooms and was smiling grandly at him.

He jumped to his feet, not certain if he should tackle his ex-patient or run in the opposite direction. Instead, he elected to hold his ground and shout orders like a general on a field of battle. "Quick! Send one of the girls for the police, straightaway! Mrs. Minnock, block the door. Good Lord Mrs. Pannade, is there any sanctuary of mine that you will not breach? Stay back, woman! Do you hear?"

Mrs. Minnock had gotten up now too, but instead of blocking the door, she crossed the room and gently took Mrs. Pannade by the hand. "It's all right, William. Catch your breath and sit down, if you please. Mrs. Pannade and I have become acquainted. For the time being she is a *guest* in this house."

Mrs. Pannade nodded. Though clearly distressed by the doctor's words, she still managed a grateful glance at Mrs. Minnock. "Oh yes, she has been amazingly hospitable to me."

Dr. Whitcraft couldn't sit; he couldn't even speak. The collision of his disparate worlds was simply too much to digest, so he stood dumbfounded, mouth agape as he looked from woman to woman.

Mrs. Minnock sensed his distress and went to his side, picked up his hand, and led him back toward the couch. "It's quite a story then, isn't it? May I enlighten the doctor, Mrs. Pannade?"

"Oh, yes, by all means."

"Well, it seems that after you left us last week, Dr. Whitcraft, one of the girls discovered Mrs. Pannade lurking in the hedge beneath my window. We don't usually have much doings with the police, so I went out and spoke to her myself. Seeing her dreadfully agitated state, I couldn't let her wander back home in the darkness, so I asked her in, to maybe chat with her and get to the bottom of why she has been following you about. We talked for hours, didn't we? Like old girlfriends who had known each other for years, we talked about everything; we laughed and laughed. I finally told her the truth about her husband, which has proven to be most liberating, don't you think?"

"Oh yes," Mrs. Pannade agreed, now tucked into an armchair with her legs kicked up on an ottoman. "I thought it was *me*! Imagine all that time when I thought there was something wrong with me."

"Oh, there's nothing wrong with you." Mrs. Minnock turned to the doctor. "Frankly, Dr. Whitcraft, I don't think she ever had hysteria. I think she just needed to get away from that ridiculous man. Look at her! She's positively glowing."

Amazement still stamped on his face, Dr. Whitcraft was indeed surprised to see that Mrs. Pannade bore little resemblance to the deeply troubled woman he had met in her parlor all those months ago. Her skin radiated color, her eyes were bright. She wore a fashionable, yet understated gown. She even looked attractive!

"After we straightened out that business, I had a long talk with her about how she must quit following you around. I told her that she was doing herself no favors, and making you absolutely mad in the process."

"I'm sorry about that, Dr. Whitcraft." Mrs. Pannade cast her eyes into her lap. "I don't know what got into me. You're a dear man, but I'm not in love with you. I guess I've never known what being in love actually meant. I am especially sorry about accosting you in the street like that and destroying your trousers."

"You what?" Mrs. Minnock turned to her friend, shocked. "What did you do to his trousers?"

She gave a shy shrug. "I certainly didn't mean to rip them so badly."

An astonished smile spread across her face, and Mrs. Minnock spun back round to the doctor. "You never told me about that!"

"Yes," he sighed. "After that unpleasantness here with Dr. Forspent on my way home. I thought I was being robbed, you know. You should have seen...I nearly got arrested."

Mrs. Minnock threw her head back and laughed, then rested her cheek on the doctor's shoulder while she regained her composure. "What Mrs. Pannade needs, more than following you around, more than hysteria treatments—is a fresh start. Rattling around in that old house of hers with that absurd man was doing her no good, so she agreed to stay here with us. She's been a perfectly lovely houseguest."

"How long have you been staying here?" he asked, not knowing what to make of this peculiar arrangement.

"It will be a week tomorrow. I find all the girls to be so cheerful, not to mention that some of the most interesting men I have ever met come through those doors. What fun it all is!"

"You're not bothered by…the ladies…their romantic—"

"Actually, I find it all rather intriguing." She sat on the edge of her chair and furrowed her brow. "Not at all what I imagined one of these places to be like."

"Hmm." The doctor was at a loss. "Does your husband know where you are?"

"I heard he's gone to Amsterdam, and frankly I don't care what he knows."

He looked at the two women, both so pleased and at home. There was really nothing else to say about the matter. He should be relieved that this peculiar episode with Mrs. Pannade appeared to have been resolved, but oddly he felt a trifle sad. As he watched her chat with Mrs. Minnock, it was indeed a little bittersweet to have lost such an enthusiastic devotee.

He sighed and glanced down at his lap. Then he said, "You know, Mrs. Pannade…you were right—about Miss Reave, that is."

The two ladies looked at Dr. Whitcraft sadly, and for a time everyone was quiet.

"William, Mrs. Pannade has had some very inspired ideas about the handling of Dr. Marplot," Mrs. Minnock said.

"I see." He stirred in his seat at the mention of that malevolent sham-artist.

"She's already gotten the wheels in motion to have him thrown out of The London Society of Physicians, writing the most inspiring letter vouching that he *caused* her hysteria with the maneuver. And didn't you say you wrote to *The Lancet*, as well?"

"Oh yes!" Mrs. Pannade's eyes danced at the remembrance. "I penned the most *detailed* accusation. I told them I was lured to their offices on the pretense of his interviewing me about my hysteria, but instead, he cornered me behind a locked door, trapping me helpless and alone, plying me with his flowery assurances, and a modicum of gin, before proceeding to…" The thrill of this revelation became too much. Mrs. Pannade's face reddened. She jumped up from her chair and slid herself onto the couch next to Mrs. Minnock. She cupped her hand around her mouth and proceeded to whisper the remaining details of the fabricated episode in to Mrs. Minnock's ear.

As she listened to her friend, Mrs. Minnock nodded with intense concentration. A half-smile crossed her lips and she laughed, but as the lengthy explanation continued, her face went blank. Then her jaw dropped open, and she gasped, pulling away from her friend. "Good gracious, Mrs. Pannade! Did you really write those things?"

"Why yes!" She threw her head back. "Yes, I did!"

Mrs. Minnock's eyes betrayed a combination of alarm and amusement. "I would guess that your rival's days at *The Lancet* are numbered, Dr. Whitcraft."

"How sweet!" He sat up in his chair, unable to conceal his delight. "That was very thoughtful of you, Mrs. Pannade. You didn't have to do that."

"Oh, well, it is the least I could do after all of the trouble I've caused," Mrs. Pannade said, blushing demurely.

Dr. Whitcraft's smile melted. "You know…I happen to know that the dastardly fiend has been up to some nonsense at The Barts. I'm not in the position to report it myself, but I know he's been doing surgery— *unlicensed surgery*—stepping in for some fellow called

Mr. Looby and showing off to anyone who would watch. If that information fell into the hands of the hospital administration…"

"Oh! I'll write them tomorrow and tell them! How wonderful!" Mrs. Pannade clapped her hands.

He envisioned his nemesis' face when the administration demanded to know why he had been using unsuspecting patients as props in his own audacious medical show. The sweet simmer of revenge tickled his fancy enough to make him giggle at the thought. "Yes, Mrs. Pannade, I'll jot down a few notes for you, so the facts will be correct."

"That's something to look forward to, then, isn't it? Who wants a drink?" Mrs. Minnock asked with a smile.

"Oh I do!" Mrs. Pannade stood and walked toward the decanter. "Doctor, let me get you a brandy and water."

****

The luncheon recess was almost at an end. Dr. Whitcraft stopped his tapping foot as he sat in the back of the courtroom amongst the spectators. Officers milled about and the barristers in their white wigs looked bored as they chatted with one another, waiting for the action to resume.

He spotted Mr. Kelter when he arrived, but the man had since disappeared and was presumably in negotiations with the judge. Dr. Whitcraft squeezed his knees together and took a breath. The humiliation of having his offenses enumerated out loud in front of all of these people would be almost too much to bear, but Mr. Kelter had assured him that he would do his very best and attempt to spare him that horror.

He wondered which spectators were defendants,

because he seemed to be the only one here who looked at all distressed. Most sat calmly, daydreaming or whispering to one another. One woman was even doing needlework. Mr. Kelter had told him that some people actually paid to sit in these seats so they could watch the drama of the English justice system unfold in front of their own eyes.

Ah, and there he was now, hastily advancing toward him from a large wooden door in the back of the courtroom. Hope piqued in Dr. Whitcraft's heart; the man appeared to be very pleased. "Good news there, doctor." He sat down. "Your case has been removed from the docket. You won't have to appear in open court at all."

"Really? That's brilliant! How in the world did you manage that?"

"I must say that Judge Ingler was very receptive to putting the whole thing aside. Very receptive, indeed."

"Thank heavens for that!"

"You'll have to pay eighty pounds or so to The Barts, which is perhaps a little more than we'd expected. It seems an artificial leg was damaged in the row, and the amputee, a Mr. George Twitchel, I believe, is unhappy with the way it handles and is demanding a new one. Still, the judge is being rather sympathetic and has agreed to waive your fine, so that makes up for it, I suppose."

"Yes, of course! Well done! This is so much better than I'd hoped!" He inhaled a large and satisfying breath as he slumped in his chair, feeling suddenly better than he had in days.

"There is one thing, though. He agreed to spare you the courtroom appearance, but he would like to have a word with you in his chambers."

Dr. Whitcraft frowned. "A word with me? About what?"

Mr. Kelter shrugged. "He wouldn't say."

"You'll be in there with me, of course."

"No. He was adamant about that. He wants to see you alone. One of the officers will come to get you when he is ready. Once that's over, you'll be free to go. I'll wait out here with you, if you like." He patted Dr. Whitcraft on the knee and drew in a large breath as he glanced around the courtroom. And then his eyes narrowed malevolently.

"Oh, why if it isn't Mr. Lorel. Look at how he struts over there. I need to have a word with that swindler. Just a moment, please."

When Mr. Kelter stormed toward him, Mr. Lorel's face dropped. It fell further when the barrister administered a rather animated rebuke.

Dr. Whitcraft sighed and looked at the floor. What the devil was he supposed to say to the judge, he wondered uneasily. Perhaps he would apologize for his profoundly unprofessional behavior. That must be what the judge wanted, to force him to be contrite in person.

"Excuse me, I didn't mean to eavesdrop on your conversation, but are you Dr. William Whitcraft?"

He turned and saw a young gentleman, rather pasty in appearance, looking keenly at him.

"Yes."

The man rolled his eyes, and cursed under his breath. "They've taken you off the docket. There goes my story. Now I have nothing!"

Dr. Whitcraft's mouth went dry. "You are you a journalist, sir?"

"Yes, yes. My name is Colin Understrapper. I'm with The Gazette. Someone gave me a tip that you would be humiliated in open court today—a doctor on trial for attacking an illustrious rival. It would have been a rather sensational story, but now…"

Dr. Whitcraft's head began to throb. "I don't suppose you would care to tell me who gave you this tip then, would you?"

The gentleman squinted. "I never reveal my sources, especially when they are such important members of the—" The man stopped, perhaps realizing he had said too much.

Dr. Whitcraft felt dizzy. That malignant snake was still at it. Would that disgusting man ever quit tormenting him? If Mr. Kelter hadn't saved him, there would have been an article in The Gazette detailing his courtroom chastisement for all of London to savor. How horrific!

He spun around, his passions inflamed once again. He crossed his arms and muttered under his breath. How ill-timed his apology to the judge would be now that he wanted to go after that swine for round two. Then an idea occurred to him. He turned back as the journalist got up to leave.

"So, Mr. Understrapper was it? You never reveal your sources, is that correct?"

"No, of course not."

"Well, then. I believe *I* may have a story for you." Dr. Whitcraft's lips curled into a smile at having said the words out loud. "It involves a most despicable act of medical negligence committed by a prominent doctor. His misdeeds have not escaped the notice of the coroner, I believe. It should be quite an interesting case."

"Oh, someone died?" Mr. Understrapper's face lit up and he dropped back down, pulling his chair closer.

"Most certainly. If I get you the details, would they be at all useful?"

"Oh yes! When can you get them to me?"

"Oh, it won't be me, but I'd look for something in the next few weeks."

"William Whitcraft?" A dull-looking hulk of a man in an officer's uniform approached the pair.

"Yes, sir." He got to his feet, but turned to Mr. Understrapper. "Keep an eye out for them. I'll look forward to reading your article."

"Thank you, doctor!"

****

Dr. Whitcraft forgot all about his fortuitous meeting with Mr. Understrapper as he sat in front of the judge's heavy oaken desk and smoothed out his trousers. The judge faced a wall of treatises—his cascading black robes and his wiry white wig made him seem inhuman as he plucked a volume from the shelf. He turned around, and without the slightest acknowledgment of his visitor, sat and solemnly cracked open the stiff leather binding. He wrinkled his nose, licked the tip of his index finger and began flipping through page after page.

Dr. Whitcraft squirmed. The anticipation was terrible. He couldn't help wonder if this silence was some kind of a test. Perhaps the man wanted *him* to speak up…perhaps he should just blurt out a profession of regret. Perhaps not. He had almost convinced himself to say something when the judge looked up and sighed. "Doctor William Whitcraft, is that correct?"

"Yes, sir." He sat up at attention. "Sir, may I begin by apologizing to his Majesty's court?"

"Oh, never mind that nonsense." The judge waved his hand. "I need to ask you a favor, Dr. Whitcraft."

"Oh…well, of course." He searched the man's face. "Are you ill, sir?"

"I suppose I am, in a sense. How perceptive of you, doctor." The judge's eyes looked tired. He hesitated for a moment before he went on. "I understand you're quite close with a *Mrs. Minnock*."

Dr. Whitcraft sat stunned, not having the vaguest notion of the appropriate answer to this question.

The judge continued blandly, as if discussing the weather. "Yes, well, I know you are. I am also an acquaintance of hers. Er, not so much of hers, but rather, one of her *apprentices*, if you understand."

Dr. Whitcraft nodded with his mouth agape, and finally managed to echo, "One of her apprentices."

"You must tell Mrs. Minnock that I've kept my end of the bargain. Please! The moment you leave this building." His eyes grew glassy and his hands trembled. "She *must* convince Missy to see me again! Missy! Do you know her? The lovely, young, auburn-haired Scottish lass."

He shook his head, too startled to imagine the faces of Mrs. Minnock's girls.

"Oh, she's a flower! A fawn in the springtime of her life. The very picture of youth and vigor…exquisite fair skin and the most dainty touch." The judge spoke dreamily, as if he had forgotten that someone was listening.

Dr. Whitcraft trembled now too. "Sir, I'm not sure what you want of me."

"To say that I'm fond of the girl would be a substantial understatement. Look. Have a look at this." With shaky fingers, the judge opened his drawer, pulled out a charcoal sketch, and handed it to Dr. Whitcraft.

Oh God, he realized it was *Missy,* sitting on the swing that hung from the linden in the back courtyard. Her head tossed back and her long hair undone and blowing behind her, kicking her legs in the air, naked as the day she was born. He nodded at the drawing with wide eyes. "That's, uh…that's quite something, sir."

"Watercolor is more of my forte, but regardless..." He took the drawing back and gazed at it. "The reason I am telling you this is because as of late, all my overtures to the girl have gone unrequited. She will not see me. I've begged Mrs. Minnock to speak to Missy on my behalf, but she says she doesn't get involved in these matters, which I thoroughly understand. But I pled with the woman to make an exception. Finally, finally she assured me that if *you* didn't have to appear in open court, and if I made the disposition of your case as easy on you as possible that she would put in a word." He set the drawing down. "For God's sake man, for all I know, *Mrs. Minnock* told Missy to stop seeing me until your case was disposed. Perhaps this is all a ploy on your behalf to get at me, and frankly it has worked! So I'm telling you now, doctor, make damn sure Mrs. Minnock keeps her end of the bargain! Do you understand? I am a desperate man!"

****

"Ah, and there he is now!" Constable Fettle proclaimed.

Dr. Whitcraft closed his front door, still reeling from the knowledge that the most traumatic chapter in his life thus far was by all appearances at an end. And what a strange ending it was. He blinked at the three apprehensive faces staring at him.

Constable Fettle sat on the edge of Miss Faffle's desk, his stubby legs dangling above the floor, his brows arched over rounded eyes. Miss Faffle, in a reception room chair, leaned forward and clasped her hands together under her chin.

There sat Mrs. Minnock, behind Miss Faffle's desk looking like she worked there. She leaned back with her arms relaxed and draped across her lap. A serene smile rested on her lips.

When he moved forward, all the players got to their feet, probably in anticipation of hearing the details of a humiliating courtroom ordeal. But the doctor remained silent as he walked past his assistant and her beau. He crossed behind the desk and embraced the knowing Mrs. Minnock.

He held her, a growing ache in his throat as he pulled her head under his chin and scooped her fair hair through his hands. He squeezed the soft ringlets between his fingers, fighting the tears blurring his eyes. "Thank you, thank you," he whispered, hugging her tighter each time he repeated the words.

Miss Faffle and Constable Fettle exchanged puzzled looks, not quite certain what to make of this extraordinary display of affection, so uncommon for Dr. William Whitcraft.

Chapter Twenty-Three

Miss Faffle had been on her hands and knees most of the morning, scrubbing away at the dotted blood trail winding its way around the office, like the flight pattern of a bumblebee.

The morning's first customer had been a construction worker, who'd arrived cupping his bleeding hand as he made his way to the reception desk and back to a chair, then to the desk again before entering the examining room, touring around a bit and finally depositing himself on the table for inspection.

Dr. Whitcraft had been delighted to pry an amazingly long wrought-iron nail out of the man's palm.

Now it was quiet again, and the doctor sat in his office with the door open, listening to the wet scuffing of Miss Faffle's labors.

"The floor is in bad shape, Dr. Whitcraft. Constable Fettle thinks the whole lot should be replaced, but I suppose that'd be rather expensive."

"I am sure it would be, Miss Faffle." He flipped a page of *The Lancet*.

"He also said he can fix those worn spots, if you like, by replacing some of the planks when he is off duty."

"Your Constable Fettle fixes floors?"

"Oh, yes. He always wanted to be a carpenter, you

know, but his father made him go into police work. He was a terrible bully. Look at how the wood is splintering under the examining table here." She picked up a rather large chunk of the floor and showed it to him. "It's worse behind my desk, where the hat stand pierced it. Well, you remember that. Isn't there a spot in your office, too?"

"I suppose." He glanced over his shoulder at the ugly hole under the stairway, certain that one day a neighborhood cat would use it as an entrance from beneath the building. He stood for a closer examination. It was a disgrace for a doctor's office to have such a pitiful looking floor. He knelt, wiggling his fingers into the cracks between the boards, wondering how many planks Constable Fettle would have to replace, but startled suddenly when a whole board lifted up in his hands, like the top of a jewelry box. He blinked, breathless as he stared into its dark compartment. It was filled to the brim.

He dropped to the floor and sat there for a long time, pondering it all while remembering the prophetic words of Mrs. Minnock. Was that woman *always* right?

After he regained himself, he called, "Miss Faffle, do we have a bag of some type?"

"What kind of bag do you need, sir?"

"A big one. And I believe I may have found your locket."

****

Constable Fettle was tucked behind Miss Faffle's desk on his hands and knees, hammering—again and again and again, rattling the office walls with every stroke. Dr. Whitcraft tried not to look up from his desk, certain his trembling shelves would snap off on the very

265

next beat and send his collection tumbling to the floor.

"How much longer?" he shouted out his open door.

The hammering stopped, and after a moment Constable Fettle appeared in his doorway looking like a happy-go-lucky day-laborer rather than an enforcer of the law. He sputtered something unintelligible, smiling past the nails clenched in his teeth.

"Pardon me?" Dr. Whitcraft asked.

He spit the nails into his hand. "Should be done in a jiffy. A few more whacks should do it, then I'll get started in the examining room. If I still have time today, I'll prepare the area there under your stairs."

"I can't thank you enough, sir," Dr. Whitcraft replied. He had thanked him yesterday when he agreed to repair his floor, and then a half-dozen more times already today. He knew lavishing him with praise was unnecessary, however, because the officer would have done just about anything if it meant he could spend the day chatting up Miss Faffle.

He commenced reading, wincing as the hammering began again. After five or so minutes, peace settled over the office and a shadow crossed his desk from the doorway.

"Miss Faffle, would you mind terribly getting me a glass of water?"

"May I come in for a moment, William?"

He looked up, startled. Miss Reave stood in his doorway. She looked like a specter, the sunlight streaming in from behind, illuminating her pale yellow dress with a glowing golden outline. He stood up to greet her, his body numb. She inched forward, her skirt brushing the floor as she moved. She hesitated before finally allowing herself to sit.

"I wanted to stop by," she began, "I haven't seen you, and I wanted to say how awfully sorry I am, that this has all turned out so badly."

He stared at her, dumbfounded. *This has all turned out so badly?* He gritted his teeth, turned and walked to the cabinet. He knelt and reached into the bottom cubbyhole, while Miss Reave continued speaking absentmindedly.

"You know, I believe you and I were mismatched from the start. Different priorities, different expectations for our lives." She paused, perhaps waiting for him to speak. After a moment, she continued uneasily. "Things aren't going that well for *him*, either. Several inquests have been opened on some of his former patients. One in particular is very troubling. They are making accusations about the safety of the maneuver. He's had to hire legal representation and is quite upset."

He returned to his desk, stiffly holding a Hessian bag. When he dropped it, it jingled and clattered. Miss Reave ignored the gesture and waited for him to respond. Finally, he spoke through clenched teeth. "He's *upset*, then, is he?"

"Wouldn't you be?" She blinked at him, the perfect picture of innocence. "If word gets out about the inquests, or that the maneuver is dangerous…it would be a disaster. That is part of the reason I came here today. To apologize, of course, but also to warn you. I wouldn't be a bit surprised if they begin calling on you next."

"Why would they call on *me*? It's the *Marplot* Maneuver, after all."

She tilted her head and a small smile spread across

her lips; the familiar coquettish expression was back into play. "Oh, now William. You certainly performed your share of them, didn't you? Edward explained to me how it was really his work with anatomy that led to the discovery of the maneuver. You only cobbled the pieces of *his* research together and—"

"Is that what he told you?"

She raised her eyebrows and set her jaw. "He told me the *truth*."

"Well, now...I see, I see." His respiration quickened. "Was it *the truth* that made you come into my office and *steal* every last reference of the maneuver from my cabinet?"

"I didn't steal anything!" she cried. "I merely collected the information he needed for the article."

"The one that didn't have my name on it?" he shouted, leaning forward.

"Oh, William." She forced a brittle laugh as she shook her head. "You have always been so jealous of him. You know *you* were the one who tried to use *his* work for yourself."

"That is a lie!" he shouted again. "The man is a soulless, maniacal..." Grasping for additional epithets, he stopped himself. Her dark eyes, the depths of which had so often bubbled over with girlish excitement when he had squeezed her hand or stolen a kiss from her cheek, were now shallow and cold, staring at him with utter contempt. An ache rose in his chest, and he strained a laugh, or was he choking back a sob when he shook his head and muttered, "I can't understand it. How in the world did he convince you to believe him and not *me*?"

Her forehead wrinkled and she looked away. She

turned back, eyes colder than before. "You know..." She tipped her head lower. "He told me you'd say that—that you'd accuse *him* of being the treacherous one. He even said that if you claimed it was *your* maneuver, then I should ask you how you came up with it. So I'm asking you, William. If it wasn't his research that inspired you, then how did you discover the maneuver?"

Several moments passed while he turned this question over in his hands like a puzzle. Dr. Marplot knew he wouldn't dare, couldn't possibly ever answer that question honestly, especially if it had been asked by Miss Reave. The editor of *The Lancet's* chess column had just put him into checkmate.

"Why the devil are you asking me that *now*?" he whispered.

Her lips contorted into a self-satisfied smirk. "He *said* you would never tell me...and it's painfully obvious now why. Because you stole it from him, William."

Anger flashed inside of Dr. Whitcraft that was so white hot, so profound, he wanted to lean in and shout directly into her face, *I didn't learn it from your precious new love, my darling sweet. I learned it from Mrs. Elizabeth Minnock, London's most famous procuress, the woman who I have been seeing for years who is superior to you in every way one woman can be superior to another. That's who I learned it from!* Those words would have flown out of his mouth if he didn't check himself and bite his lips shut.

"Regardless of who came up with the silly thing," Miss Reave continued impatiently, "I think you, better than anyone else, know that the profession needs the maneuver, and that it must be defended no matter who performs it. I am certain if you told those inquest people of its value, and that it is perfectly safe and could never harm anyone, all this unpleasantness might just go away."

Dr. Whitcraft put both hands on the bag, pulled the string tightly over its opening, and spilled its contents on to his desk.

Miss Reave's smile vanished into a thin-lipped look of horror. Spoons, hair clips, silver baubles, inkpots, any variety of pilfered trinkets were all on exhibit in front of her, like a table at a gypsy bazaar. He watched her face, making sure his own was expressionless.

"Would you care to claim any of your souvenirs, my dear? Better do it soon, because there is an officer of the law in the next room. Or better yet, perhaps I should save all this for your father."

She jumped to her feet. "I don't know what you are implying with this display."

"Maybe the floor boards in *his* office are loose, too. So why don't you take them, take them. I gave Miss Faffle back her locket, in case you miss it, but the rest are yours. Have at them."

She stood in front of him, mouth agape before slowly bringing her lips back together. For the first time, her eyes looked desperate. She whispered, "Please don't tell Papa."

"If you ever, ever come back here again and speak to me on behalf of that devil, I will expose all this nonsense to your father. I may even tell him about your inappropriate dalliances with that charlatan...and *me* for that matter!"

"You and I never had any inappropriate dalliances!"

"He doesn't know that, does he?" Her eyes grew wider still. "You think he was tough on your governess? Why don't you wait and see what happens after I've finished talking to him!" In his heart, he knew he couldn't possibly tell such appalling untruths to her father. Never in a million years. But it felt so wonderful to see the look of sheer terror on her face.

"What do you want me to do?" she muttered, eyes dancing over the collection of items on his desk.

"I want you to get out, my dear." He shoveled the clutter back into the bag. "And take all this nonsense with you."

****

Mrs. Minnock was nearly trampled by Miss Reave fleeing out the front door holding a large brown bag in her arms.

"Oh my! Was that..." she started to ask Miss Faffle, but it was Dr. Whitcraft who stepped out of his office.

"Yes, it was. It was."

"I can see it has been an exciting morning. Hello, Miss Faffle." Seeing Constable Fettle on his hands and knees in the examining room, Mrs. Minnock called, "Oh, and hello there, Constable Fettle." He glanced up from his sanding and waved. She turned back to the doctor and placed her hand on his wrist. "Are you all right, William?"

He grasped his temple. "Frankly, I'm not certain."

"I believe this should do wonders for you. Have a look." She handed him a large bundle of documents. He was not particularly in the mood for reading any more, but glancing down at the lacy script, several words jumped right off the page.

Subject of Inquest: Dr. Edward Marplot.

"How wonderful! How did you get these?"

She smiled, but said nothing.

"These are official?"

"Of course…I thought you might want to see."

He giggled. "Oh Miss Faffle! Miss Faffle, I need you to do an errand for me."

Miss Faffle scurried around her desk past a woman slumped in the corner chair, surrounded by a semi-circle of crumpled shopping bags.

"Good Lord," Dr. Whitcraft whispered, noticing the woman for the first time. "Mrs. Anile? Mrs. Anile. She's left, you know."

But Mrs. Anile did not respond or even stir when Miss Faffle had flashed past.

He sighed as he turned to Miss Faffle. "I'll need you to bring these documents to a Mr. Understrapper, down at The Gazette. He should be expecting them…and oh, wait a moment, I have another letter for him, too, on a different matter."

He disappeared into his office and then came out again, carrying an envelope. "Please take this to him as well." He grinned at both ladies as he walked toward Mrs. Anile. "I believe it's going to be a lovely day after all!"

Miss Faffle was about to put her hand on the front doorknob when Dr. Whitcraft's dispirited voice stopped her. "Oh…oh good Lord. Miss Faffle, wait a minute."

He pulled his hand back from Mrs. Anile's neck and glanced distastefully at Mrs. Minnock. He breathed a long and most profoundly defeated sigh.

"Miss Faffle, can you make another stop…before The Gazette? We'll need someone here from the coroner's office, then."

Chapter Twenty-Four

Dr. Whitcraft picked up the oil lamp and was about to ascend his staircase for the evening when he heard an urgent knock on his front door. Irritated, he put down the lamp and walked into the reception area. The unkempt form of Mr. Gamon stood atop his stoop, swaying and pounding on the door with an open hand.

"What do you want?" he shouted at the slovenly greengrocer.

Mr. Gamon furrowed his considerable brow and pantomimed for the doctor to open the door. He sighed, imagining this man likely wanted to discuss the rather pointed letter he had sent to Mr. Understrapper some weeks ago regarding the unclean condition of his grocery.

The journalist had done a splendid job at taking the details of his letter and running with them publishing a most shocking three-part series detailing the numerous violations of public trust perpetrated on his hapless customers.

But it appeared Dr. Whitcraft was about to pay the price for his civic-mindedness. Dread filled his heart as he approached the door. Mr. Gamon was even more disheveled than usual. He was hatless and his thick brown hair was matted and mussed, and his apron was a filthy palette of produce smears. And, he was making greasy handprints all over the glass. I'll have to remember to have Miss Faffle clean those off in the morning, he thought while fumbling with the lock. He cracked opened the door and at once smelled a combination of fermented fruit and alcohol.

"Sir, I have no business with you." The doctor went to shut the door. But Mr. Gamon was nimble and put fingers in the crack, prying it open just enough to slide in his foot.

"Oh, is that right? I should flatten you right here, you stodgy son-of-a-bitch! You made it your damn business. You're like an old woman, writing letters of complaint to the newspaper. Why'd you do it? I'm out of business until I make the repairs and clean up my place."

Dr. Whitcraft pursed his lips. "I should expect so. As a servant of the public health, I believe I have done each and every one of your unfortunate patrons a service in seeing that you clean that disgrace up."

"The only reason you did it is because of that whore who works here. She's the reason your patients left you, you know."

"Sir, remove your foot at once! I'll not stand here and listen to the drunken ravings of a filthy beast such as yourself!"

At that, Mr. Gamon's brutish face distorted with fury and he threw himself through the front door, growling as if to confirm the doctor's diagnosis. Dr. Whitcraft stepped back, nearly tripping over his own feet while gauging the situation. He had the distinct feeling that he was about to be thrashed, and right in his own reception area.

"I'll squash you like a bug, you effeminate prig," Mr. Gamon proclaimed, staggering toward the doctor with his fists waving. "How are you going to mend yourself when I break your knees, then…eh?"

Mr. Gamon grabbed the hat stand by its base with both hands and heaved it off of the ground.

The doctor dove behind Miss Faffle's desk and peeked out as Mr. Gamon managed a few heavy steps forward. He wore a most repulsive and triumphant grin.

Then, in a singular act of dexterity and skill, Mr. Gamon fixed his stance with trembling knees and tipped the hat stand on its side, grabbing it with evenly spaced hands like a weightlifter. He elevated it high above his head.

Dr. Whitcraft gasped in awe at this herculean feat, and for a fleeting moment wondered why he hadn't thought to hold it like that when he had needed a weapon some months ago.

Just then, the door of the examining room swung wide, revealing Miss Faffle standing frozen in her nightclothes. The sight of the hat stand-wielding debaucher towering above the cowering doctor was too much for her to bear. She let loose a shriek so shrill, so painfully unpleasant, that Mr. Gamon winced, hunching his shoulders to stop the offending frequency from piercing his eardrums.

Whether it was the shriek, the change in posture, or his general drunken clumsiness, it was at that moment Mr. Gamon lost control of the hat stand. He juggled it for a split second, dancing underneath its weight before it slipped through his hands and drove him to the floor like a hammer to a nail.

Dr. Whitcraft rose from beneath Miss Faffle's desk, arching over to see the crumpled Mr. Gamon. He lay motionless and bleeding, his limp arm draped over the hat stand. He looked like a wounded soldier at right shoulder-arms.

Miss Faffle looked ashen. She stared down at Mr. Gamon with her hands covering her mouth. She and Dr. Whitcraft stood there for quite some time, each lost in their own thoughts as both contemplated the dealings that had led up to this eventuality.

Finally, Miss Faffle spoke up, in an uncharacteristically low and serious tone. "He's bleeding a lot, doctor."

"Yes. He is, isn't he?"

"His nose..."

"I would gather that it's broken."

Then Miss Faffle began to cry. "Oh, I'm so sorry! This is all my fault."

"No, no...now don't start that." He held up a hand, trying to gather his thoughts. "We need to get the police here. Eventually he's going to wake up."

"Constable Fettle! He's on duty tonight, patrolling by Piccadilly Circus. I can run and get him! Oh he's very keen to arrest him, Dr. Whitcraft."

"You will do no such thing! I can't allow you to go wandering in the streets, a vulnerable young woman at this time of night."

"But one of us needs to stay here with him. If I stay and he wakes up there's no telling what he might try to do."

The doctor stared at the man on the floor. He could envision any number of things. "Yes...all right. I see your point," he reluctantly agreed. "You know where Constable Fettle will be?"

"Oh yes. I know I can find him. You need to stay here to treat him anyway, I think he is in trouble there, his nose is—"

"Yes, yes. It looks terrible, doesn't it?"

****

Dr. Whitcraft rolled the hat stand off Mr. Gamon. He judged that the majority of the man's bleeding had finally stopped, though his nose was unquestionably broken. It seemed to have spread across the middle of his face like a fanned-out deck of cards, but there was really nothing to be done about that. There were certainly no prizes for beauty in his future. The doctor stood back up and wiped his hands with a handkerchief. Constable Fettle should be arriving soon, and he would just wait and let the man lay there sprawled on his floor.

He grunted as he righted the hat stand, pausing for a moment to inspect its prongs for blood, when out of the corner of his eye he was startled by a figure ascending his steps. It wasn't Miss Faffle or Constable Fettle. It was, in fact, the unmistakable visage of his tormentor—tall and patrician. Dr. Edward Marplot stood at his front door.

He had wondered for weeks how he would react to the inevitable encounter with this man, always imagining it occurring at a random social occasion or perhaps in the chaos of the city streets. But he had surely never expected him to come calling at his own home.

Seeing him through the glass was enough to make Dr. Whitcraft's pulse triple. But a second look revealed something new. He appeared changed somehow. The calm, paragon of arrogance looked haggard, his face lined with worry and exhaustion. Dr. Whitcraft's heart sang at the transformation, but he didn't dare betray his feelings. Instead, he acknowledged his visitor with a rigid nod.

Dr. Marplot opened the door and stepped in, glancing at the body on the floor. "A patient?"

"He is now, yes," Dr. Whitcraft replied, trying to mask the myriad of emotions racing through his heart while he walked behind Miss Faffle's desk and sat down. "To what do I owe this pleasure, doctor?"

Dr. Marplot straightened himself and tucked his hair into place. "Please excuse the lateness of the hour. I was in the neighborhood, you know." His lips puckered as he spoke. "So, how have you been, *doctor*?"

Dr. Whitcraft silently considered the man standing before him. Marplot so desperately sought to conceal his agitation, but it was there. Ah, yes. It was most certainly there. "What do you want?"

"Well, now. You are direct, indeed you are. I thought it may interest you to know that as of this evening, my membership in The London Society of Physicians has been *revoked*."

"Really?" Dr. Whitcraft struggled against issuing a smile. "That *is* a shame, isn't it?"

"Yes, it is. It is a shame. What I can't figure out is *why.*" He stepped closer. "So that's one wickedness that has befallen me as of late, and while I'm on the subject, here's a second. The coroner has suddenly made it his business to investigate the deaths of all of my *female* patients...but curiously only those who died while I was making the treatment of hysteria a priority."

"Hmm." Dr. Whitcraft nodded, flattening his lips.

"Yes. Hmm is right. So you can imagine how utterly taken aback I was when a third act of villainy revealed itself...that rather large article in The Gazette,

I wonder if you saw it. It delineated every aspect of the coroner's inquests, details privy to no one but the coroner and myself. Puzzling how something like that could have gotten the newspaper's attention, don't you think?"

Dr. Whitcraft blinked, feeling like a boy on Christmas morning.

"And then, let's not forget the fourth calamity—*Mrs. Pannade,* with whom I believe you are familiar. Why do you think she has taken it upon herself to inform the fellows at *The Lancet* that I have been using their offices as a hunting ground to seduce and corrupt married ladies? I cannot even speak of the *perverse* undertakings she has described. It's just shocking." A vein danced at the man's temple, pulsating as his words grew increasingly loud and agitated.

"And finally, the *coup de grace*, if you will. I discovered in this morning's post, that Mr. Boodler has finally concluded that it was *my negligence* as a physician and not the *bloody carriage* that killed Mrs. Fussock!" Dr. Marplot took a step over Mr. Gamon and gripped the edge of the desk. "The licensing board has scheduled a hearing, you know, to determine if I should be even allowed to continue practicing medicine! *And there you sit!* Do you think it would be way off the mark if I were to conclude that perhaps *you* had something to do with all five of these atrocities? *All of five of them?*"

Dr. Whitcraft tilted his head down and looked over his glasses at his opponent. "Well," he said, surprising himself with the cool tone of his voice, "that seems unlikely now, doesn't it? How in the devil would *I* have managed to do all of those *terrible* things?" The question was asked, and it hung in the air for a time before the faintest smile crept across his lips.

Dr. Marplot's face contorted and he gasped, "I knew it was you! I told Catherine and she said you didn't have it in you, but I told her! So you think your five-step plan is going to ruin me? Is that what you think?"

An electric thrill charged through Dr. Whitcraft; a sensation not terribly unlike that of being shocked by the voltaic pile, although this effect was instead rather euphoric. Seeing this man so compromised was the fulfillment of countless nights spent agonizing at the ceiling, imagining how he should suffer for his misdeeds. It was all right here, right now, playing out so perfectly in front of him, in his own office where the excitement about his maneuver had begun. Dr. Whitcraft shut his eyes and inhaled a long and satisfying breath. Justice had finally been restored to his world. Almost.

When he opened his eyes again, they were glimmering with devilish joy, and he couldn't resist the impulse to offer a word to the man stridently inflating and deflating in front of him.

"I wish you good luck at your hearing, *Doctor* Marplot. Or perhaps I should call you…*Mister* Marplot."

At that, Dr. Marplot lunged at the desk like a man possessed, clearing its contents with one sweep of his long arm, sending Miss Faffle's trinkets crashing to the floor.

Dr. Whitcraft anticipated the move and jumped to his feet, grinning as he ducked around the desk and sped toward his examining room. But he had forgotten about the body of his most recent patient sprawled on his floor, and in mid-stride, Dr. Whitcraft's foot lodged under Mr. Gamon's upper right thigh, propelling him up, over and down, ultimately landing face first into the waiting arms of the unconscious greengrocer.

Dr. Marplot wasted no time crossing around the fallen men. Like all other mischief-minded people in this office, he too grappled with the hat stand. In a flash, he emerged overtop both men, brandishing his weapon like Thor with a lightning bolt. Dr. Whitcraft gasped from the floor and covered his eyes, bracing himself for what was sure to be a fatal blow.

"Dr. Marplot, I presume," Constable Fettle sang out from the doorway as Miss Faffle peeked over his shoulder. "Why don't you put that down and take two steps back, so I can arrest you for the vicious assault of those two innocent gentlemen."

There was a considerable crash when the hat stand hit the floor, splintering three new holes in its brittle wooden planks. Constable Fettle glanced down, probably considering the lengthy repairs this would require, but remembered himself as he looked back up into the shocked face of his culprit.

"The assault of *two* men?" Dr. Marplot shrieked, positively spasmodic as he pointed at Dr. Whitcraft. "*That man* there is innocent of *nothing*! You should arrest *him* and the other, well I had absolutely nothing to do with that man's—"

"Yes, look at that poor bugger, his face all smacked in like that. What a pity." Constable Fettle's chin doubled as he spoke in a sad and serious tone, although his grin remained constant. "The problem is, Dr. Marplot, that you have three witnesses here that will testify otherwise, don't you know."

Dr. Marplot's eyes searched the ground, stricken. He straightened himself to his full height, and gave a regal tug at his ascot before thrusting his chin in the air. "For the record, officer, I heartily dispute harming that unfortunate individual on the floor, there. I testify that I haven't the faintest idea who that gentleman is. For all I know, Dr. Whitcraft was in the process of murder when I came upon the scene. That duly noted, I certainly understand the necessity of you taking me into custody so that we may resolve this matter at the police station. I will not do my reputation any further damage by refusing the machinations of justice."

Miss Faffle dashed to her boss, reaching out with two hands and pulling him to his feet.

"I'm glad to see that we are both in agreement, Dr. Marplot," Constable Fettle said, having adopted a more professional countenance. He made a sweeping gesture toward the door.

Dr. Whitcraft watched, awestruck by the whole affair, unable to shake the distinct feeling that he might awaken in his bed to find that this glorious turn of events had only been a most wonderful dream.

Dr. Marplot stepped toward the exit, but stole a glimpse back at his rival. Dr. Whitcraft relished the intensity of his searing glare, the wheeze of his accelerated breathing, the lovely shade of umber his complexion had attained—oh, it was all just delicious! He giggled to himself, rubbing his hands together as if preparing to sit down to a holiday feast.

Dr. Marplot broke his stare with a jerk of his chin, gathered himself and proceeded calmly out the door, followed by Constable Fettle.

Dr. Whitcraft and Miss Faffle walked to the door and watched the pair descended the stairs. The two appeared to be in the midst of the most benign discourse, when without warning, Dr. Marplot made a run for it, leading by his right shoulder as he bolted across the street in between passing carriages.

The enraged constable's shouts could be heard even inside the office. Miss Faffle threw open the door, watching her beau give his best attempt at a chase. But Dr. Marplot's speed only increased, until finally he disappeared like a phantom into the cold London night.

Chapter Twenty-Five

Several Months Later

Dr. Whitcraft looked over his shoulder, wondering what had become of Mrs. Minnock. She had just been there, right next to him, but must have stepped away to speak to someone. Or maybe she needed some air because it was oppressively hot inside of the church.

He slid into a pew in the center of the sanctuary; it didn't matter where he sat now anyway because someone would surely summon him when the bride was ready to walk down the aisle. Until then, he took a deep breath, smoothed out his trousers, and prepared for what was sure to be a long and ponderous ceremony.

He scanned the rather motley assemblage: a surprisingly good turnout. Most of the guests still milled around, convecting the hot church air this way and that, while others languished in their seats, softening like wax in the humidity.

The pew in front of him was occupied by three dowagers crowded tightly together in spite of the heat, looking like peahens as they gazed sharply over their noses at the crowd. It was difficult not to be mesmerized by their fascinator hats, unquestionably purchased from the same proprietor given the similar corkscrews, danglers and feathers suspended from each.

He looked over his shoulder again for Mrs.

Minnock, but swiveled back around when he heard one of them speak.

"My sister is still reeling. Her hysteria has returned and the poor dear is crippled."

"At least she escaped that criminal's hands unscathed."

"Oh, I know! It could have been *her* lying dead in the mortuary instead of Mrs. Fussock. Clearly, the Lord saw fit to preserve the ones he *really* cares about."

"Amen to that."

"You know, I heard Mrs. Fussock couldn't be bothered to volunteer at her league's autumn bazaar."

"Disgraceful."

"Incredibly selfish."

"Mmm. Anyway, my sister told me that they're never going to catch that terrible man. He's living under an assumed identity and treating patients at a hospital in Paris."

"Paris? Well, that's not what I heard at all. My neighbor, Mrs. Randle, insists her butcher saw him on the stage in Prague, stealing the show in the role of the Count's gardener in a rather low adaptation of *The Marriage of Figaro*."

"Are you talking about *Eugenia* Randle? Oh, she doesn't know what she is talking about, and I certainly wouldn't trust her butcher."

"Well, you both are wrong. Everybody I know agrees that Dr. Marplot boarded a ship bound for America, of all places, to become a surgeon. Oh, how I shudder to think of the poor afflicted souls in the New World laying helpless in his hands."

"Here you are," Mrs. Minnock sang with a smile as she glided along the wooden pew next to Dr. Whitcraft.

"Shh." He brought a finger to his lips and cocked his head toward the women. She raised her brows and leaned in to listen.

But he didn't have to listen. He knew the true version of events. After evading the grasp of Constable Fettle on that most glorious evening, Dr. Marplot had managed to return home, clean out his most precious effects, and promptly vanish. Warrants were issued, thorough searches were made at his home and offices, but no confirmed sign of the man was ever detected in London again.

"You know, I heard that girl of his helped him plan his escape, buying tickets, securing passage. She's just as guilty as he—"

"That's not what I heard at all. I heard he ran off *because* of her. He would've faced the charges in court but *she* was such a shrew about the whole matter."

"Well, you both know of course, that other doctor…her jilted fiancée, the one he tried to murder, what was his name? Dr. Wit something."

"William Whitcraft."

"Yes, him. He's giving away the bride today. From what I heard, *he* had the last laugh on *her*. *She* came crawling back to him, but he threw her out like yesterday's stale bread. Good for him!"

Mrs. Minnock winced and Dr. Whitcraft squirmed in his seat.

Miss Reave had indeed appeared in his office, her fair skin more pale than usual, her normally mischievous dark eyes ironed over and lifeless. She sat across from him, murmuring, unable to meet his gaze, never mentioning the disappearance of her new beau, or much of anything else, really. After a time she rose, whispered some kind of nonsense about something or other, and departed from his office in a blur.

Later, he discovered that Dr. Reave had demanded she make a final attempt at reconnecting their relationship, knowing it would be the only way to repair her scandalized reputation. Because that attempt had so utterly failed, however, he elected to have her sent to the Scottish countryside where his dowager sister lived on a remote estate.

Dr. Whitcraft could think of nothing more torturous for his former fiancée than spending hour after hour gazing at the rolling green hills without any parties to dress for, gossip to spread, or trinkets to pilfer. He had been a victim of that scoundrel, but so had she, and she had paid an awful price. He couldn't help almost feeling sorry for her.

"I heard he's over her, though," the fattest one laughed wickedly, fascinator wiggling like antennae as she cackled. She dropped her voice to a whisper. "Do you know who Mrs. Brade said that doctor's taken up with? You wouldn't believe it if I told you."

"Oh I know exactly what you're going to say! He even walks around the city *with* her!"

A flustered church marm scurried up to the doctor's pew and leaned over, out of breath. "Dr. Whitcraft, sir, they're just about ready to begin."

The three women turned around, mouths agape as he got to his feet and sidled past Mrs. Minnock. He turned back and offered a tip of his hat to the stunned ladies before following the old woman down the aisle.

The gossip didn't bother him. Not any more. A few months ago he would have been mortified to hear such tales bandied about in public like that, but it all seemed so frivolous to him now.

The church marm stepped out of the way, and Dr. Whitcraft inhaled as he caught a glimpse of the bride for the first time. Miss Faffle was a blushing vision dressed in a blue and white gown borrowed from Mrs. Minnock. It billowed out and back like a ship's sail as she walked toward him, smiling brighter with each step. Her hair had been neatly collected, wound and dotted with daisies, and her cheeks blushed rosy-red from the staggering heat of the church. She looked positively angelic.

"Oh, Miss Faffle," he breathed, surprised at the paternal pride rising from his breast. "How wonderful! Don't you make a most lovely bride!"

****

Constable Fettle beamed as Dr. Whitcraft delivered his bride to the altar. When the doctor turned to make his way back to his seat, the eyes of the entire congregation followed him, measuring his every step with breathless attention. He swallowed hard, the fodder of so much bawdy talk in London's high and low circles alike. He tried to appear nonchalant when he slid into the pew next to Mrs. Minnock who dabbed at the corners of her eyes with his handkerchief.

"I wouldn't have guessed that you'd cry," he whispered.

She sniffed. "I'm just so pleased for her…and relieved. It all could have gone so wrong and look how happy she is now."

Miss Faffle *was* happy, deliriously so. She gazed adoringly into the eyes of Mr. Fettle. The preacher droned on and on about the sacred institution of marriage. Even her mother had forgiven her. The woman sat proudly in the first row, sporting a giant mum on her chest, nodding in agreement with each of the preacher's cautions.

Mrs. Minnock whispered, "That was almost *you* up there."

He looked at her over his glasses. "It most certainly was."

"Are you happy it's not?"

The answer was complicated. Miss Reave had been the epitome of everything he thought that he had wanted. The lovely, well-connected final accouterment necessary to complete his life serving the hysterical throngs of London society. Would that life have made him happy? In giving up the idea of her, he had lost more than a fiancée. He had lost the certainty of exactly what he wanted from his life.

Finally, as he stared into the quizzical eyes of Mrs. Minnock, he smiled. "I am happier than you can imagine."

He had said it too loudly. Several irritated guests turned around and frowned.

"Shhh!" An angularly prim woman scowled at them both.

Mrs. Minnock giggled softly.

"You *shhh*!" Mrs. Pannade glared at the woman, who at once shrank back into her seat. Mrs. Pannade may have been cured of her relentless pursuit of the doctor's affections and was seemingly rid of her hysteria symptoms, but she still could throw a most fearsome stare if she wanted to.

She turned and nodded at Mrs. Minnock and the doctor, and sat back to watch Miss Faffle struggling to slide the golden band on to her new husband's finger.

****

The three gossips huddled together in a corner and whispered as Dr. Whitcraft passed by. He nodded at them before joining Mrs. Pannade and Mrs. Minnock. Everyone waited for the commencement of the wedding breakfast.

"What are the both of you grinning at?" He looked from woman to woman.

Mrs. Pannade glanced at Mrs. Minnock. "I just found out how Miss Faffle and Constable Fettle managed to pay for this lovely affair."

Dr. Whitcraft frowned at Mrs. Minnock.

She shrugged. "You shouldn't be so modest, Dr. Whitcraft. There is no shame in chivalry."

He looked down and kicked some dirt off his shoes. "Well, Mrs. Pannade, after Dr. Reave felt compelled to pay me back for what I've spent over the years on his daughter, it seemed like a proper use for the money, I suppose."

Mrs. Minnock squeezed the tips of his fingers. "Mrs. Pannade, did I tell you what a lovely dress that is?"

"Oh, why thank you!" She arched her back then twirled for her audience. "Corrine selected the style. That girl knows exactly what flatters my figure." She glanced at Dr. Whitcraft as her hand slid down the side seam. She brought her chin to her shoulder and posed. Remembering herself, she straightened and turned back to Mrs. Minnock. "Say, now that Lilly is leaving, have you decided who will share Corrine's room?"

"Brigitte has wanted to be downstairs for ages, so I suppose she will move."

"Lilly's leaving?" he asked.

Mrs. Pannade and Mrs. Minnock exchanged glances.

"Yes," Mrs. Minnock said. "I was going to tell you about that later. I hazard to say, you may find the reason a little startling because it deals directly with your recent unpleasantness."

He waved his hand. "I'll manage, I'm sure. What is it?"

"It seems a judgment of negligence has been handed down against..." Mrs. Minnock paused and glanced at the gossips who had inched closer. She lowered her voice. "Against you know who, and because the man has disappeared, the court saw fit to seize that empty house in St. James Square. They've handed it over to the Mrs. Fussock's next of kin...*Mr. Fussock*."

"Mr. Fussock?" *His* former dream house, now in the hands of Mr. Fussock? He wasn't sure how to feel about that bizarre development.

Mrs. Minnock continued, "The acquisition has apparently proved inspiring to the man, and has been just the carrot he needed to lure Lilly away from us. The two were married yesterday."

"Good Lord," he said. "Now *she's* Mrs. Fussock?"

The bride and groom scuttled past swept along by a crowd of well-wishers. Mrs. Pannade sighed with pleasure as she watched them. "Ah, one never knows who will end up with whom. Lilly with Mr. Fussock. Mr. Pannade is out of my life now, thank God and Dr. Whitcraft is rid of that uppity adolescent. And the new Mrs. Fettle will never have to hear from that awful greengrocer again. I never heard what happened to him."

"The harshest sentence for any similar crime within the last ten years of English justice, Mrs. Pannade," he said. "Fifteen years."

Mr. Gamon had never been aware that his unconscious body had played such a pivotal role in the debasement of Dr. Marplot. But he did learn that the name Dr. William Whitcraft carried a certain cachet with the judge assigned to hear his case—the Honorable Judge Ingler. After announcing his sentence, the judge paused and glanced across the courtroom, appearing to seek Dr. Whitcraft's blessing. When he nodded, the gavel crashed down, sealing the man's fate.

"It's too bad that Dr. Marplot isn't in there with him," Mrs. Pannade said. "But regardless, now that he's gone…isn't it *your* maneuver again, Dr. Whitcraft?"

He shrugged again. "Frankly, anything remotely associated with him is now tainted beyond repair. I'm afraid the maneuver is destined to become a footnote in medical history."

"You could move out of London and do it somewhere else, where no one knows about it. Or you could call it something else," Mrs. Minnock suggested.

"What? Like The Five-Step Plan? No, somehow I've lost my taste for that business. When I was in Paris, I learned that hysteria strangely doesn't seem to be as big of a problem in other parts of the world as it is here in England. Who knows why that is. But that's neither here nor there. I believe I'll have to become inspired by something else, perhaps move my practice in another direction. Maybe I don't want to practice any more. Maybe I should teach, or write. I don't know."

Mrs. Minnock was quiet for a moment and then said, "William, I had no idea you'd been thinking of this. It's funny you'd mention a change in careers. I've been thinking about the same thing."

Now that he was watching, she and Mrs. Pannade were looking intently at one another, sharing something between them seeming to have great import. Finally, she threw up her hands. "Oh, shall we tell him, Mrs. Pannade?"

Mrs. Pannade nodded wildly and burst into a highly charged grin. "I'm going to be taking over Mrs. Minnock's duties. *Me!* Can you imagine?"

"You're *what*?"

Mrs. Pannade's eyebrows raised while her grin grew larger still. "Me!"

Mrs. Minnock smiled at Dr. Whitcraft and shrugged.

He grabbed her by the elbow and pulled her toward the wall, away from the other guests. "Why didn't you tell me this? I mean, this is quite the news, isn't it?"

"Which? About me or Mrs. Pannade?"

"About *you*! I can't fathom that business about Mrs. Pannade, for heaven's sake...but you! What are you going to do?"

She sighed, pulling him away even further. "William, that night everything happened, when you arrived at my house all bleeding and disoriented...that disgusting man from Parliament was with me. I had to send him off so I could tend to you. Well, that was it for me, my last evening out." But after thinking about it for a moment, she put her hand to his ear, cupping in the sound so it was only for him, and whispered, "Except for you, of course." She smiled.

"I had no idea."

"Of course you didn't. There was no reason for you

to know. It's my choice. My life. I've done all I'm going to do with this life. It's time for me to turn the damn thing over to Mrs. Pannade, like Mrs. Pettish turned it over to me. I've made a little money." She shook her head. "That's not quite honest. I've made a fortune, actually. My frugality and good business sense have paid off and now I have the luxury of being able to do whatever strikes my fancy."

He paused, and finally said, "I'm very happy for you, of course. It's wonderful, really. I've always despised the idea of you in that way..."

"Unless it was with you, of course."

He winced, and quickly asked, "You'll move then, I presume. Where will you live?"

"I haven't gotten that far yet. I'm seeing about some other places."

"But, you're not leaving London. You can't possibly—"

She threw her arms around him and held on for a time. He stood stiff and bewildered when she finally whispered, "William if I stayed here, I would be nothing except what I am now—Elizabeth Minnock, famous London procuress. No matter where I go or whom I talk to, everyone knows me. What I am. I want to go where I can be anonymous."

He pushed her back with a look of urgency just as Mrs. Pannade descended on them both, crying, "Oh, don't they make a lovely couple!"

For a moment, Dr. Whitcraft thought she was talking about them, but then saw the bride and groom over his shoulder.

"Yes. Yes they do," he whispered.

****

Dr. Whitcraft quietly descended his stairs holding a lit candle, lost in thought. He hadn't been able to sleep because his mind had been in a whirl since he had returned from the wedding. He placed the candle on his desk, sat and opened the top middle drawer. There sat an unfolded letter, its edges worn from the multiple times he had handled it. He adjusted his glasses and read it over again, the silence in his office heavier than usual.

Still clutching the letter, he looked up into the darkness. He thought about Miss Faffle's empty desk for a time, and then remembered some of the faces of the scores of patients he had seen over the years…trying unsuccessfully to dismiss all notions of sentimentality arising in his heart. He took a deep breath.

"Why not?" he said aloud, and then smiled.

****

"Get up! I want you to read this." He had brought the letter and the candle upstairs.

Mrs. Minnock squinted at him sleepily. "What? Right now…?"

"Yes. Please."

She sat up and took the letter from his hand. In the flickering candlelight, she read it. When she finished she looked up and shrugged.

"I met those fellows in Paris. One of their students introduced me…they liked my research on electricity, as you read, and offered me a job the last day of the conference. Sent this letter out to me shortly afterwards. Of course, I couldn't consider it because of the maneuver, but now…why not? Why not, indeed?" He placed his hand on her shoulder and squeezed. "I want you to come with me. Let's just go, Elizabeth."

She looked up at him, her blue eyes wide with wonder. "This is rather spontaneous of you. Isn't it rather out of character?"

He smiled and shrugged. "Not very stodgy then, I suppose. What do you say?"

She giggled and jumped into the arms of her formerly stodgy ex-client, tossed her head back, and cried, "I say, *Oui, Oui!*"

Afterword

Given that the tale of *The Five-Step Plan* is one of obsolete medical techniques, it seemed only fitting to carry that theme to my character's names. Every fictional character in this story possesses a last name that is an obsolete English word. What follows is a list and their definitions.

The Key Players

Dr. Whitcraft (witcraft): Logic…argumentation

Dr. Vorago: Gluttonous waste-gut and spendall

Miss Faffle: Busy work

Mr. Gamon: Deceive, tell lies

Miss Reave: To take away

Dr. Marplot: Spoilsport

Mrs. Minnock: A favorite darling, the object of one's affection

Mr. and Mrs. Pannade: The prancings of a lusty horse

Constable Fettle: To arrange or mend

Hysteria Patients

Mr. and Mrs. Wedfellow: Spouse

Mrs. Brabble: Quarrel

Mrs. Snaggs: Large teeth

Mrs. Junters: The state of being sulky

Mrs. Fussock: A fat lazy old woman

Mr. and Mrs. Meecher: To act by stealth / clandestine lover

Mrs. Princod: Fat round plump person / pincushion

Mrs. Chankings: Slightly masticated spit-out food

Patients

Mr. Brim: To be in heat

Father Benison: Blessing

Mr. Lask: Afflicted with diarrhea

Mr. Buzznack: An old organ out of order and playing badly

Mr. Twitchel: Childish old man

Mr. Larking: Sex with a woman's breasts

Doctors

Dr. and Mrs. Smatchet: A small, nasty person

Dr. Forspent: Weary

Dr. Scamble: Cheat to get free food

Dr. Hurple: A shrug one does in inclement weather

Dr. Chimble: To gnaw like a rat

Dr. Clowclash: A state of confusion

Dr. Naffin: Almost an idiot

Dr. Encraty: Mastery of the senses or an abstinence from pleasures

Dr. Sangrado: Quack

Mr. Looby: An awkward, ignorant fellow

Dr. Prinking: Dressed nicely

The London Society of Manners

Mrs. Uppish: Testy, apt to take offense

Mr. Fustian: Bombast language

Mrs. Foyce: Gas from an old woman blamed often on the small dog in her lap

The Police / Justice System Figures

Sergeant Draffsack: A big paunch or lazy glutton

Constable Duffart: A dull, soft fellow

Mr. Boodler: One who takes or offers bribes

Judge Ingler: Passive participant in anal intercourse

Mr. Jarkman: Vagabond counterfeiter of documents

Mr. Kelter: Money

Supporting Characters

Mrs. Anile: Old womanish

Mr. Caxon: An old weatherbeaten wig

Mr. Varment: Dashing

Mrs. Pursy: Fat and short of breath
Mr. and Mrs. Drumble: Confused
Mr. Grannows: Streaks of dirt left in underwear after washing
Mrs. Harridan: Worn out old woman, harlot
Mr. Smittlish: Infectious / contagious
Mr. Flepper: Upper Lip
Mrs. Pettish: Passionate
Mrs. Shardborn: Born or residing in excrement
Miss Drizzen: A low mournful sound like a cow
Mr. Understrapper: Inferior fellow in any office
Mr. Lorel: A dissolute person
Mrs. Randle: A set of nonsensical verses
Mrs. Brade: Fraud

A word from the author...

I grew up in Ohio and went to college in Salem, Massachusetts, before moving to New Orleans in 1996. I worked in marketing while my husband attended medical school, but left when my first son was born. I am proud to be a stay-at-home mom for my two sons, but now that they are older, I have plenty of time for my true passion, which is researching and writing historical fiction.